Platonic?

Platonic?

Nick Waugh-Bacchus

Matador
5 Weir Road
Kibworth Beauchamp
Leicester LE8 0LQ, UK
Tel: (+44) 116 279 2299
Fax: (+44) 116 279 2277
Email: books@troubador.co.uk
Web: www.troubador.co.uk/matador

ISBN 978 1848 764 675

British Library Cataloguing in Publication Data.
A catalogue record for this book is available from the British Library.

Typeset in 11pt Bembo by Troubador Publishing Ltd, Leicester, UK

Matador is an imprint of Troubador Publishing Ltd

Printed in Great Britain by the MPG Books Group, Bodmin and King's Lynn

To my wife Dawn, children Holly, Jessica and Ben – thank you for your love and patience.

To all those who, over the years, have inadvertently influenced the writing of this book – thank you for the inspiration.

Preface

We all travel down our own paths. Sometimes the path we are on can cross or run so closely to that of someone else that it allows us to peer over upon it just to see if it's one we would like to tread for a while. Sometimes we find ourselves at a junction where two such paths meet at their end. One route takes the two paths along together and the other route divides them once more. It's at such forks in the road where life defining decisions are often made.

Scary Mary

"I don't normally do blind dates," Mary paused, albeit briefly, to allow the lump of sweet and sour chicken, stabbed so mercilessly with her chopstick only a few moments earlier, to fall into her cavernous pit of a mouth and tumble down into what was clearly an even huger stomach, "but sometimes you just have to go with the flow, don't you think Jack?"

Jack was trying to subtly remove the piece of batter that had shot across the table from Mary's mouth as she had obliviously continued with her sentence whilst still devouring the poor piece of poultry. The thought did occur to Jack that the batter might just have jumped in an effort to escape the acidic fate that awaited it in the pit of Mary's ample belly.

"Jack?" Another piece of batter hurtled in Jack's direction. Instinctively he winced as the desperate morsel clattered into his eye.

"Jack? Did you hear what I said?"

Jack hadn't, but then Mary seemed happy to ignore her projectile spittle so Jack didn't feel too much guilt.

"Sorry Mary, I must have been distracted. You were saying?"

Mary leant forward giving Jack a full view of the remaining semi-masticated chicken floundering around in her mouth. Jack found himself edging backwards slightly, the voice in his head nervously suggesting that if he got too close he might inadvertently get sucked in the next time Mary took a breath.

"I was saying that I don't normally do blind dates, but that sometimes you just have to go with the flow, do you think?"

Jack didn't normally do blind dates either. However sometimes, he agreed, you do just have to go with the flow. This didn't mean to say of course that going with the flow meant that the direction in which you were flowing was necessarily the right one. Indeed from the moment Jack had walked into the restaurant and felt the air squeezed from his lungs by the ferocity of Mary's welcoming hug, even the most optimistic side of him, a side that saw the good in everyone, had shaken its head and uttered "Oh Fuck!". An appropriate exclamation as the realisation crashed down upon him that he had travelled thirty miles after a hard day's work to fork out his hard earned cash on a romantic liaison with Jabba the Hut's sister.

"Absolutely, sometimes you just need to go with the flow." Jack forced a smile in the hope Mary would respond and therefore close her mouth. To his relief she did and then, to his greater relief, she excused herself and disappeared towards the hot food stands that stood in the corner of this particular 'All You Can Eat' restaurant. The respite, even if only fleeting, was most welcome.

Jack sat back in his chair and let out a large audible sigh of relief. He took the opportunity of surveying his surroundings in the hope he might find something nicer to look at than the view to which he had been unfortunately subjected for the bulk of the evening to date. Jack did feel a twinge of guilt that he should think such a thought but, in order to put this feeling into perspective, he had to temper this with what he knew about himself.

Jack was not a shallow person. He was not one to be swayed by a low cut top, long legs and a perfectly formed backside. Actually, that's not quite true, Jack was a bloke after all. However, if these very favourable qualities weren't backed up by a personality then the aesthetic only appeal would quickly wane. On the other hand if a woman had a personality that reached out and grabbed you then Jack would always find that there would be something else attractive about them as well, whether it be something as simple and yet as vital as a great smile or beautiful eyes.

Taking all this into consideration Jack knew that he was not going to enjoy tonight. Mary, on the evidence presented to him so far, was sadly lacking in both the appearance and personality stakes. Jack, though he claimed to be 'no oil painting', wasn't an ugly guy by any stretch of the imagination. However, he was humble enough to recognise that looks weren't everything and that it was what you said and how you acted that really defined who you were.

It was for this reason that Jack decided to largely ignore the little waves coming from a table of three extremely attractive young blonde ladies who had caught his eye as he looked around. Ironically he had looked around hoping to see something attractive but, as he was technically on 'a date', he knew that 'looking' was all in which he could allow himself to partake. Such nobility, whilst highly commendable, was a bit of a pain in the arse. It had haunted Jack from his early teens and had no doubt cost him the opportunity of many a carnal encounter over the years. Jack drew little comfort from the fact that this affliction had, on occasions, also undoubtedly saved him from what would have been some extremely regrettable exchanges of bodily juices.

The peace and quiet his momentary solitude had offered were once again shattered as Mary returned to her chair with a bump and a grunt.

"Wow," Jack couldn't help but comment, "that's one hell of a plate full you've brought back there Mary!"

"I love Chinese, and they'll happily take our cash at the end of the night," was as much as Mary could say before sending a large prawn to the same fate as the sweet and sour chicken, "so why not, that's what I say." Jack had started to edge backwards during the latter half of Mary's sentence and in doing so had put himself just out of range of the latest batch of food particles desperately trying to flee from the black hole occupying the majority of the lower half of Mary's face.

"So Jack, you work in a bank then?"

"Yes." Jack did work in a bank, but didn't really like to make that too public. It was right up there with Traffic Warden or Tax Collector in his eyes.

"So, you're a bit of a 'banker' are you?" Mary laughed at her intonation.

"Well I work in a bank." Jack had heard the 'banker/wanker' reference so many times before which was one of the reasons he stopped telling people what he did for a living.

"Yeah, so you are a wanker, oops, I mean banker!" As she belly laughed at her deliberate faux pas Mary almost choked on the mouthful of noodles she had just sucked up from her plate.

"Oh don't choke!" fortunately Jack's complete lack of

4

sincerity was lost on Mary as she tried to ease her coughing and spluttering by forcing another wedge of food into her mouth.

"Seriously don't choke." Jack's sentiment second time round was somewhat more genuine as the terrible prospect of having to attempt the Heimlich manoeuvre upon Mary suddenly loomed into sight. Standing behind a bent over Mary and squeezing her was very much the last thing on Jack's agenda.

"I'm okay, I'm okay," Mary's solution of force feeding herself seemed to do the trick, "hey, do you know what I do for a living?"

"Eat?" Jack hadn't meant to say that out loud but he needn't have worried, Mary wasn't actually listening.

"Well, I work in the 'Adult' industry!" Mary raised her eyebrows suggestively towards Jack. Jack's dinner raised itself suggestively in his stomach but fortunately managed to stay down.

"I see," was all Jack could manage.

"A bit more interesting than banking don't you think!"

Jack was speechless. He cast his eyes around the restaurant looking for either some hidden cameras or the nearest escape route.

"I don't mean I make porno's."

Jack wasn't sure how to take this last remark either. His brain had ground to a shuddering halt with the words 'Adult Industry' and was working extremely hard to avoid any images of Mary in this particular line of work entering into his head lest it cause him irrevocable long term psychological damage. This had, so far, protected him from delving too deep into the possibilities of exactly what Mary did within the

Adult Industry and, even though she had now specified that it wasn't making pornographic movies, his mind was now having to do all it possibly could to block out the images of what such a movie would look like should it, God forbid, ever be made.

"Do you want to know what I do?" Mary leant forward to whisper to Jack. Jack tried so hard not to lean back but couldn't help himself. Fortunately his movements were subtle; however the more he leant back the more Mary leant forward. If he didn't stop quickly there was a real chance she would topple over on him and, as this would quite possibly result in instant death, Jack couldn't take this chance. He therefore reluctantly pushed himself to lean in to hear what Mary had to divulge.

"I'm a dominatrix!"

Mary sat back and picked another king prawn off her plate and seductively toyed with it around her mouth.

Jack sat back and prayed that this was all a bad dream. If Mary had hoped that her admission and subsequent show of sexual intent with the large pink shrimp would stimulate the man across the table then she would have been most disappointed if she could see the contents of Jacks pants at that particular moment – his genitals having shrunk to a size they had last been on the day he burst out of the comfort of his mothers womb, in the hope this would aid them as they desperately tried to disappear back up into his body.

"Wow, that's," Jack was searching for words other than 'scary', 'terrifying', 'stomach churning' and 'enough to bring up my dinner', and, after a slight pause, settled on "different!"

"Different?" Mary had hoped for a bit more of a reaction than just 'different'.

"Yeah, well, it is isn't it?"

"Well it beats being a banker – although I have beaten a few bankers!" Mary started to choke on her joke once more. Jack couldn't help but smile – thinking that the prawn was clearly fighting back.

"So," Jack waited until Mary had regained some composure, "how did you get into your particular field?"

"I was a bit of a Goth in my younger days."

Jack wasn't quite sure how that link worked. He had known a few people who had gone through their black and purple phases and none of them, to the best of his knowledge, had made the transition from moping around bemoaning that their parents didn't 'understand them', listening to Marilyn Mansun and trying to convince everyone that Robert Smith from The Cure was actually good looking, to dressing up in leathers and beating middle-aged businessmen with leather whips.

"Is that part of the training then?"

Mary looked puzzled so Jack continued.

"Well, did you go to the careers advisor and tell them you wanted to be a dominatrix, and they said the way to get into that particular line of work was firstly to be a Goth?"

Jack could tell by the slightly bemused blank look staring scarily back at him from across the table that he was beginning to dig himself into a hole. Nethertheless he kind of felt that if he dug deep enough he might just be able to hide in it. "You know, it's like going to get your A levels and then your degree if you want to be a teacher, but for a dominatrix you have to go through a gothic phase, have a natural tendency to beat people, learn how to tie knots – so I guess if you've been in the Girl Guides or Scouts that's a bonus, study medieval

7

torture, and finally perhaps go on an over-assertiveness course!"

"What? Don't be stupid. We don't have to do any of that."

Jack, of course, realised this; however he had hoped that Mary would have also realised he was joking. As it was, he was now becoming increasingly concerned that she was about to produce some form of spiked club from her leather handbag with which to beat the living crap out of him.

"You're looking very stern Mary," Jack tried another deflecting tactic, "is that part of your dominatrix role?"

"No."

"Oh."

"I'm not at work now am I."

"No - but it's beginning to feel a little like that to be honest!" Jack tried to smile but the lack of emotion from the woman in front of him was making this difficult.

"If I was at work I'd be charging you £200 for my time."

"£200!!" Jack was a little shocked by this.

"£200 - for an hour." Mary's mood had lightened as she saw the amazement in Jack's eyes.

"£200!!" Jack was genuinely amazed, "for an hour?" He couldn't help but wonder who on earth would pay that much money to see Mary dressed in rubber and high heels and have her whack them with sticks or whatever it was she did.

"What on earth do you do to get that much money in an hour?" Now, Jack hadn't actually meant to let that last question slip out, but it was too late to claw the words back. Fortunately, or unfortunately, Mary was only too willing to let him know.

Five minutes later Mary finally stopped talking and sat back in her chair. Jack didn't quite know where to look. He had tried to keep as much eye contact as he could during the whole torrid tale that Mary had bestowed so enthusiastically upon his unwitting ears so as not to appear rude, however, he now felt extremely uncomfortable and, if truth be told, more than a little scared.

"Ha ha, you're shocked aren't you?" Mary chuckled approvingly from the other side of the table, clearly, and obviously not too surprisingly, enjoying the discomfort in Jack's startled face.

"Erm, yes, a little." Jack tried to force a laugh but unfortunately it fell out of his mouth as a nervous stammer much to the further amusement of Scary Mary.

"Well don't be," Mary started to lean forward again which actually caused Jack to involuntarily jump back in his seat, "all that's what I do for work. I only do that for my boyfriends if they want me to."

Jack nodded nervously and was momentarily distracted by some giggles from the table of the three attractive women who, it seemed, were equally enjoying watching Jack's discomfort.

"Some of my old boyfriends actually liked to tie me up." Mary raised her eyebrows with alarming suggestiveness. "Is that something you think you might like to do," up went the eyebrows again, "Jack?"

Jack felt that Mary did indeed need some kind of restraining, but wasn't sure if he would be able to convince the local authorities that Mary represented a true threat to society.

"I'm not sure that we've quite reached that stage in our relationship, and besides I'm not very good at knots." Jack, as was his wont, tended to make jokes when he was nervous.

"You weren't in the cub scouts then," Mary's look of mischief was most unnerving for poor Jack, "you obviously haven't got your knot tying badge."

"Er no."

"You haven't got a woggle I could play with either then?"

"Fuck no, I mean, no, no, I haven't." Jack berated the voice in his head that had inadvertently bleated out the word 'fuck' in panic as a natural flight or fight instinct to keep his woggle well and truly out of Mary's clasp.

"Fuck no!" Mary, fortunately, was laughing loudly as she continued to enjoy Jack's discomfort. "I think I could teach you a lot Jack," she leant forward sending her heaving bosom collapsing into the mix of wontons, egg fried rice, ribs and spicy chilli beef strips laid out submissively awaiting their fate on her plate, "and I think you'd quite like me to give you a lesson."

Mary sat back up, the remains of a barbequed spare rib clinging on to her breast.

"It's really kind of you to offer," Jack lied.

"A free one of course." Mary reached out her hand and caressed Jack's twitching fingers before retrieving the rib from her chest and ruthlessly devouring the meat from the bone. This in itself was enough to cause Jack's penis to invert itself once more.

"Again, another kind offer Mary," Jack's words were slow as he watched her continue in her decimation of the poor rib, "but I'm not sure that's the right thing for us at this stage of our relationship." Jack was attempting to let Mary down gently. This was a rather unfortunate misjudgement as the reality was that the only thing that could let Mary down gently was a winch and harness.

"What!! Are you fucking joking?"

The whole restaurant turned to face Jack's table. Jack's eyes widened and his jaw fell open at the sight of Mary's face, without any warning, suddenly balloon up and turn crimson with rage.

"W-w-what? What?" the words slipped limply out of Jack's pathetically quivering lips.

"Are you fucking joking?" Mary folded her arms. "I've offered my services, free of charge," at this point Jack was cowering back in his chair in the vain hope that this would somehow give him the mystical powers of invisibility, "and you're not interested? What are you? Some kind of fucking weirdo, or arse bandit?"

The silence in the restaurant was deafening and only interrupted by the rhythmic flapping of Mary's nostrils.

"Er, I'm not trying to be rude Mary, it's just.."

"Are you fucking joking!" the woman was now shouting at the top of her voice, "don't you know how to treat a lady?"

Jack was in a state of shock and did a quick double take to see if he could see any sign in Mary's eyes that this might be some kind of wind up.

All he saw was madness.

It was fucking scary, pant soilingly scary.

"Are you okay Mary, is this some kind of.."

"Some kind of what?" Jack was convinced he actually saw steam start to come out of Mary's ears and let out a sigh of relief when he realised it was just a tray of sizzling beef being offered to a table behind her. "Are you listening to me?"

Jack hadn't meant to be distracted by the smoke.

"Yes, yes of course," he started to try and lower his voice in the hope she would follow suit, "let's just calm down, I think we must have some crossed wires or something."

"Crossed wires!! Crossed wires!! I don't know about any fucking wires, but I'm fucking cross, fucking livid!!"

Jack was genuinely scared, and the relief of the possible back up provided by the hasty arrival of the restaurant manager far outweighed the embarrassment he was feeling knowing that it was his table that was causing all the commotion.

"Is everything all right ladies and gentleman?" was the rather stupid question that prompted both Jack and Mary to look at the poor chap, Mary in utter disbelief, Jack in disappointment that the man just hadn't produced a gun and put her down.

"No it's fucking well not!!" barked Mary.

"Please, please, no more bad language my lady." The man did his best to exert his authority, not easy to do when he was crapping himself.

"Don't have a fucking go at me!! It's him you should be having a fucking go at!" Mary pointed pointedly towards Jack.

"Please, ladies and gentleman, you must calm down or I ask you to leave."

"You'll do WHAT?" Mary's roar drew actual gasps from the tables in the immediate vicinity and prompted a rapidly assembled gathering of terrified Chinese waiters whose illusion of strong support for their manager was somewhat undermined by the fact that they all hid behind him.

"You can't fucking ask us to leave, I haven't finished my fucking dinner."

Jack was so stunned he just sat there, his mouth as dry as the desert.

"No, you must leave now." The manager, against his natural instincts, started to move towards Mary to usher her out.

"Don't you touch me!!" the warning was sufficient as Mary got up, "I'm perfectly capable of getting up and leaving myself!"

The communal sigh of relief that echoed around the restaurant woke Jack from his temporary state of paralysis, as did the hand on his arm from the manager escorting him to the restaurant door in Mary's wake. Just before he got to the exit Jack turned to make his impassioned plea,

"Don't send me out to her!"

It fell on deaf ears and suddenly Jack found himself standing outside the restaurant on the opposite side of the narrow road to a strangely smiling Mary.

"Come on then," she started to turn to walk down the road, "let's get a kebab."

"What?" Jack hadn't been in such surreal surroundings since a dream he had a few weeks earlier where he was washing his boss's hair in a bath tub in the middle of the town centre whilst dressed in a pixie outfit.

"Come on, there's a great kebab van down the road." Mary seemed completely normal - in so much as she was hungry which seemed to be her normal state of affairs from what Jack had surmised on their date so far, well that and her psychopathic sex-talk-induced rants of course.

Jack looked at Mary, and then at the restaurant, and then back at Mary who had stopped in her tracks and was beckoning Jack towards her.

"Haven't we just eaten?" was the best Jack could come up with.

Mary laughed.

"That was just starters," she rubbed her belly as the thought of a kebab on a rotisserie drifted into her head, "and, hey, did you like the way I got us out of paying the bill?"

Jack found himself open mouthed yet again, much to the amusement of Mary.

"That was," Jack looked back at the restaurant and then back at Mary, "that was just so we didn't have to pay for our meal?"

"Yep!" there was something altogether very unattractive about the smug look that had sat across Mary's face. "Works every time. Now, get your arse over here. I want a kebab and then, if you're lucky, you can have mine."

Jack felt his dinner begin to rise.

"Ah, that's a very kind offer, again, Mary, so thank you," Jack shifted uneasily on the spot and fumbled under his shirt sleeve for his watch, "but I think I should probably look to get to the station now."

Mary, who was still stood a few feet away, started to turn crimson again.

"You are fucking joking aren't you!"

Jack didn't stop running until he reached the station.

Hayley

The answer phone clicked on.

"Sorry, I would pick up the phone at the moment but my arms have just fallen off. I am sure you will appreciate that this has come of a bit of a shock and is a little painful. The next sound you will hear is the bleep to cover the sound of me swearing quite graphically after which please leave your name, number and brief message of concern and support."

The answer phone had seemed a great idea at the time but had he, for one minute, known how much the desire to leave the perfect message would drive him to the brink of madness he would have never taken the bloody thing out of the box. Clearly he had not yet achieved his goal.

"Hi, Jack," came over the crackly speaker, "it's only me. I just wanted to see how it went. Call me, bye."

Jack smiled warmly. Hayley sounded so optimistic. She always did, that was one of the things he loved about her.

Hayley had been Jack's closest friend for what seemed like an eternity although the reality was that they had only met a little over eighteen months ago. One of the reasons it felt that they had known each other for so long was because they had clicked straight away and almost immediately fallen into the comfort of each other's friendship. Theirs was a relationship where it felt as if they hadn't stopped laughing since their first meeting, although technically they obviously had otherwise their throats would be more than a little sore and they would almost certainly need some extensive counselling.

As the answer phone message clicked off Jack couldn't help but smile to himself as the memory of the first time he had heard Hayley's voice flitted into his mind.

It had been just past mid morning and Jack was sitting at his desk pondering over yet another major dilemma – should it be the cheese or possibly the roast chicken roll that he should buy for his lunch. Marjorie, the normally patient sandwich lady, was trying to chivvy him along.

"What's it to be Jack?"

"It's not that simple Marg," was the rather serious response.

"What d'you mean, 'it's not that simple'," retorted Marjorie in, Jack thought, quite an unbecoming tone, "how difficult can it be? Do you want the cheese…" Marjorie thrust the roll no more than what could have been three inches away from Jack's somewhat startled nose, "or…" as she grabbed the other roll, "the chicken?"

The chicken lunged with an alarming ferocity even closer to Jack's nostrils than had the cheese roll moments earlier. Jack instantly comforted himself with the thought that Marjorie, the normally placid and sweet sandwich lady, was evidently going through some kind of latter age women's crisis. Fortunately Jack, in a moment of surprisingly good judgement unbecoming for him in situations like this, decided not to mention his theory. In the same way that you should never wake someone who is sleepwalking you should never aggravate a menopausal woman armed with food snacks.

Having avoided saying the worst possible thing he could,

Jack still, true to form, managed to ramble down a path best left untrodden.

"The flippin' butter's oozing out of that one now! Christ Marg, if that was a small animal you'd have just crippled the poor bugger."

Marjorie looked Jack deep in the eyes as she ruthlessly squeezed the last breath out of the poor roll and dropped it defiantly on his desk in front of him. For a moment Jack was sure he noticed a small pair of horns begin to protrude in the corners of her forehead.

"I'd go for the cheese if I were you," sounded a pleasant new voice. Jack looked up to see Martin, his boss, giving his 'introducing somebody new' smile, and the beneficiary of his smile and owner of the pleasant voice.

"Hayley, Jack," pointed David, "Jack, Hayley."

"Good choice!" smiled Jack after an initial momentary pause essential for his brain to acknowledge the pretty new stranger but prevent him from going as far as eyeing her up and down to obtain a full first assessment, no, plenty of time for that. In Jack's own experience the full body check is much more easily achieved from a safe distance and without anyone else noticing.

Jack re-assessed his current predicament.

"Marg, my mind is made up, it has to be the cheese. You've murdered the chicken and eating the evidence would make me just as guilty."

Marjorie's horns shrank back behind her wrinkled brow, in shock no doubt, and her startled expression, described in the pub later by Jack as "priceless, bleedin' priceless", genuinely was bleeding priceless, particularly when Hayley then took a napkin from the poor woman's basket and gently covered the prostrate roll, gravely pronouncing,

"There's nothing to see here, please move along."

So Marjorie did. Jack didn't and instead, as Hayley walked on to the next introduction, he took the opportunity to undertake the essential full body check. Hayley was of slightly above average height, 5 foot 4ish was Jack's guestimate, quite slender but with, importantly, nice hips, a potentially award-winning arse and, from what Jack could make out without staring too obviously, a perfectly adequate pair of breasts. Not too big – nothing worse than worrying about suffocation if a woman with huge breasts decides to go 'on top'.

Jack had only once been with a girl with huge tits and, to put it frankly, it had scared the crap out of him. Her name was Mandy and she seemingly had elected to use her giant assets as weapons. Jack had fought back the temptation to ask her if she needed a licence to carry them. In truth he hadn't even really fancied her and had it not been for the fact that (a) he was pissed, (b) he felt obliged to as she'd made such an effort and had started sobbing when he said he had to go home, and (c) 'Bonk a girl with Big Tits' had been on his New Year's resolution list made only a few hours earlier (whilst getting pissed – see point 'a'), he would not have gone for it. He wished he never had.

Mandy had assumed that Jack was pretend wrestling as he grappled helplessly trying to get out from underneath her phenomenally huge mammaries. Just as he thought he would make an escape which Houdini himself would have told his grandchildren about, Mandy grasped her left breast in her hands and whacked him round the head with such force Jack was convinced that he momentarily lost consciousness. It was almost as if she was pillow fighting but armed with her own super charged bionic pillows. There was only ever going to be one winner and indeed Mandy came first...Jack was a gentleman like that and, besides, he was genuinely scared. It's a well known technique used by all men whilst 'on the job' that if you're getting close to the point of no return you should think of something dull or wholly unattractive. A few of Jack's favourites included 'Formula One Racing', 'Esther Rantzen' and 'Grandma Puts on her Tights.' He had to stop using the last two after the 'Grandma' one had actually completely lost him a major erection that could not be raised despite stringent, and very generous, efforts by the unfortunate woman. The 'Esther Rantzen' had, to Jack's immense concern, caused him to shoot almost immediately on the last two occasions he had used it. Jack, to this day still couldn't reconcile whether he was too close prior to thinking about her or whether he had some kind of deep rooted 'teeth fetish'.

On this occasion with Mandy, and her two large wobbling friends, Jack didn't need to resort to such tactics. As he lay there staring upwards, wincing with every 'wwhoosh' as her breasts swung back and forth closer and closer to his face and to what, Jack was sure, would be instant decapitation, Jack didn't feel an ounce of excitement. He was just relieved that his manservant was scared rigid as well. Had he not been able to perform, had the cries of "Yes!!Yes!!" suddenly turned to "No, No, No!!", he was convinced he would have been either smothered or clubbed to death.

That was Mandy, but the girl who by that time was being introduced to one of the managers over by the fax, the girl with the amazing dark eyes and the most stunningly warm smile, was Hayley.

Jack smiled again, gave a little fond shake of his head as he let the memory of that first meeting slip out of his mind, heaved himself up from his chair and went over to get the phone.

"Hello?" answered Jack's ring.

"Hi trouble," smiled Jack, "how are you my darling?"

"Sod me Jack, how did IT go, did you like her, are you seeing her again, did you, you know..." came the avalanche of excited questions.

Jack said nothing but took in an audible sigh just to build up some tension.

"Jack!! Come on, spill the beans, or did you spill them last night?" laughed Hayley.

"Well.." another audible sigh.

"Come on!!"

"Well...sorry what was the question Hayley?"

After a brief giggle and audible sigh of her own, Hayley continued,

"How...did...your...date...go...last...night...Jack?"

"Oh!!" replied Jack trying unsuccessfully to sound surprised,

"It...went...really..really...shit..Hayley."

"Oh No!!" Hayley sounded shocked.

"Oh..yes..it..was..shittier...than...a...big....pile...of smelly...shit."

"Oh Jack, I'm so sorry," Hayley tried to sound a little sincere, however couldn't contain herself and burst out laughing, "Really, was it that bad?"

"It wasn't good."

"What went wrong, my sister told me this girl was perfect for you."

"Your sister?" Jack was a little surprised, " I thought you knew Mary?"

Silence.

"Hayley!!" Jack tried to sound stern, "I went on this blind date because you told me you knew this perfect girl for me!!"

Silence. Followed by a little giggle.

"Hayley!! You bitch! You've never met Mary have you!!"

"Jack!! I don't remember ever actually telling you that I knew her, I'm sure that I said I 'knew of' the perfect girl for you." Hayley's second attempt at sincerity floundered as had the first.

"I hardly know your sister, I've only met her a couple of times!"

Hayley paused and reflected, "I guess that's true, and come to think of it I don't think you made a particularly good impression."

"Why?" Jack was curious and more than a little indignant.

"You weren't exactly 'over' compassionate about her guinea pig."

"I thought I was exceptionally understanding and sympathetic." Jack clearly was trying to convince himself that this was the case,

"Understanding and sympathetic Jack?"

"Absolutely," was the resolute reply.

"You got the DJ to announce, 'This one goes out to Tricia, sorry your guinea pig's dead.'"

"Exactly, how much more sympathy could a girl want?"

"You got the DJ to play 'Who Let the Dogs Out' you callous bastard!"

"Ah, great song, and besides, I thought she'd see the funny side," protested Jack knowing full well he was digging his customary hole.

"How could anyone see the funny side of finding the back legs of their guinea pig hanging out the side of their next door neighbour's dog's mouth?"

Jack shrugged, not that Hayley could see this of course.

"Well it is a little bit funny, in a surreal kind of way."

"Jack!!" Hayley was trying not to laugh herself, "Think of the suffering that guinea pig went through!"

"You're right, having to live with your sister. Do you think it could have been suicide?"

"You are a sick bastard Jack Matthews."

"Don't think complimenting me is going to make me forgive you for setting me up on a date with Godzilla's ugly sister."

"Was she that bad?" Hayley's attempt at sounding sorry was wholly unconvincing.

"Bad! Bad? I thought she was going to eat me!"

"Wow, lucky you on a first date!"

"Seriously, she said she had previous boyfriends and when she opened her mouth I'm sure I heard one of them shouting to get him out."

"Ah, she couldn't have been that bad!"

"Worse, my friend, worse!"

Hayley laughed. They both did and carried on their conversation until a knock on Hayley's door brought a close to proceedings with a promise to 'do lunch' the next day.

Lost Charm

Jack wandered casually up to the doors of the bank. He had been day dreaming most of the way into work, reliving the events of the weekend. He afforded himself a wry smile and pushed the front door bell. Staring back at him through the glass was David Cox.

David was one of the 'old school' type of bankers. He had cursed the day that cashpoints were first used and, rumour has it, actually wore a black armband when decimalisation came into force. He was a man totally devoid of humour and with a chip so huge on his shoulder that you could almost physically see it. He also rather unfortunately suffered from dandruff and this had often prompted enquiries as to whether he was actually trying to salt the aforementioned prize-winningly proportioned chip.

David's problem was that he had failed to move with the times. He had maintained his beliefs that, if members of the general public were careless enough to encounter financial difficulties, they should then understand that the correct manner to adopt was one of contrite inferiority and seek the forgiveness of the bank. If they grovelled sufficiently, and ideally had some equity and a bias towards the Tory party, then a suitable penance would be arranged and salvation in the form of a short-term overdraft would be granted. This belief had seen him plummet down the internal rankings of the bank at the same time as people such as Jack, fortunate enough to be living in the 'real world', were rapidly climbing the banking ladder having successfully understood that if the general public want to borrow some money then that was fine providing they understood some basic rules. These rules were:

They had to take out some form of insurance policy, or

They had to agree to see a Financial Advisor, or

They had to have a nice pair of tits (only required if your bank manager was a heterosexual bloke.)

Suffice it to say, Jack was not one of David's favourite people. Jack knew this, however he couldn't immediately figure out why David was scowling back at him, shaking his head and gesticulating for Jack to go away.

In a completely shallow attempt to wind David up as much as possible Jack started to perform some elaborate sign language akin to something you would see on an early Sunday morning television programme for the hard of hearing. As he did so he slowly articulated his actions,

"Da…vid… I… can…'t… hear… you… you… are… clearly… a… distur… bed… old… man."

David continued to point Jack away with increasing frustration and annoyance.

"Da…vid… do… you… want… to… dance… You… look… like… John…Travolta."

At this point, with Jack in full creative flow, his manager walked up to, and past him. There was no eye contact, just a word of advice as the boss walked over towards where the rest of the staff were congregating waiting for David to complete the opening security drill.

"Jack, we're a bank, not an old people's home".

Jack sharply stopped his act, which was a shame as he was

quite enjoying it, as were the rest of the staff who had decided against calling him over in the first instance. As the smile drained away from his face it suddenly appeared on the other side of the glass on David's.

Jack decided against one final piece of sign language and walked quickly off to regain favour with his manager.

Once inside work Jack sat down at his desk and checked forlornly through his diary. His despondent sighs did not go unnoticed by his colleague Ken as he plonked his briefcase loudly on the adjacent desk.

"Don't tell me," surmised Ken as he sat down, completed one swivel on his chair and then fumbled around under the seat before managing to release the lever which saw his chair reclining to an angle more regularly seen at a dentists surgery, "the same old sorry faces, no-one you haven't sold everything under the sun to already, no decent totty, no decent visits out.."

"That's right Ken, my old mucker," interjected Jack, keen to halt Ken's long winded, but, it has to be said, extremely accurate summary of Jack's appointments, "my diary holds about as much surprise and promise as one of those so called 'lucky bags' you used to be able to get when we were kids."

"Shit! Is it that bad?"

"I think so, but probably worse." Jack held his diary up for Ken to admire.

"You see Ken," Jack stood up and wandered over to his colleague's desk, "with a lucky bag you always had the anticipation of not knowing what was inside. The reality was, though, that the only thing lucky about it was the fact that your initial optimism was maintained to the point where you

25

ripped the bag open on account of the fact that somehow you had somehow forgotten that all that was ever inside was some kind of crappy four piece jigsaw puzzle, four shitty broken crayons kindly provided so you could try and colour in an equally shitty picture of some scene from a TV cartoon show that was vaguely popular ten years previously, a small lolly that not only tasted shit but broke your teeth when you finally realised that you could probably go on sucking it for a week and it wasn't going to get any smaller so you'd have to try and bite the bleeding thing, and finally," Jack paused to draw a long overdue breath, "finally there would always be a weirdly coloured rubber that didn't actually rub anything out, it just smeared bits of itself all over whatever you were trying to rub out making it far worse than if you'd just left it alone in the first place."

"Blimey, who got out the wrong side of bed this morning?"

"I don't know, my bed's up against a wall so I guess that rules me out."

"You do know that in your little outburst there you said you used to go on sucking it for a week and it didn't get any smaller?" Ken smirked to himself.

"Ha ha, look, the thing is, is that with a lucky bag you end up with two big disappointments. Firstly, you realise that there's nothing 'lucky' about the bag at all, so it's just one big lie," Jack held up one finger, "and secondly, everything inside the bag is shit." Another finger rose in confirmation that indeed it was a double disappointment.

"However, a lucky bag would be preferential to my diary today Ken. I have three appointments, Mr Douglas, Mr Donovan and Mrs Martin. Shit, shit and..er..shit," three fingers waved emphatically proving that his diary was indeed worse than a lucky bag, "and if that is not bad enough, it's only Monday morning and my diary shows no signs of getting any better for the rest of the week. So Ken, if you have any suggestions, and I mean any that are remotely sensible, I'm all ears."

During Jack's rant Ken, whilst managing to maintain a passing interest in his friend's plight, had also been struggling fiercely to return his chair to an upright position. He had succeeded just as Jack finished his impassioned speech but his immense satisfaction at achieving this was short lived as he suddenly realised that he was expected to respond to whatever Jack had just said.

"Well, er, Jack," Ken leaned back in his chair, clasped his hands together, took in a deep sigh, looked at Jack, raised his eyesbrows and gave a reassuring nod of his head whilst making a small 'tutting' noise, "mmmnn, it's a difficult one Jack. I don't envy you mate."

Ken turned to his desk hoping that the same reassuring nods and 'empathetic' body language he used on his customers when he wasn't listening would work on Jack.

Jack stood motionless for a moment.

"Jesus Ken, you really need to work on your bull-shit skills."

Ken nodded his agreement and Jack wandered pathetically back to his desk and stared at the customer appointments scribbled in his diary in the somewhat misguided hope that if he did so long enough they might just somehow mysteriously disappear. His wonderings were interrupted by a sharp flick to his ear as Hayley walked past.

"Morning Mr Matthews..good weekend?" the latter half of the sentence was accompanied by a wry smile.

"It was most splendid Miss Smith."

Hayley sat near enough opposite to Jack, the wisdom of which they occasionally questioned as it undoubtedly meant that they would not get as much work done as the bank would no doubt like them to and, due to their close friendship, prompted a fair amount of unwarranted gossip in the huddled corners of the staff rest-room. Hayley would re-assure Jack, well, tease would perhaps be more accurate, that he needn't worry too much as most of the Chinese whispers that worked their merry way round decided that Jack was in fact 'gay' and not 'knocking off Hayley'. Jack obviously thanked Hayley for this reassurance and would then subconsciously adopt the guise of a 'true lad', deepening his voice, making unnecessarily long – to the point of slightly psychotic – eye contact with any woman that would dare to look back, and reminding anyone who would listen that he had slept with women in the past and lots of them too. That last bit was a bit of an exaggeration but Jack felt it would help his defence.

"Did you get up to anything interesting Mr Matthews?" came the enquiry from across the table.

"Funny you should ask, Miss Smith, as some supposed good friend of mine set me up on a blind date."

Ken was walking past at this point,

"Was he any good?" his laugh followed him as he headed back to his desk.

"Very funny Ken, Ho-di-bloody-ho-ho."

"He was a Ho Jack!" Ken feigned shock extremely well, far better than his earlier bullshitting episode, "you should stay away from those male prossies Jack."

Jack smiled the kind of smile that ended with the word 'off'.

"No, seriously Jack," continued Ken, "you've got to be careful 'cos as soon as you turn your back…"

"Alright Ken I think we get the picture, one that clearly you are very familiar with yourself. To be honest Ken, the sooner you find your way out of your little closet the better for us all."

"Ahh, classic closet behaviour Jack," Ken had put on his psychiatrist's hat, "you are attempting to deflect the unquestionable questionability of your sexuality onto someone else. Methinks you doth protest too much." A cautionary finger waggled in Jack's direction.

"Methinks thou should ask thy sister Ken, for I was once in a closet with her," Jack paused briefly to ensure the implication of his remark had registered before raising his mug of coffee in a toast to his silenced friend, concluding, "and methinks she did not protest too much."

"Ignore him Ken," defended Hayley, "he's just miserable because his magical charms have mysteriously deserted him… again."

Jack sat back in his chair pondering Hayley's observation. He knew Hayley was waiting expectantly for his next clever response but he suddenly realised that Hayley was dead right. He had lost, or at best mislaid, whatever charm he had previously possessed. The winning smile, the glint in the eye and the killer line had been replaced by an uneasy grimace, a rather scary stare and a stumbling fumbled stream of corny one-liners that, if they were ever successful, Jack would have to call an immediate halt to the proceedings on the grounds that any woman desperate or stupid enough to fall for them would almost certainly have escaped from some kind of institution. Jack's increasingly furrowed brow at the realisation of his loss of powers had not gone unnoticed by Hayley.

"Jack, are you alright?"

Jack stared helplessly back at his friend.

"I don't think I am Hayley."

Lunch

The lunchtime hustle and noise of over-excited children, screaming babies and spotty, badly-dressed young college students, eager to show each other that they could use the word 'fuck' in every sentence, made it very hard for Jack to understand what the young lad behind the counter was saying.

Jack leaned further over the hurriedly stacked trays and cupped a hand round one of his ears adopting the international body language for "I can't hear or understand a bloody word you're saying."

The young lad, 'Tim' as his name badge claimed, stared back and slowly recounted Jack's order,

"Lard fries, lard strawrary rilk shrake and a ropper with cheese."

Jack mused, ever so briefly, that he appeared to have stumbled into an episode of the 70s sit-com 'Mind Your Language'.

"Tim, that sounds great, but please go easy on the lard, I've got my stunning figure to think of." Jack patted his belly, a belly that was showing the first worrying signs of peering over his belt. Tim, also rather worryingly started to pat his own belly and smiled enthusiastically back at Jack whilst making 'mmmnn' noises.

"I think he wants to eat you Jack," whispered Hayley.

"Tim, could I also have a Big Mac meal for my friend as

well, but go easy on the lard as I quite like to think about her stunning figure as well."

Tim stared blankly back at Jack and then frantically started to check the menu for 'lard'. Hayley came to the rescue advising Tim that she would like a 'number 6' from the menu. The Lard meal and Rumba Six were served up and Jack and Hayley took their seats upstairs overlooking the shopping precinct.

Jack picked up one of his fries and danced it around the rim of his pot of barbeque sauce.

"So, what's up Jack?"

Jack's chip gave an elaborate dive into the sauce and thrashed around helplessly for a brief moment before sinking to the bottom of the pot. Hayley peered thoughtfully into the pot,

"Jack, I think your chip's drowned." She carefully picked it up and took another chip from his tray. She held them both up and, in true puppet theatre style, addressed the fries:

"Are you okay Mr Fry?" "Not really," Hayley's French Fry voice wasn't that convincing but it raised a smile from Jack, "I'm a bit sad at the moment," the chip nodded towards the other sauce-ridden fry, "and my mate's really pissed off too."

Hayley stroked her chin and delivered her verdict,

"I was wrong Jack, your chip hadn't drowned but clearly your chips are down."

Jack laughed out loud,

"Hayley, that was possibly the worst joke you have ever told."

"I know," she smiled warmly, "but seriously, you're not your normal self. You're still irritating and smell a bit strange obviously, but other than that you're not 'Jack'." An exaggerated look of panic fell across Hayley's face as she dramatically enquired, "My God, are you really Jack? Or are you some miserable bastard who's eaten him and taken on his rather odd form? Tell Auntie Hayley!"

Jack took in a sigh and afforded a smile and a shake of his head in acknowledgement of Hayley's performance. In truth he hadn't really got as far as working out what was wrong at the moment, well not in any great detail. He knew he seemed to have lost any previous ability to encourage women to want to sleep with him but couldn't quite understand why this was making him feel as low as it clearly was.

"Do you ever get one of those feelings," he began with the air of someone who was about to deliver some searing insight, which was a little optimistic if truth be told, "when you're merrily going along with life when, suddenly, wham, it hits you. I don't know whether it's a sudden recognition of your own mortality, or that there must be more to life than this. You're stuck with the same routine day in, day out, you're basically really going nowhere and not even going nowhere fast, no, you're going nowhere in one of those crappy old people's buggies that trundle along the kerbs at 5 miles per hour, only your buggy was made in Eastern Europe in the seventies and you have to pedal it, but there's only one pedal, and the bloody thing is broken anyway..."

Hayley listened, her brow gradually furrowing as she began to reach her diagnosis, but she allowed Jack to continue on a little.

"..so you can't even pedal it. You have to get out and carry the thing on your back, but it's made of that material they use to make shell suits so the bloody thing just slips off and lands on your foot so now you can't even walk somewhere, you have to limp.."

"Shit Jack, is this all because you need a shag?"

"Yep, that's about the long and short of it."

Hayley sat back in her plastic chair, "and there was me thinking it was something serious."

"It is serious Hayles," Jack was slightly aggrieved that his life shattering problem and detailed explanation was being belittled by his best friend, "it's not just about the 'need for a shag'," Jack reflected momentarily, "although that would almost certainly help."

"Honestly Jack, if it will help why don't you go out tonight, tank yourself up and use your charms to seduce some unsuspecting young lady. I'm sure you'll feel much better in the morning."

Jack shrugged his shoulders and sighed again. It wasn't just about a shag.

"Failing that, go home and have a good old wank!" Hayley giggled as she sipped her coke.

"Hayley, do you mind, not all blokes do that you know." Jack was crap at lying and didn't know why he had bothered to try and defend himself.

"No I'm sure you're right Jack, it's probably only the ones who have dicks."

Jack smiled, conceding the point, and sat back in his chair. He reached for another chip and peered out thoughtfully at the lunchtime crowds busying themselves in the precinct.

Hayley sat back in her chair and gave the same thoughtful stare towards the world outside. 'People watching' was one of her favourite pastimes and, after years of practice, she had become extremely good at it. 'People watching' is, of course,

34

not a talent peculiar to Hayley. 'People watching' is a natural gift that God, in his wisdom, bestowed upon all women. Word is that God gave them this gift in order to punish Adam for eating the apple. The fact that he was the only person Eve could 'person watch' must have irritated the crap out of Adam – particularly as it was Eve who gave him the apple in the first place. However 'and Adam did sayeth unto Eve – "Will you stop staring at me woman, haven't you got some washing to do or something?"' hasn't appeared in the more recent translations of the early Bible text, and this possible explanation is therefore subject to some scepticism by respectable historians, even if they have been unable to come up with any other plausible reason as to why most women are so damn nosey!

Of course 'people watching' isn't the fairer sex's only natural gift. Jack had met a few women who possessed the gift of unwavering self belief that they are always right even when wrong and a few more who also had the ability to convince themselves that it's a poor fitting pair of jeans which make their arse look big as opposed to the possibility that their arse might actually be on the more weighty side of the big-arse scale. Fortunately this latter gift didn't apply to all women and certainly not to Hayley whose arse was proportioned quite perfectly.

"Jack," she sat forward, her attentions concentrated on the crowd below, "look out for that bloke there in the flasher's mac."

Jack peered out trying to show some interest.

"What bloke?" He was failing somewhat in the 'interested' stakes.

"That bloke there!" Hayley pointed, rather over-excitedly

Jack thought, "the bloke with the long mac, over there, by the library."

Jack finally managed to sum up enough interest to focus on the man in the street.

"I see him," Jack watched intently for a few seconds waiting for something to happen. He waited a few more seconds during which time the man had checked his watch and stared at his shoes. Jack looked at Hayley who was transfixed on the man below, "Hayley…what exactly am I supposed to be looking for?"

Hayley sat back in her chair and stared Jack in the eye. Clearly Jack had no idea about people watching.

"You're such a bloke Jack," Hayley tutted and looked outside once more.

Blind Date

Jack was not sure he was doing the right thing. This was not an unusual thought for Jack, and indeed "I'm not sure I'm doing the right thing" had plagued him from his early childhood, through his teens, early twenties and was still there now banging the same old gong in his conscience.

The reasons for the same old thought had obviously changed over the years ranging from 'I'm not sure I should be doing a poo on mummy's quilt', to 'I'm not sure I should be having a wank' (a repeat offender since his early teens) through to 'I'm not sure I should have done that – she is asleep after all.'

On this occasion, as he walked hurriedly through the precinct, the thought was based around "I'm sure this is possibly the worst idea EVER".

A blind date! The Ghost of Scary Mary was still haunting his nocturnal dreams to the point where he was considering calling an exorcist. How he had let Hayley talk him into going on another one was a question he had asked himself over and over again for the last couple of days. Hayley's re-assurances that she did actually know this particular date and that the location for the rendezvous was closer to home had somehow swayed his judgement.

Judgement swayed, Jack now found himself walking through town. He stopped briefly outside Marks & Spencer's window to check his appearance. This he did in a flickering of the eye. It was the checking out of the mannequin's nipples protruding pertly through a skimpy top that took just a little longer. Satisfied that he looked okay and that it would indeed be a bonus if Jackie – the girl Hayley had set him up with tonight – had equally as pertly protruding breasts as the temptress in the window, Jack went on his way to his destination.

'The Hogs' was not one of Jack's favourite drinking establishments. It was one of those places he could take or leave but Hayley had insisted this would be a good choice as Jackie knew it well and would feel 'comfortable'. It had recently turned into one of the trendier venues in town in which to drink and with that had come the influx of teenagers, tarts and terrible music. A pub where you could previously have had a few beers and a good laugh with a group of your mates was now somewhere you could view the largest collections of acne and poorly applied lip-gloss in the Southern Counties. It was no use, however, to try and tell any of the poor souls as they couldn't bloody hear you on account of the aforementioned terrible music which was played at a volume only fractionally below the point where your ear drums would implode.

Fortunately there was a small upstairs area where you find some brief sanctuary. However, in order reach this comparatively peaceful haven you would need to ascend some awkward winding steps which shuddered from the relentless thump of the base speakers adorning numerous points along the pub walls. Once up the stairs this metronomic thud could still be felt but the terrible 'music' that had surrounded its beat had mercifully eased leaving the strangely soothing effect of someone having just plugged a stethoscope into the PA. It was up these steps that Jack was walking now.

"She'll be in black and she's got short blond hair," Hayley had told him, "and I'll tell her to be at the bar."

"Any other clues?" Jack had asked, "I'm a bit concerned I might mistake her for a pint of Guinness."

"You can't miss her, she's," Jack noticed a somewhat worrying slightest of pauses, "unique." concluded Hayley.

"Unique?"

"Yep, you know," Hayley had playfully punched Jack on his arm, "unique, one of a kind, different!" Another playful punch followed. Jack had smiled and forced a laugh out at the time but as he turned at the top of the stairs and walked towards the bar he was recounting this conversation with more than a little concern.

The bar was reasonably quiet. There were a couple of people sat on stools, one of whom was indeed dressed in black and had short blond hair. However this particular woman was absolutely gorgeous and Jack knew that this immediately ruled her out as his prospective date – he simply wasn't that lucky. The other occupant of a stool was a middle aged bloke in a polo-neck sweater sipping half a bitter and staring blankly back at his own reflection in the mirror behind the bar. Jack assumed that this chap either must have wandered in by mistake, couldn't find his way out or was some pervert waiting for the tarts to arrive, or possibly even a combination of all three.

Jack wandered over to the bar and took the decision to stand next to the good-looking girl – it seemed quite considerably the better of the two options – the eternal optimist within having decided to cling onto the remote possibility that this could indeed be his blind date. He said nothing initially other than to request a pint from the bartender. Out of the corner of his eye he couldn't help but notice how gently the good-looking girl was caressing her bottle of Alco-pop. Jack smiled to himself as the voice in his head remarked that he wished Jack's last conquest had been so attentive.

"Hi," he found himself saying after a quick inspection of the head on his pint which was taking a little while to settle.

No response. Well, a raising of eyebrows and a disapproving glance aside, no response.

"Hi," tried Jack again with an accompanying wave of his hand and the best smile he could muster.

"Hi," an acknowledgement of sorts.

"Are you waiting for someone?" Something in their briefest of initial dialogue had told Jack that any further correspondence was going to go nowhere so quite why he wanted to carry on the conversation he didn't know, but still, nothing ventured..

"I am actually, so if you don't mind, I'd rather you went away."

The coldness of the sharp retort stunned Jack into momentary silence. He wasn't used to such an early rebuke, normally he would have been talking to a girl for at least a couple of minutes before she would reject him. Wishing to keep this record intact Jack decided to continue.

"But we've only just met."

"I know, and already I feel we've grown apart. So," the girl walked two of her fingers across the bar, "Go," the fingers walked onwards towards the bars' edge, "Away!" and her fingers plummeted downwards – a quality Jack often admired in a woman but Jack was more struck by the fact that rarely had he come across a girl so far up her own arse.

"I can't I'm afraid. I'm waiting for someone too. I would go away and talk to the other guy at the bar," Jack nodded towards the polo-necked one and whispered, "but I'm concerned he may be a serial killer."

"Well," the girl stared Jack right in the eye, "all the more reason for you to fuck off over there."

Jack recoiled again. Rejection was not an uncommon occurrence for Jack but he couldn't ever recall actually been told to 'fuck off' within one minute of starting a conversation with a woman before. Now Jack was not a man who welcomed confrontation. However, equally, he wasn't a man who welcomed being sworn at, well at least for no reason anyway. Therefore, he decided he wasn't going to lie down easily and allow the she-devil to trample all over him.

"I could be wrong," Jack sipped the froth away off the top of his pint, "and I'm no expert," another sip, "but are you coming on to me?"

The girl picked up her bottle, took a lingering sip, licked her lips, placed the bottle slowly down on the bar making sure to slowly run her fingers from its very tip down to its base, and stared deep into Jack's, now somewhat fearful, eyes.

"I think we both know the answer to that one, dick-head, but if you want to hang around and wait for my boyfriend and his mates to turn up, we can ask them. Or…you could just Fuck Off!"

"Wow," Jack took a further sip of his pint and, although somewhat relieved that this latest piece of information suggested that this was indeed not his blind date, continued, "wouldn't your boyfriend be cross when he turns up and sees you coming on to me?"

"I think he might be cross when he turns up and sees you coming onto me, dickhead." Jack couldn't tell if her tone was mellowing or not, he suspected not.

"How cross would he be if he turned up and saw that I was coming onto you, but that you," Jack extended his index finger away from the grip on his pint towards the blonde girl, "were kind of coming onto me as well?"

"Well that won't happen will it, because I'm not coming onto you. I'd rather have the bloke at the end of the bar." She nodded towards the serial killer.

"Really?" Jack exaggerated his look of surprise. "How cross will your boyfriend be when he finds out you want to shag Hannibal Lecter?"

"Ha,ha, you're such a comedian." No mistaking her tone this time. Sarcasm, like rejection, was not an uncommon acquaintance of Jack's on evenings out.

"Thank you." He beamed across at the increasingly grumpy face opposite.

"I was being sarcastic. You're about as funny as a dead dog. Only you smell worse."

Jack managed to stifle a laugh. He hadn't heard that particular put down before.

"Ah, you've been sniffing me. If that's not a sign that you fancy me then I don't know what is?"

"It's hard to mistake the smell of bull-shit, and, as I said, my boyfriend is on his way so why would I fancy you?"

"Just because you have a boyfriend doesn't mean that you couldn't technically fancy me. You don't have to actually do anything about it," and Jack would have run a mile by this time had she changed her mind, "but I think it would be good for you if you were honest with yourself."

"Weren't you supposed to be meeting someone?"

The words 'Oh Fuck' emblazoned themselves across Jack's mind. He was indeed due to be meeting someone. He looked around to the staircase and then to the various seats to see if anyone had silently arrived in the last few minutes whilst he had taken on the challenge of trying to make the Ice Maiden smile. No-one was there.

"There was a girl there a few minutes ago – but she saw you and left." The girl at the bar took great delight in relaying this tale and turned away from Jack to stare at her own reflection in the mirrored bar.

Jack took a couple of swift glugs on his pint before placing the half empty glass down on a fresh bar mat. He stared briefly at the reflection in front of him and glanced briefly at the reflection next to his and the look of triumph on the young woman's face.

"Well, it's been a delight meeting you." Jack nodded towards the woman and she, not surprisingly, ignored him completely.

Jack checked his watch and decided that enough was enough. He walked towards the stairs pausing only briefly to let the serial killer know that the girl at the end of the bar fancied him. Blind dates, he surmised, were not for him. Even the ones where the blind date doesn't turn up are a disaster.

Once down the stairs Jack edged his way through the throng towards the big glass doors and freedom. Once he had managed to squeeze his way through to the exit he inexplicably stopped. Perhaps it was because he knew that he would never return to that pub again that he decided to stop and survey the bar for one last time.

A heady cocktail of barely covered seventeen-year-old

legs and boobs, and foundation-encrusted desperate middle-aged spinsters were eyeing up the hairy backsides that peered above the poorly fitting ripped jeans of the teenage dickheads and sad old gits who, in turn, were eyeing up the legs and boobs and russet plastered skin of the aforementioned women. The DJ introduced, or more accurately mumbled, the next number and the staggering sad bastards on the dance floor cheered, seemingly oblivious to the fact that it sounded exactly the same as the noise that had been pumping all bloody evening. A barman inadvertently slipped, sending a diligently collected stack of pint glasses crashing to the floor to a chorus of delighted whoops and roars from the masses.

God, Jack felt old.

He nodded to the bouncers as the door shut mercifully behind him.

Worms

Jack stared intently at the clock on the bottom of his PC. He had started staring at it when he noticed it flicking from 8.23 to 8.24. Since then he had been trying to predict the exact moment it would flick over to the next minute.

It was now 8.47.

Twenty-three times he had failed so far and the situation was now threatening to get out of hand.

He had tried lots of techniques, "one Missisippi...two Missisippi, "three elephant, four elephant..." and, as desperation stuck in, he had now resorted to, "four fuck it, five fuck it."

All he wanted to do was to check his appointments and now he was locked in a bitter battle with his PC clock. It had already cost him his cup of coffee. The coffee that had accompanied him over to his desk content in the knowledge that it was to fulfil its worldly purpose by being drunk (a purpose many of the young people from the Hog's the night before also shared), but a coffee that had been left, neglected to grow cold and lonely and now faced the inevitable prospect of being cast away down the sink, rejected just like the many other coffees Jack had spurned over the years.

Not only had it cost him his caffeine boost, but his epic battle had also cost him the opportunity to join in the latest office sweepstake on how long it would take Sharon from the Cashiers to announce to anyone who would listen, including customers, the most recent sexual position she had tried with her new lover Marco. Yesterday's winning time being 9.17 am (she starts work at 9.15, and was a couple of minutes late) and had begun with "he just flipped me over and grabbed my legs..," after which point Jack's ears mercifully shut off.

Now, Jack found himself staring doggedly at the screen once more,

"Forty-eight, fuck it..forty-nine fuck it..."

"Jack.."

Jack barely heard his name and, in a moment of surprising focus, ignored it completely.

"Fifty-one, fuck it, fifty-two, fuck it..."

"Jack!"

Jack again maintained focus despite taking in the somewhat more impatient use of his name.

"Fifty-four, fuck it, fifty-five, fuck it.."

"Jack!"

"Fifty-six fuck it..," he recognised the owner of the voice as Hayley, "fifty-eight fuck it,"

"What happened to 'fifty-seven fuck it?'"

Hayley's enquiry overlapped Jacks 'fifty-nine fuck it' and caused sufficient turmoil within his brain at this oh so critical stage that in a reflex action he momentarily glanced away from the screen. Regaining his senses in a split second he turned his gaze away from the laughing Hayley and back to his screen where the clock was staring smugly back at him with the figures 8.48 shining brightly.

"Fucks are no good," Hayley reassuringly patted Jack on his shoulder, "you should try elephants."

"Well, I'm not sure I would want to do that to an elephant, but hey, I'll take your word for it." Jack managed to raise a smile before making a mental note not to look at the PC clock again, ever.

Hayley took her seat opposite Jack.

"Oh, your appointment's here Jack," Hayley took a sip from her non-neglected coffee, "she's a bit early but we've sat her in the room."

Momentary panic followed. The twenty-four minutes of clock watching had not only given Jack slightly blurred vision but had also stopped him checking his diary.

He hastily tried to sign on to his workstation, thumping the keys inaccurately in a frenzied attempt to type his name, before accompanying each thud on the Return button with, "Why..won't...this...bloody...thing...work..."

Hayley, who had come around to his side of the desk to watch the ongoing panic at close quarters, leant over and slowly removed his hand away from the battered and bruised keys.

"I think the problem is that you appear to be trying to sign on in the name of 'Jas Mattjes'!"

Hayley smiled as she started to type in Jack's correct details.

"Jas Mattjes is my code name you know." Jack nodded and attempted to raise his left eyebrow.

"No," Hayley clicked on the Return button, "'Jas Mattjes' is what Bob Marley used to light up his joints."

Jack looked a little confused.

"He didn't use a lighter.." Hayley paused to allow the penny to drop, which it didn't, "he used ," and in her best Bob Marley impression, "Jas Mattjes."

Jack laughed, "he made them with Jammin' you know.... It made them taste..sweeeeeeeeet." Jack puffed on an imaginary spliff and swivelled around on his chair narrowly missing the striding legs of his manager in the process.

"Haven't you got an appointment to go to Jack?" said the voice as it walked through the office in the knowledge that no eye contact was necessary.

Jack swivelled back round and clicked onto his diary.

"You're seeing Miss Michaels," interjected Ken who had been munching his way through a packet of crisps since his arrival, "you lucky bastard." The empty packet dropped into Jack's bin as Ken made his way towards the kitchen.

"Thank God for that." Jack was relieved.

Sarah Michaels had been one of his accounts for a few years and, as well as being rather attractive, had bought the odd insurance policy from time to time. Jack gathered up his 'Look at me I have an important looking folder' folder, bid his farewells and headed off to the interview room.

Jack, folder in hand and well practised look of confidence upon his face, strode purposely through the sanctuary of the 'behind the cashiers' glass bit' of the banking hall.

Jack liked this space.

The tranquil surroundings of 'behind the cashiers' glass bit' could often be a peaceful haven. A quiet space, away from the bizarre Customer Reservation that lurked beyond the spy hole in the security door. A calm unruffled place into which no customers, particularly the ones who had just advised Jack that he was in fact a 'tight heartless wanker', could chase him.

Jack stood by the door and squinted through the spy hole. The door was at the end of the row of cashiers, all of whom turned in unison to watch Jack squint once more in a vain attempt to see through this tiniest of holes unaware, as were all the staff, that the glass on the outside of the door had in fact been coloured in seven months ago by a bored six-year-old waiting for his mother to change up the £24.57 they had collected in a large plastic imitation coke bottle over the course of the previous eighteen months.

A few moments earlier Sharon had been recounting her previous night's sexual adventures to her colleague Molly. Molly was the one person who always seemed to have time to listen to Sharon's stomach churning lurid confessions, mainly on the grounds that she was practically deaf and blissfully unaware for the most part that Sharon was even talking to her. Now Sharon, who had mercifully cut short her tale which had begun with the phrase, "You wouldn't believe what I did with a roll-on deodorant last night" in order to watch Jack peering through the door, averted her gaze once more. She looked out onto the banking hall through the huge glass windows – the security door being practically the only non-transparent fixture within the line that separated the baying customers from the sanctity beyond the cashiers. The hall, as it had been in the previous three minutes since they opened, and with the exception of Jack's appointment who had arrived early, was completely empty.

"There's no-one there Jack."

Jack pulled his aching eye away from the door and nodded to Sharon,

"You can never be sure Sharon." He tried to sound serious as he walked out into the empty hall.

Sharon turned to Molly,

"He's right, I guess," she thumbed through a pile of twenty-pound notes, "if we were ambushed by a gang of pygmies crawling on their bellies there is a chance we might not see them."

"Eh?" Molly looked a little shocked and walked off in what can best be described as a 'huff'. Her impaired hearing had led her to somewhat misconstrue Sharon's last sentence and Molly was now convinced that Sharon had in fact been gang-banged on her belly by some pigmies. Fortunately she did not tell Sharon this; it would, after all, be foolish to put ideas into her head.

Jack opened the door of the interview room and smiled his way in.

Sarah Michaels was sitting patiently. She had a warm smile and, Jack liked to convince himself, was always harmlessly flirtatious.

"Hi Sarah," Jack offered his hand which was taken and politely shaken as Sarah briefly half stood up, "you alright?"

"Great thanks Jack," they both sat down, "how are you?"

"Oh, I'm fine thanks." Jack wriggled in his chair as he tried to get comfortable whilst still trying to maintain a remotely professional air.

"Is that apart from the worms?" Sarah mimicked Jack's erratic chair aerobics much to both of their amusement.

"No, the worms are doing just fine," Jack smiled, "besides I find it's a lot cheaper than having to buy my budgie all that bird food."

Sarah's nose wrinkled, quickly followed by the rest of her face as the image created by Jack's last comment flashed across her mind.

"I see," she regained her smile as the image passed with fortunate speed, "that's possibly a little too much information but thankfully I haven't eaten yet today!"

Jack, having already realised the words had left his mouth fractionally before he could claw them back, felt himself turning a delightful shade of crimson. In an attempt to rescue an embarrassing situation, sadly the best he could come up with was,

"Well I guess you won't be having noodles for tea."

Luckily for Jack this comment drew a laugh.

Sitting still at last in his chair, and composure restored, Jack continued,

"So, what can I do for you today Sarah?"

"I need a temporary overdraft Jack."

Normally requests for overdrafts are not made with an enormous smile; however, Sarah's grin in this instance was so large it was contagious and prompted the obvious question from Jack as to why she seemed so happy to be asking to borrow money.

Sarah clearly was desperate to be asked and rocked forward on her seat, her pretty face alive and animated as she explained,

"My boyfriend is back this week and wants to take me away for the weekend," she took a gasp of breath, composed herself, and beamed across to Jack. "He's been talking a lot recently about how long we've known each other, and basically," another pause and another beam, "I think he's going to propose."

"Hey," Jack's own beam was genuine too, "that's great Sarah." Sarah enthusiastically nodded her agreement. "Ah, well done, I'm really pleased for you."

Back at his desk, after telling all about his appointment and being a little disappointed that no-one else seemed to share his excitement, Jack found himself staring through his PC screen.

He had been delighted for Sarah. She was a really lovely girl, sweet, funny, intelligent and it had felt so good to see someone like that so happy. So why was his mood suddenly feeling so crushed? He briefly entertained the prospect that it was because he really quite fancied Sarah, which was true to a degree, but he had always known she was out of his league and besides, he enjoyed their banter far too much to risk making things awkward by asking her out. The fact that she had a boyfriend in the navy also made the whole 'asking her out' idea rather risky.

Jack peered down at his keyboard and pushed the Enter key until his computer started to beep, prompting some abuse from across the desk. The fact was that his mood had nothing to do with his attraction towards Sarah. It was, and he was almost ashamed to admit it to himself, simply jealousy. In that one brief moment when he stared across his desk he had witnessed genuine happiness in someone else's eyes. It was a beautiful sight and Jack had been swept along with it.

His face scrunched up as he realised that if anyone of his colleagues had come back from an interview bursting with happiness just because one of their customers was happy, he would have thought they were on some kind of dodgy medication that should really prevent them from handling scissors or driving. He physically winced as he imagined how he must have looked to his friends and was sure that he had not done himself any favours in trying to alleviate some of the gay rumours that Hayley had teased him about.

He closed his folder shut and stared at his PC.

Unfortunately he stared at it just at the very moment the clock flicked over from 9.35 to 9.36.

"Fuck-it," he thought, followed by, "two fuck-it, three fuck-it.."

Happy Hour

The bar was buzzing with early evening revellers eager to ease the stresses of work in the way they knew best – drinking themselves to a state of paralysis. This they would do to the point where any indiscretions during the night would either be completely lost in the time their alcohol-induced haze would steal away from their memories never to return, or, heaven forbid, if time did in its wisdom allow recall of their misdeeds that they could lay the blame fairly and squarely on the evils of drink.

The time was only 6.30 but already a swift glance around the bar would enable you to hazard a reasonable guess as to who would be getting drunk first, who would be getting chatted up first, who would probably be thrown out first and who would almost certainly throw up first.

Lloyds Bar, Happy Hour, Friday night – a haven for people watchers everywhere. Little surprise then that Hayley had arrived. The noise as she walked through the door was in sharp contrast to the dullness of the familiar walk from the bank and swiftly the clinking of glasses, the choir of excited voices battling to be heard over each other and the cackles of laughter brought a warm feeling of belonging to Hayley who peered intently through the crowds to try and see her friends.

In the corner three smartly suited ladies were discussing their respective weeks.

"Er… crap… boring… more crap… and more boredom… followed by another helping of crap and not to be outdone," the lady dressed all in the black power suit paused briefly to sip on her Spritzer, " a final generous dollop of boredom."

"You say that every week Jackie," laughed her pretty young friend in a generously revealing top, "surely something exciting must happen to you occasionally?"

Jackie shook her head and took another sip of her drink.

"Hey," the third lady, Karen, sat up tall in her chair as if preparing to deliver some devastating news, "weren't you due to be meeting Hayley's friend this week?"

"Oh yeah!" beamed the pretty one. Her name was Michelle and she had been Hayley's best friend since they went to school together. "How did that go?"

Jackie stared back at them quite coldly, her week of crap and boredom clearly wasn't quite ready to submit to an evening of girly chit chat.

"It didn't go anywhere as the prat didn't turn up."

"Really? What did Hayley say?" Michelle seemed a little surprised.

"Nothing – I haven't spoken to her since Tuesday, but," Jackie finally allowed herself to break into a smile as she saw Hayley waving excitedly as she made her way through the crowd towards her friends, "I guess I'll find out now."

"Hi all!" Hayley slumped down into her chair and took a large swig from her large glass of wine, "God I needed that!"

"Hiya!" chorused her friends.

"Oh Jackie," Hayley picked up her glass once more and took another slightly smaller gulp this time, "I'm really sorry I didn't ring you, I've been so busy. What happened on Tuesday night, Jack said you didn't show?"

Jackie's jaw dropped and the smile that had briefly crossed her lips disappeared to be replaced once more by the frown that had slapped itself across her face for the majority of the evening to date.

"I didn't show?" her raised voice took all three of her friends aback. "An hour an a half I waited at that bar for him to turn up and rescue me from the nonentities that kept on trying it on with me."

"How do you know that one of them wasn't Jack?" enquired Michelle with a mischievous grin.

Jackie paused to take a breath, "Because none of the drongos who tried to chat me up were dressed all in black."

As this little interchange developed, an inkling of the possible truth had been quickly dawning upon Hayley.

"When did you say that he had to wear black?"

The table fell silent as all eyes turned to Hayley.

"When you set me up for the date I said he should dress all in black."

"I thought you said that you would be all in black?"

"I always dress in black!" Jackie's voice rose once more but this time it was coming from the beginning of a smile.

"I know!" Hayley's tone mirrored that of her friend, "I thought at the time you were being funny?"

"Funny?" Jackie turned to her friends, smiled, then turned back to Hayley, "what's so funny about dressing in black?"

"Nothing," Hayley looked at her friend, "black suits you," the look in Jackie's eye suggested that Hayley needed more than just 'suits you', "you look stunning in black, and with your beautiful blonde hair.."

Hayley started to laugh prompting several smiles and calls of "What?..what?..what's so funny" from the other girls and a stern look from Jackie.

Hayley composed herself, "It's just when I described you to Jack as wearing all black with blond hair he was worried he'd mistake you for a pint of Guinness!"

That was it, Michelle and Karen doubled up in their seats and after an initial look of extreme indignity Jackie joined in the infectious laughter.

The first to stop and gather herself was Hayley.

"So you were probably there when Jack was," Hayley looked thoughtful, "but it's weird he didn't come and speak to you."

Hayley reached into her pocket and pulled out her mobile.

"You're not going to ring him are you?" Jackie looked genuinely concerned as the distinct possibility that Jack was indeed one of the men who had spoken to her dawned upon her, as did the memory of some of the put downs she had delivered.

"Absolutely, he only told me you didn't show, he didn't mention trying to chat someone else up."

"Mind you, would he?" Michelle began, "I mean, if your friend sets you up on a blind date and you end up chatting someone else up it's hardly the sort of thing you're going to tell your mate who set you up!"

She had a point.

"Jack!" Hayley's face lit up as she heard his voice, "hey, listen, I'm at the pub with Jackie.." Hayley turned to Jackie, "Jack says 'Hello'"

Jackie waved back nervously.

"Jackie's waving to you…" another look to Jackie, "Jack says he's waving too."

"Oh good." Jackie was now beginning to feel a touch awkward.

Hayley turned her full attention to the phone conversation,

"Listen, Jackie says she was there on Tuesday, did you definitely go to the right place?….Yep, that's right, the bar upstairs," she turned to Jackie to obtain the confirmation that the bar upstairs was where Jackie had been waiting. Jackie nodded and felt the colour drain from her face. "So did you see any blond women dressed in black there?….You did?.."

Hayley nodded and listened intently, occasionally laughing as Jack recounted the story of his eventful conversation. As he did so, Hayley peered over to her friend who was hiding her face behind her hands in embarrassment.

The silence was broken as Hayley passed on a question from Jack.

"Jackie," she paused to ensure that she had the full attention of the entire group, "Jack wants to know if you were the sexy woman at the bar who told him you were waiting for your boyfriend?"

The colour had returned to Jackie's face, albeit considerably more crimson than had been the case when she first arrived.

"Yes," she muttered and forced an embarrassed smile, "can you ask Jack if he was the guy who I told to fuck off and talk to the serial killer at the other end of the bar?"

The girls' stunned silence enabled them all to hear Jack's laughter at the other end of the phone.

Hayley finished her call, apologising dramatically for her friend's somewhat irrational behaviour and all eyes were firmly in Jackie's direction.

"He wasn't wearing black!" was the best excuse Jackie could muster.

"I can't believe you Jackie!" Hayley took another sip of drink, "what were you thinking?"

Jackie was struggling to come up with an excuse that would have warranted her behaviour.

"I'm not sure, I guess I didn't want to be chatting to another guy when Jack turned up."

"Well if it's any consolation," Hayley smiled at her friend, "Jack said he would have asked if you were his date but he thought you couldn't be as you seemed to be way out of his league."

"Ahh," chorused Karen and Michelle who had been enjoying the spectacle of watching Jackie writhe with embarrassment.

"He sounds nice Jackie," Karen began, "was he cute?"

"He was all right."

"Jack's lovely," confirmed Hayley

Michelle turned to her friend,

"You're always telling me how lovely Jack is, I don't know why you just don't ask him out yourself."

Now it was Hayley's turn to feel all eyes around the table focus on her.

"Oh don't be ridiculous, Jack's my best mate."

"Thanks very much!" Michelle sat back in her chair and tried to look as if she was hurt by this remark.

"Well, apart from you guys obviously," Hayley appeased her friends, "but he is. It's so nice to have a bloke for a mate."

"Why's it so good?" Michelle seemed to be developing a knack for asking pertinent questions.

Hayley had to think for a moment. It wasn't as if she had ever actually intended to find a man to have as a best friend. There hadn't been a specific incident that had led her to decide that Jack had warranted such a title. In many ways her friendship had formed with Jack just as her friendships had formed with the girls sitting around the table eagerly awaiting her answer.

"I guess it's good to have the male perspective sometimes." She sat back in her chair and took a sip of her wine. Her three friends sat motionless staring at her. "Is that it?" Karen's indignant tone voiced the general consensus.

"Well, yes, and, no I guess," Hayley was struggling a little, "the weird thing is that I don't really look at my friendship with Jack in terms of he's a bloke and I'm a girl. We're just mates."

"Nah, there's more to it than that," Michelle spoke in a very matter of fact manner, "you talk about him far too much for it to be just that. I bet, for example, that you don't say to people, 'Michelle's lovely' and look all gooey, well at least I hope not!"

Karen and Jackie laughed and nodded their agreement.

"I do not look 'all gooey' when I talk about Jack," her friends looked at each other and raised their eyebrows much to Hayley's annoyance, "oh I don't know, I can't explain it."

"Sounds like love to me!" Michelle smiled teasingly.

"Ha ha ha," Hayley was becoming a little tired of her friends' questioning around a subject about which she was suddenly feeling a little uncomfortable, "It's not love, only I guess in the same way that I love you girls. He makes me laugh, we share the same sense of humour and we're just on the same wavelength."

There was a pause as her friends slowly nodded as if fully accepting Hayley's point. It was only, however, a brief pause.

"Do you flirt?" Karen joined in the inquisition.

It was Hayley's turn to pause. The fact was that she and Jack kind of did flirt but it was all harmless. Wasn't it?

"No not really." Hayley decided this was the safest answer to give.

"Well that's no fun, you should at least flirt with the guy."

"Well I guess we do to a degree." Hayley hadn't meant to let her defences down but she had been thinking about it when the question was asked and had been caught a little off guard.

"Told you," Michelle raised her glass in affirmation of her theory, "It's love."

"No it's not!"

"Well you don't flirt with us." Jackie had a point.

"Of course I don't, you're my mates."

"So's Jack."

"But you're my girlfriends."

"So does that make Jack your boyfriend?" Michelle smiled but, sensing that Hayley was no longer enjoying this little interplay, continued, "Oh Hayles, you're so easy to wind up."

"Look," Hayley felt the need to have the final word on the subject, "Jack is a really really great guy. We get on really well. I trust him and I know he cares for me. But that's as far as it goes. He wouldn't go on these blind dates I've been setting up for him if he had any intention of going out with me, would he?"

"Well, he does tend to screw them up doesn't he."

Hayley's attempt to have the last word obviously failed.

"He could be screwing them up deliberately in the hope that eventually you'll be the only woman you know left for him to go on a date with and then he'll pounce!" Jackie was kind of enjoying the fact that she was no longer the one at the table turning pink.

Hayley took an audible deep breath.

"Right," she finished the last mouthful of her wine and began to edge her chair back as she then started to stand up, "who's for another drink?"

Her friends stared up at their friend.

"Oh come on Hayles," Michelle felt a little guilty, "seriously we're only winding you up," she reflected briefly, "well kind of."

Another sigh from Hayley who was now standing, arms folded, waiting for the next joke at her expense.

"Oh sit down for God's sake," Michelle had prefaced this comment with her own audible sigh, "Jackie will get these in, won't you Jackie?"

Jackie was so surprised at this that she just nodded her agreement and stood up,

"No problem, same again girls?"

They all nodded and Hayley slowly sat down.

"I'll give you a hand," Karen smiled and she and Jackie left Michelle and Hayley alone.

Hayley tried to avoid eye contact for a moment, just to convey her annoyance.

"Tell me you're not sulking?" Michelle stared intently making it impossible for Hayley to avoid her eyes without smiling at the realisation that she was indeed sulking.

"I might be…a little!"

Eye contact was regained.

"Look I'm sorry," Michelle genuinely was, "it's just that you do go on about Jack a lot and," she instinctively reached out and gently touched Hayley's hand, "what if this guy is actually the one for you? I mean, Christ, he sounds like all you could want from a bloke. He's funny, he's kind, he's good looking and if he's on the same 'wavelength' then surely we're talking soul mate territory here?"

Hayley squeezed Michelle's hand in thanks for her caring words,

"He is great Michelle."

"But?" Michelle sensed there was a 'but'.

"But.. I just don't feel that extra thing that would tip the balance."

Michelle grinned,

"You could ask him if you could feel the extra 'thing'?"

Hayley laughed.

"I'm pretty sure if I offered to feel his 'thing' he'd let me but tell me he was only doing it as 'a friend'!"

"Ah, you see, there is the dilemma, he may be a good friend but at the end of the day he is basically a bloke and is therefore, by definition, ruled by his cock!"

Hayley laughed,

"Actually, I may have been doing him a disservice. I don't think he would with me."

"Well," Michelle's eyes sparked, "there is one way to settle this little quandary isn't there?"

Hayley frowned.

"And what is that then?"

"You could ask him on a date."

"I'm not asking him on a .." Hayley hadn't realised Michelle hadn't finished her sentence,

"Hold on, hold on! I was going to say, you could ask him on a date that isn't really a date as such, but that was something which would mean you would spend time socially together as a couple."

Hayley scrunched up her eyes as her brain frantically tried to work out what her beaming friend was going on about.

"What?" was the best she could come up with.

"You should go out with him as a couple but without there being any assumption that you are a couple and see what happens."

Hayley's eyes were no longer scrunched but wide open in bemusement.

"Nope, you've kind of lost me still."

Michelle took a deep breath.

"Look," she spoke slowly in the hope her message would sink in this time, "I think you should ask him out in such a way that it means you will spend time together as a couple but without the pressure of it really being a date, and from that you'll hopefully be able to know whether he is just a friend or whether there is possibly more to your relationship with Jack than you actually believe there to be."

Hayley was finally beginning to grasp her friend's idea.

"Oh, and how do I do that then?" was her response, delivered with a hint of sarcasm.

"Well, you've got your niece's Christening next weekend, what better opportunity?"

Michelle smiled, raised her eyebrows and then her own glass before swallowing the last few drops and raising her eyebrows and a smile once more for good measure.

Fill Up A Bucket

Jack braked hard as the traffic lights turned to red.

"Bollocks!"

This was the third set which had lulled him into a false sense of security beaming out their green "Come on, accelerate a little harder and you're bound to make it in time!" signal from the distance as he and Hayley hurtled towards them. As they did so, the lights then had a change of heart and beamed out their orange "Actually…thinking about it again.." message before the swift red affirmation of "Ha Ha, burn rubber, sucker!" brought Jack's faint hopes that they might actually make up some time to a literally screeching halt.

Jack turned to Hayley who was haplessly fumbling around with a large open map of the local area. The annoyance and frustration that was etched on his face eased away as he realised how ridiculous she looked.

"So," he waited until he felt that he had just a smidgen of her attention.

"So," he tried again only a little louder. His initial 'So' had failed to register in Hayley's brain as she turned the map up one way, her eyes wildly scanning the squares looking for the slightest clue as to where on earth they were, before turning the map upside-down and making another desperate scan.

Still no response.

"Hayley," a smile began to encroach on Jack's face, "oh Hayley?"

The map was turned once more.

Jack decided to try a different tack.

"What the F..?" Hayley nearly jumped out of the seat as the horn wailed out, succeeding in its mission to obtain her attention. She slapped the map against Jack who had taken great delight in the sight of Hayley's complete and utter shock.

"Thank God the sun roof's not open or I could have lost you then!" Jack laughed as he pulled away past the green light that had decided they had waited long enough.

"You bastard," Hayley hit him again, "I was about to find where we were you prat."

"Of course you were."

Another playful smack.

"Yes I was actually." Hayley tried to sound convincing.

Jack looked over to her and didn't need to say a word, his facial expression sufficient to tell Hayley that both he and she knew she was never going to find where they were. Well, actually, the truth was that Jack knew she was never going to find out where they were as he had noticed some time ago that she was looking at a map of the Woking area when, in fact, the church they were looking for and indeed the road Jack was now travelling down, were in the Wokingham area. Jack had thought about telling Hayley she had got it wrong but it had been far too much fun watching her getting more and more lost in the mass of paper. This had initially grown slowly but had began to spawn at great speed as Hayley looked further into the pleats of this smallest of neatly folded map books before the print had finally cascaded out in a raging torrent of ordnance adorned sheets. Besides, as Jack had watched Hayley become more and more frustrated it had quickly dawned on him that an admission that he knew it was the wrong map could seriously put his health at risk, a thought justified following his assault after honking his horn.

"Well the good news," he broke the momentary silence, "is that I think we're on the right track now. I saw a sign for the village at the last junction. Just five miles to go hopefully."

"Thank God for that," Hayley attempted to re-fold the map but this too proved quite a difficult task, akin to trying to put a sleeping bag back into its cover after you've first used it, in short, impossible. Her attempts were brought to a premature climax as she scrunched the map into a ball and hurled it over her shoulder into the back of the car. Just prior to the rather hastened scrunching she had noticed the front of the booklet began with the words 'Woking and Surrounding Area'. She had, in a fraction of a second, made the decision that Jack did not need to know about her discovery. After all, he'd been driving around following her directions for a while and she convinced herself that it would be upsetting for him to feel he'd been led on some kind of wild goose chase. Yes indeed, and the decision not to bring this to his attention had absolutely nothing to do with the fact that ten minutes earlier she had told him just to 'keep your eyes on the road and let the brains in the car direct us where we need to go'.

Jack had watched as Hayley had hastily hurled the map into the rear of the car.

"You could have folded it neatly Hayley – we might need that when we have to find our way home." Jack tried hard not to force a smile.

"Oh, I'm sure you'll remember the way!" Hayley tried hard to force a smile.

Hayley decided it was time to change the subject and there were some key issues she felt she needed to discuss with Jack before they arrived.

"Right, Jack," she paused briefly, "I need to debrief you on certain members of my family so that today goes nice and smoothly."

Jack let out a stifled laugh.

"You make it sound like we're going on some kind of military exercise."

"It's worse than that," Hayley, much to Jack's growing concern, seemed serious, "honestly Jack, they say you can't choose your family and if you could then, well, you know when you're a kid and you have to pick teams so everyone lines up and you pick the best kids first," Jack was nodding and smiling, "and the kids who are picked last are the useless ones?"

"That's your family is it?"

"No," Hayley stared intently at Jack, "you wouldn't even ask my family to line up in the first place."

Jack wasn't sure whether to continue smiling or not. On the one hand he found this all rather amusing but on the other hand he was only a few minutes away from meeting these people. He decided to reserve judgement.

"They can't be that bad Hayles."

Hayley slumped back into her seat.

"Some of them are alright."

"Your mum's nice."

"Yeah she's normal, but she's bound to go on at you a bit."

Jack laughed.

"Does she still think we're secretly going out?"

Hayley nodded. This was a topic that she and Jack had found very amusing in the past but today she felt a little different. The fact that she had agreed with her friends to ask Jack along, in their eyes as some form of bizarre date, had suddenly made her acutely aware of any suggestion that there was more to her friendship with Jack than, well, just friendship. She mulled this over in her mind but knew that she could have easily asked Jack along without that conversation with Michelle and that neither she nor Jack would think anymore of it. Indeed when she had asked Jack if he fancied coming with her he had agreed straight away without seeing this as anything out of the ordinary at all.

Hayley's thoughts were interrupted by Jack cursing at another approaching set of traffic lights.

The car stopped.

"So you were going to debrief me," Jack turned to Hayley, "well you'd better be quick as I think the church is literally about two hundred yards past these lights."

Hayley sat upright in her seat and pulled down the sun visor on the windscreen to check her appearance.

"You look lovely dear," Jack smiled.

"Thank you."

"So who do I need to look out for then?"

Hayley's mind suddenly went into panic mode. Their car was now pulling into the church car park and her head was full of images of the more eccentric elements of her family.

Jack turned off the engine and looked once more at his friend,

"So, who do I need to look out for then?"

Hayley looked sternly back.

"All of them."

She turned, opened the door, and got out of the car.

Jack stared briefly out of windscreen.

"Oh good."

A knock at his window prompted him to get out as well.

The car park was pretty much full but there was no-one to be seen.

"How late are we?" Jack asked as he lengthened his stride in order to keep up with Hayley as she scurried along.

"Oh, fifteen minutes or so. But don't worry, we can probably sneak in at the back and no-one will notice."

They reached the large wooden doors and Hayley took a brief moment to compose herself, taking in a couple of deep breaths.

"You're not going to hyper-ventilate on me are you?" Jack's smile was swiftly removed from his face by Hayley's reciprocal scowl.

"Come on, and be quiet."

Hayley pushed on the doors.

They didn't move.

She pushed them again, only a little harder this time.

They didn't move.

Silence.

Jack was desperate to say something but felt it safer to say nothing and avoid any eye contact. He also thought it would be really good if he could somehow manage to lose the smile that was slowly and uncontrollably spreading across his face.

Hayley knew Jack wanted to say something because this situation was exactly the sort of situation that Jack would. She too wanted him to say something as this would give her a good excuse to vent some frustration by thumping him again.

She waited briefly, avoiding eye contact as well, but still Jack held firm.

In her frustration she thumped into the door this time but still to no avail.

"Oh Fuck it!" Hayley uttered rather more loudly than you would perhaps want to at the doors of a Place of Worship.

Jack's smile had now spread fully across his face and he could hold his vow of silence no longer.

"I don't think 'Fucking It' is the answer."

Hayley turned and landed a couple of smacks on Jack's arms which he had already wisely raised in order to protect his beaming face. After the initial assault he peered out from behind his hands to see Hayley standing, hands on hips, foot tapping, and desperately trying to stop her own smile from forming.

"Well, Mr SmartyPants, have you got any suggestions?"

"Well, you've pushed it hard enough, I think we're both really against the idea of fucking it..so what about," Jack grabbed the handle, "pulling it instead."

The door started to move and Jack started to smile. His smile, however, did not last too long as the door not only creaked with the kind of deep chilling echo of a creak you would expect to hear in 1970s horror film as our two heroes enter some dark deathly Gothic castle in deepest Transylvania, but it then seemed to get wedged against something and wouldn't open more than about 10 inches.

Hayley couldn't help but laugh as Jack started to yank at the door repeatedly, his best efforts moving the door the smallest of fractions on each occasion.

"Muscleman!" Hayley posed much to Jack's amusement.

Jack pulled the door twice more before deciding on a different attack.

"Sod it," and he pushed, well almost slammed, the door shut.

Both Jack and Hayley froze and the grins that had been present moments earlier fell from their faces.

"Did you hear that?" Hayley asked.

Jack didn't need to answer as the door slowly opened.

A tall elderly man in white robes stood before them. He beckoned them inside with his left hand. His right hand was trying to stem the flow of blood from his nose.

"I'm so sorry," Hayley was contrite with embarrassment, "let me see that." She started to try and prise the man's hand away from his face but the left hand that had kindly beckoned them inside swatted her hand away.

"Oh God, I'm really sorry." Jack joined in the apology.

Hayley nudged him hard to his ribs, whispering, "You can't say 'God.'"

"Oh Christ you're right." Jack genuinely didn't mean to blaspheme again.

The man in the robes pulled his hand away to inspect the damage. Both Jack and Hayley winced at the sight of the rather dis-figured nose that hung on the poor bloke's face.

"You've got blood on your robe," Hayley found herself pointing at his cuffs, "but, I guess, you can see that." She felt perhaps she should humour him a little as his continued silence was a little unnerving. "You'll need to put that on a boil wash and put some Oxy Action in with it." Now she felt that she should perhaps ask Jack for a shovel, either so she could dig herself a bigger hole, or possibly just to bang over the guy's head.

"Is everything alright?" echoed a voice from within the church.

The man in white ushered the two inside and smacked Hayley's interfering hand away from his nose once more. He then went outside.

Hayley and Jack briefly composed themselves, paused as they heard the wail of pain emanating from just outside the door and took this as their cue to hurry into the church.

"Sssh, go quietly," Hayley grabbed Jack's arm, "they might not notice us."

Somehow they both knew this simply wouldn't be the case.

They pushed through the inner doors into the chapel and were met by the turned heads of the entire congregation.

"Come in, don't be shy," boomed the priest, Father Kieran, who was standing by the font with the immediate family gathered around him. This was accompanied by a little feedback from his microphone. He tapped it a few times sending a dull thud echoing into the roof.

Hayley waved and nodded her acknowledgement. She guided Jack to the nearest pew and they went to sit down.

"Don't sit down there love."

Hayley found her complexion turn rosier as her mother's words echoed around the large walls.

"Hayley," her mother, who was standing at the front dressed in a truly ghastly floral dress, shouted once more, "come and sit at the front with your father."

The prospect of standing up and walking to the front of the church past the gaping multitudes really didn't appeal to Hayley at that precise moment and her continued embarrassment left her rooted to her seat.

"Hayley!" her mother called again. "Maurice, call her over."

Hayley's dad stood up from the front row where he had been previously enjoying some anonymity and beckoned his daughter with pleading eyes, clearly feeling the embarrassment nearly as much as her.

Hayley started the move and at that exact same moment the baby started to cry. An audible 'tut' spread through the congregation as if clearly the tears were entirely down to the young lady walking, head bowed, up the centre aisle. Jack walked a few paces behind her smiling and nodding at anyone who made eye contact.

They reached the front pew and Hayley mouthed the word "Sorry" to her sister who was rocking her baby, rather quickly Jack felt, in an attempt to stem the tears.

Through all this Father Kieran had stood with a huge, unfailing toothy grin.

"Friends, family, fellow Christians. We are all gathered here today for a very special reason," he began and surveyed his audience, "and what is that reason?"

The priest paused.

The pause went on.

Jack shuffled around in his seat and looked at the congregation. All had their heads bowed. It was very weird.

"So, my friends, what is that reason, who can tell me?" continued the priest, his cordless microphone hard against his lips.

Jack shuffled around to face the priest again, perhaps not the wisest of things to do and maybe he should have picked up on the fact that no-one else was looking at Father Kieran. Now, as things stood, he had confirmed eye contact with the preacher and there was nothing he could do about it.

"Young man," the priest walked over to Jack, "stand up now."

Hayley buried her head in her hands.

Jack just wanted to bury himself.

"Come on now," laughed Father Kieran, who Jack was swiftly coming to the conclusion was really a frustrated closet game show host, "stand up and tell everyone your name."

Jack fought against every sinew in his body and forced himself to stand. He jolted backwards as the microphone was thrust towards him and then withdrawn as the priest continued,

"So what's your name son and where're you from?"

Jack was convinced be briefly saw madness in this man's eyes.

"I'm Jack, and I'm from not very far away." He tried to smile a charming smile.

The priest pulled the microphone away and re-addressed his audience,

"Everybody, this is Jack. He's from not very far away, and he's going to tell us why we are all here today."

Before Jack could think he, once more, had the mike back in his face.

"Er…"

Jack felt the hairs on the back of his neck stand on end as the eyes that had been hidden by the bowed heads felt safe enough to come out into the open and descend upon him.

The priest nodded at Jack expectantly and thrust the microphone further towards his nostrils.

"Er…" continued Jack, "we are here to celebrate," his words were slow and deliberate as he maintained eye contact with the preacher hoping that if he started to go wrong he would be given some kind of sign, "something…very…special," the priest nodded encouragingly.

Jack nodded back and started to sit down.

"Go on.."

Jack really didn't want to, the sanctity of resting his arse on the pew was only a few centimetres away.

"And what is the special thing we are celebrating today?" The address was to the congregation but the microphone was thrust back towards Jack who was easing himself back up from his previously crouched position.

"Um, we are celebrating..the..um..birth?" the priest nodded and smiled, "of..Jesus?"

There was a gasp from the seats behind and a shake of the head from the priest.

"Oh, and, how from the birth of Jesus, we also celebrate the birth of his children," Jack was trying desperately to turn this around, "and welcome them into his church?"

Jack's relief at Father Kieran nodding again was almost audible, and, as he would reflect later, he really should have left it there and sat down,

"Because, we are all God's children, and we will all, one day, sit on his right hand next to the Holy Ghost, actually no, that can't be right, that sounds a little painful."

The embarrassment of the second gasp emanating from the crowd behind him was fortunately more than offset by the relief of the priest pulling the microphone away from Jack at breakneck speed. Jack turned to Hayley and whispered,

"I think that went well?"

Hayley was quite honest in her reply.

"Yeah?"

"Friends, family, fellow Christians, we are indeed here to celebrate welcoming Jesus's children into God's family." The priest moved back to the font and took the baby from her mother's arms. The baby responded by bursting into tears once more. Father Kieran held her up and began to pull a string of quite frankly extremely disturbing, rather than funny, faces in the misguided belief that this would alleviate the tears. The reality was that if the baby would retain any memories of this man into later life, there would be a good chance she would grow up with a deep-rooted phobia of Men of the Cloth and could quite possibly turn to some mild devil worship by way of therapy. At the very least the world was assured that in thirteen year's time there would be one more Gothic clad teenager bemoaning how depressing their lives are and hanging on Marilyn Mansun's every word. As if to back this up the baby momentarily jerked and then let out a resounding belch that was exaggerated ten-fold by the marvellous acoustics and, in doing so, sent forth the contents of the bottled milk and tinned spaghetti bolognese, digested only a couple of hours earlier, back into the world and over Father Kieran's face, hands, robes, even his ears.

Sat on the front pew, enjoying this spectacle immensely, Jack reflected that it is truly amazing just how much sick you can get out of such a small baby.

Hayley too was impressed.

"Do you think I should mention the boil wash and Oxy?"

Jack thought about this.

"Why not?"

He got up and followed the members of Hayley's family who had rushed over to help the vomit encrusted preacher as he held the baby at arm's length and tried to subtly spit the few drops of bile, that had hit him centrally in the face, away from his lips.

The reception after the Christening was in the adjoining church hall.

"I can't believe you told him he should put his clothes in with the other guy's."

Hayley bit into a small thin slice of pizza.

"It seemed like a good idea at the time, how's your pizza?"

Jack picked up the second piece that sat on Hayley's paper plate.

"Mmnn, cold and tasteless," he continued and took another bite, "delicious."

Hayley looked out into the hall. She had taken up refuge in the far corner in the hope that she and Jack could go unnoticed for the next thirty minutes or so before making a get-away.

Hayley had, however, not taken into account her Achilles heel. To remain anonymous it's a real advantage to avoid eye contact but it's very difficult to avoid eye contact if you are staring at everybody.

Her eyes wondered to the centre of the hall where her sister was rocking the baby gently in front of the grandparents, all of whom were making all the usual grandparent noises, cooing, commenting on how they remember when their kids were christened, remarking what a lovely service it was.

This last remark drew a sharp "hur" from Hayley's sister who peered out into the hall herself and almost immediately caught Hayley's eye.

Hayley smiled weakly and gave a shallow wave that was acknowledged by a frown and upturning of her sister's nose.

It didn't take a rocket scientist to work out she was cross.

Hayley turned to Jack who had just stuffed the largest prawn vol-au-vent he could find into his mouth.

"I think my sister's pissed off with you again."

Jack started to mumble "why?" but had to abort before he splattered his friend with filo pastry.

"Why do you think?"

Jack finished his mouthful, dabbed his lips with a napkin, and gave Hayley his best "what I do?" look.

"It wasn't my fault that the baby puked on the priest."

"I know, and I think Mary knows that as well."

"What then?" Jack picked up another slightly smaller vol-au-vent.

"You had to laugh didn't you."

Jack started to laugh again.

"Ah come on, you should have warned me."

Hayley smacked his arm playfully.

"What was there to warn you about? Why would I even suspect that you would find the baby's name so amusing?"

Jack was struggling not to laugh any more.

"Oh come on, you can't say you didn't laugh the first time they told you the name."

Hayley smacked Jack again, something she had found herself doing a lot over the last hour or so.

"No I didn't laugh, I think that Philippa is a lovely name."

"It is," Jack put the vol-au-vent into his wide smiling mouth, "but not if your surname's Bucket."

"Their surname's pronounced 'Bouquet' like that woman on the telly."

Jack had to let some of the pastry go this time.

"The priest said 'bucket' so it's official and besides even Tricia's husband says it's Bucket! Now every time someone calls his daughter she'll get confused and go and piss in a pot. Seriously how can you call someone Philippa Bucket, it's like calling your son Dwain if your surname's Pipe, or Russell if it's Sprout, I mean come on!"

Hayley's smile let Jack know that she had to agree with him. However, her expression was short lived as she saw her mother and grandmother approach. In truth the first thing she saw approach was her mother's ghastly dress, its floral pattern clearly inspired by her own parents' wallpaper from the early 1970s. Her Gran didn't look a lot better either, but then Grans never do. It would just seem wrong for a Gran to turn up to a Christening in anything other than a dress that they first wore when they were in their thirties. Indeed Jack had a theory that once Grans reached their thirties they were forced to settle on the one dress that they would have to wear for the rest of their lives and never take off, never, not even when they had to go to bed. This, he thought, helped explain why they smelt of wee.

"Nice outfits!" Jack whispered as they approached, faces on full beam.

"Hayley, darling," her mother spread open her arms and hugged Hayley as if she had not seen her for months.

"You alright mum?" Hayley pulled herself subtly out of the embrace.

"I'm fine my love," she paused just long enough to take in sufficient air to carry on, "oh wasn't it a lovely service! Oh it's so nice to see all the family together…."

As she spoke Jack stood motionless trying to smile back at Hayley's Gran who was staring up at him with the fixed slightly mad gaze that the onset of senility can bring. Jack didn't know whether he should say anything but was a little worried that if he did he might startle her and the last thing he needed now was to bring about the sudden cardiac induced demise of one of the elders of the family. He tried nudging Hayley who, herself, was trying to look interested in what her mother was saying.

"Oh, and Jack," Hayley's mum turned to Jack who was now able to avert his smile, "I thought your little speech was lovely."

"Really?" Jack was surprised,

"Oh yes, we are all God's children aren't we."

Jack didn't want to get into a deeply philosophical religious conversation with Hayley's mum, indeed he didn't want to get into a deep philosophical conversation with anyone ever. He had mistakenly gone down that route before with a customer who was a Jehovah's Witness. Jack hadn't been doing the job long and thought he was 'building rapport'; however, two hours later he could take no more and the interview came to a rather abrupt end when Jack concluded that 'it's all a load of bollocks isn't it Mr Brown'.

So rather than start down the road of "Yes we are all God's children aren't we," Jack opted for a diversion instead.

"That's a lovely dress you're wearing Mrs Smith."

Mrs Smith looked suitably flattered.

"Well thank you Jack, yes I love it too." Jack briefly made

eye contact with Hayley in time to see her jaw drop. "Do you know, I wanted Hayley to have worn a matching one but she refused," Mrs Smith looked genuinely dumbstruck, "can you believe it?"

Jack turned to Hayley whose jaw was still lower than usual,

"Hayley, why didn't you go for a matching dress, that would have been," he noticed her eyes narrowing, "lovely!"

"Ah, Jack, you're so nice." Mrs Smith grabbed his arm, "Oh Hayley when are you going to snap this young man up?"

"Mum!" Hayley sounded like an embarrassed teenager.

"Oh, you'd make such a lovely couple," her mum was now gushing.

"Really, Mrs Smith, Hayley and I are just best friends," Jack made his rescue attempt, "honestly, your daughter is far too good for me."

"Ahh, Jack you're so sweet, isn't he Ma?" Mrs Smith turned to her mother who was still maintaining her exact position and fixed inane grin.

No response.

Just a grin.

Jack looked on, shuffling his hands with mild embarrassment, as Mrs Smith leant down and practically shouted into the ear of her mother in a deep slow deliberate voice,

"Mother! I said Jack's so sweet isn't he? Don't you think he and our Hayley make a nice couple?"

The old woman nodded and stretched up towards Jack beckoning him to lean down to hear her speak.

He obliged, but really needn't have taken the trouble as this tiny woman possessed a voice that carried right up into the roof of the hall and into the ears of the chattering guests.

"So, do you want to give her one?"

You could hear a pin drop.

Jack froze, his brain uncertain what instruction to send to his face in order that an appropriate expression could cross it, and completely lost for what words to send to his mouth that perched nervously ajar on top of his lowered jaw.

Mrs Smith and Hayley were equally stunned and unable to voice anything other than a couple of nonsensical murmurs and panicked glances, looking for the nearest available exit.

Jack could do no more than remain transfixed by Hayley's Gran but noticed her eyes seemed suddenly alive. Jack sensed a change in the old woman as the spark in her eyes grew brighter. He almost jumped when, suddenly, she winked at him.

"So, are you going to give her one," she paused briefly, just long enough to hear another gasp from the other side of the hall, before concluding, "of your vol-au-vents?"

There was a simultaneous sigh of relief from around the hall. Jack found himself nodding admiringly at the little frail lady in front of him as she winked once more and promptly helped herself to one of the vol-au-vents waiting expectantly on Jack's plate.

"Come on Ma," Hayley's mum felt it an opportune time to beat a hasty retreat, "let's go and look at the baby."

"Again?" Rather ironically the old lady sounded just like Jack did as a child at the thought of having to visit his own Grandma. She turned to follow her daughter before turning back to face Hayley and Jack for one last time. Fortunately she was a little more discreet this time.

"If I were 50 years younger I'd give him one!" she cackled

mischievously and hurried away in pursuit of Hayley's mum.

"I'm so sorry Jack." Hayley was almost doubled up in embarrassment, "I think she's gone a bit, you know, do-lally!"

Jack couldn't help but watch the little old lady walk away to re-commence her assumed role as daft old biddy.

"Your Gran's fantastic!"

Hayley wasn't quite expecting that.

"Really?"

Jack smiled and let out a low snigger as he watched her Gran steal a vol-au-vent off an unsuspecting guest's plate,

"Yeah, she's utterly mad."

"Gran?" Hayley looked over in the direction Jack was staring, just in time to see her Gran turn to them and point at the back of the elderly aunts who were fussing over the baby. She raised her extended palm in front of her face and mimed an overtly bored yawn.

Robin Hood

Hayley smiled at the cashiers and mouthed 'Morning' as she made her way through the office on her way to start another week of tedium at the bank.

She was just relieved that after eighteen months she had managed to get into a routine whereby as her alarm clock clicked onto 7 am, the radio blared forth, that she also clicked, albeit just, into autopilot. Her brain was able to remain largely disengaged having sent out its pre-programmed instructions for her to get out of bed, wander bleary-eyed to the shower, put too much shower gel into her hands resulting in some spillage and a mild cursory "fuck it". She would then rub her aforementioned bleary eyes until they reached the status of 'not-so-bleary' before slouching back into her bedroom to put on the clothes she had sensibly left out the preceding evening. A light coating of make-up was followed by an equally light helping of the latest fad cereal claiming to possess the power to help Hayley maintain her figure and health (as long as used in conjunction with a calorie controlled diet obviously). Finally she would sip from a cup of herbal tea before dispersing the majority of it down the sink, which is where it truly deserved to be, and then proceed to wander outside and clamber into her car to make the ten minute drive into the town centre car park.

From there she would walk past the string of shops offering various deals on various similar looking garments which she would decide she liked one day but about which by the end of the week would have changed her mind on at least three occasions. Next she would turn a corner into the pedestrianised town square where autopilot was finally turned off as the bank came into sight and it was too late for her to change her mind and turn around.

This morning had followed this usual course and now she found herself trying to convince herself that, even though it was Monday, it would soon be the weekend.

"Morning Hayley." Ken was already sitting at his desk.

"Morning," Hayley responded and sat herself down.

"You're looking a bit smart today Ken." Hayley couldn't help but notice Ken was wearing a new suit and was adjusting an equally new brightly coloured tie. The suit was hard to miss and, although clearly 'new' and no doubt from a designer label as was Ken's style, was perhaps a little outdated and the like of which hadn't been seen in a bank since Miami Vice was the biggest draw on television. Hayley decided against passing any judgement over the suit and instead led with the more obvious, "got an interview?"

"No," Ken continued to adjust his tie, "don't you remember? Mr Horsefield is visiting the office today."

Mr Horsefield was the Area Director. He would swan in from time to time with a huge false grin emblazoned over his smug face and words of wisdom for the poor unfortunate members of staff who hadn't been either clever or quick enough to find creative ways of avoiding having to listen to him.

Had it not been Monday morning Hayley wouldn't have forgotten the visit. Had it been any other day then the Office Manager would have been around to each section the previous evening reminding them of the importance of 'creating the right impression' and of 'being positive'. Hayley felt that he would gain far more respectability if he would simply be honest with the staff and remind them of the importance of 'don't let on how crap we're all feeling' and 'please lie to him and don't call him a wanker to his face'.

"Oh good," Hayley let out a deep sigh, "how wonderful."

"Yep," Ken sat up and straightened his tie once more. "well, got to look the part haven't we."

Hayley stared at Ken as he checked out his appearance in the reflection from his blank monitor.

"My God," Hayley started to get up, "you're serious aren't you."

"Yep." Ken, finally happy with his appearance, decided to actually turn his monitor on. "Certainly am - oh, and coffee two sugars if you're going."

Hayley was and made her way slowly to the kitchen in search of a strong coffee to give her a caffeine induced kick-start to the day.

The kitchen, although a glum, bland room, was a popular place in the bank. Despite the obscene profits that they turned over year after year the bank had taken the decision that to invest in a coffee machine would be just too costly. This decision had given the branch staff the opportunity to while away numerous hours 'getting the coffees in'. The most expert exponents could often spend in excess of 40 minutes in the kitchen if they managed to canvass enough requests for a drink. These experts would also be able to convince everyone that they were doing them a favour by quenching their thirsts whilst they carried on working when in fact, had the experts just stayed at their posts to share the burden of the work, then everyone could have probably spared the time to actually get away from their desks for a proper break themselves.

"Morning gorgeous!"

Jack grabbed his mug from the cupboard and placed it next to the two waiting patiently by the warming kettle.

"Hiya," Hayley stifled a yawn, "you alright?"

"Not bad," Jack opened the cutlery drawer and handed Hayley a spoon, "are you going to use this today – I hate it when you just use your fingers, as my ex-girlfriend once said to me!"

Hayley took the spoon and shook her head at Jack.

"Is that why she is an 'ex' and not a current girlfriend then?"

"Nah," Jack pulled the lead from the kettle that was bubbling away, "she's an 'ex' because I hated it that she only ever used her fingers!"

"You're such a bloke aren't you!" Hayley took the kettle and started to fill the mugs.

"Ah, I'm only joking." Jack wondered if he had offended Hayley.

"So was I." Hayley stirred the drinks and handed Jack his coffee.

The two friends slowly made their way back to their desks where Ken had just about finished preening himself yet again.

"Morning Ken." Jack sat himself down before realising that there was something different about his colleague this morning. He sat back in his seat, put his hands behind his head, and squinted towards Ken as he tried to work out what the difference was.

Ken was tapping away at his computer initially oblivious

to the stares being directed his way. His attention was soon obtained however as Jack started to make humming noises and rub his chin.

"What?" Ken huffed as he felt obliged to stop his typing.

Jack continued to rub his chin.

"There's something different about you today Ken."

Ken tutted and went back to his typing.

Hayley sipped at her coffee and put Jack out of his misery.

"It's a new suit Jack."

"Aah," Jack nodded before concluding that, "no that's not it."

Ken huffed once more as he again felt forced to stop what he was doing. He looked crossly over at Jack,

"Yes, it's a new suit, so go on, say something funny about it then."

Jack raised his palm in his defence,

"No, no Ken. It's a lovely suit. It suits you."

Ken didn't trust his friend and started to move his hands over his keyboard.

"I just wish next time you want us to have an 80s theme day you let me know in advance."

"Ha ha," Ken didn't know why he had even started to continue with his work, "Jack, the trouble with you is that you have no appreciation of true style and fashion."

"That's true I guess." Jack wasn't the type of guy to get too worked up over designer clothes although he also wasn't the type of guy to look like he bought all his clothes from the market stall, "I haven't got your sense of style. And I think it's great that you've chosen to wear that today. I'm a big Duran Duran fan as well."

Ken shook his head in pity at his friend.

Jack responded by bursting into a chorus of 'Her Name is Rio.'

Ken carried on typing as he waited for Jack's rather tuneless rendition to end.

"I'm glad you're smiling at the moment my friend as the word is that Horsefield's visit today is to see us."

Jack too had forgotten about the visit but wasn't unduly concerned.

"Ah that's okay, I'm doing alright at the moment. I had a good week last week."

"Ah, but the word is that his visit is because we are coming under some scrutiny over the quality of our lending as opposed to how much we're selling."

Ken smiled to himself and enjoyed the silence from across the desk.

The thing is that Jack was a good salesman. He could close a deal but what made him good was that he also didn't look to rip any one off. So, to be more accurate, Jack felt he was a good salesman because he got good results and kept some degree of integrity. The bank, however, felt that Jack was an average salesman because yes, he got good results, but he also attached too much importance to the concept of 'integrity' and therefore did not maximise his selling opportunities.

Lending, however, was perhaps not an area that Jack should be working in. It wasn't that Jack didn't grasp the basic concepts of sound basic lending; after all, this was essentially straightforward – if you lend someone some money are they going to be able to pay it back? Jack understood this perfectly and his decision making on this was really actually exceptionally good. The problem he had was that he was a nice bloke. Being a nice bloke and having to decide whether to lend people money that isn't specifically your money can present an interesting moral dilemma. Jack had found himself in the middle of this dilemma on many an occasion and he had, on more than one of these occasions, decided to show great faith in his customer's promises at the expense of his professional opinion. This had in turn led to some mockery from his colleagues when a number of these decisions didn't quite pan out as well as Jack would have hoped. By the same token a fair percentage of them did turn out right and it was these that enabled Jack to justify continuing with his particular method.

"You're very quiet Jack," Ken had enjoyed the silence, "should I 'save a prayer for you now'?"

Jack found himself having to acknowledge Ken with a smile.

The phone ringing disturbed Jack from his thoughts.

"Jack."

"Morning Martin how are you?"

His boss ignored his attempt at social chit chat.

"Jack, you're seeing Mr Horsefield at 9.30, Hayley's due at 10.30 and Ken will be after lunch."

Jack was a little taken aback by the impending nature of his meeting.

"Do I need to bring anything?"

"Just plenty of excuses I would suggest."

Jack was left holding the phone to his ear as it went dead. He was touched by Martin's words of encouragement. Jack wasn't quite sure where Martin had perfected his motivational techniques; he was, after all, not old enough to have actually served in the Third Reich.

"You've gone white Jack," Hayley observed from her desk.

"Oh, I've got to see old Horse Face at 9.30."

"Shit."

"Yep – and you're due at 10.30."

"Shit." Hayley felt herself losing some colour although, to be fair, it may have been that anyone would have looked pale when in close proximity to Ken's tie.

"When am I seeing Mr Horsefield?" Ken was now happy to join in the conversation.

"He doesn't want to see you Ken."

Ken's face dropped, much to Jack's amusement.

"What do you mean he doesn't want to see me?"

Jack eased himself up out of his chair and slowly stretched his arms towards the ceiling, giving Ken plenty of time to sit open-mouthed awaiting the reason for the Area Director's decision to spurn him.

" I don't know," Jack moved his head around his shoulders to ease some of the tension that had suddenly appeared in the last couple of minutes, "but I don't think it's about lending."

Ken's expression changed to one of surprise.

"It's not?"

"Nope."

Jack motioned as if to carry on but decided it would be more fun just to sit down and say nothing.

Ken watched in dismay as Jack did just that and coolly started to thumb through his diary.

"And he doesn't want to see me?" Ken was more than a little perplexed. "Are you sure Jack?"

Jack looked over at Ken's furrowed brow and couldn't help but think that its creases were exaggerated by his unnaturally smooth crinkle-free suit. He stood up and gathered his folders.

"Well actually, apparently he does want to see you but he's just waiting to get Head Office to deliver his time machine so he can go back to 1983."

Hayley couldn't help but laugh at Ken's inability to avoid splurting out "Oh Fuck off" as Jack walked past him, patted Ken's head with his folders and trudged off to what would prove an awkward and uncomfortable sixty minutes of attempted misdirection, relentless bullshitting and hastily improvised excuses. All this culminated in Mr Horsefield expressing his concern that Jack would appear to see himself as something of a modern day Robin Hood. Jack was actually quite impressed with the astuteness of his Director's summary; however, in a moment of unusually good sense Jack opted to laugh off this suggestion making some remark about 'tights not being his thing'.

Jack sat in the corner of the staff room, his feet resting on the wooden coffee table, and stared into space as he slowly munched his way through his sandwiches. He wasn't thinking about much in particular, his thoughts seeming to dash from one subject to another with no real logical pattern.

His attention was diverted as Hayley made her way over to join him.

"How did it go?" Jack moved his legs away so Hayley could get past and sit down in the comfy chair next to him.

"Okay," Hayley sighed as she took the lid off the Tesco's pre-packed prawn and pasta salad, "but, I have to tell you, he didn't compare me to any folk heroes at all."

Jack laughed.

"Honestly, he told me to send Maid Marion down to see him!"

Hayley gave him a fake disbelieving look and started to eat her lunch.

"I'm a bit upset he compared me to Robin Hood," Jack continued. "I think if he was going to go down the 'folk hero' line he could have gone one step further and gone into the 'superhero' genre. That way he could have compared me to Batman or Superman!"

"Yeah, cos' they were shit at lending as well." Hayley paused her eating and reached for the carton of orange juice she had placed on the table.

"Okay, well, perhaps I could be 'Bankman' – he's like Batman, but his costume's not quite as extreme."

"You mean you don't wear your pants on the outside of your trousers?" Hayley smiled as she peered into the plastic container in front of her looking for a prawn to harpoon with her plastic fork.

"Yes, that would mean too much pressure to ensure I have clean underwear on every day. And I guess I wouldn't have a Batmobile either, or a Bat mask, or," Jack was coming to the conclusion that perhaps this initially amusing idea was fundamentally floored, "a Bat utility belt."

"Ah," Hayley finally speared a prawn that had been hiding behind a pasta shell and cucumber cube, "but you could wear one of those masks the footballers wear when they've had eye or nose fractures, and, you may not have a utility belt, but you have a pouch where you can keep all the bank door and safe keys and that go onto your belt."

Jack thought about this image for a moment.

"Nah, actually, Bankman's shit!"

"Yep," Hayley nodded as she took another sip of drink, "who wants a superhero whose main weapon is that he can sell you house insurance?"

"True." Jack nodded and picked up his cup of coffee.

"Hey, thanks for a good time at the weekend by the way, it was a good laugh."

Hayley put the empty container down on the table.

"Yeah, it was, how should we say, interesting!"

"No it was good," Jack smiled at his friend, "seriously, I think your family are great."

"Thanks, they love you don't they." Hayley was relieved at Jack being so nice about the weekend as at times, during its course, she had wanted the earth to open up and swallow her. "Honestly, all I heard last night was my mum going on about you and what a fine son-in law you'd make."

Hayley laughed an embarrassed laugh.

"That's terrible," Jack put on his best 'shocked' face, "your sister's already married and has just had a kid!"

"Ha ha!" Hayley smacked Jack on his arm, "don't worry, I told her we were best friends, just like you did on the day."

This was a remark Hayley would, until a week or so ago, have made without a second thought. But today, and much to her concern, she found herself waiting to critically analyse Jack's response, listening out for any slight variation in his tone or inflection that would perhaps suggest in some small way that he may just might view their relationship as potentially more than just the best friends that they both already knew they were.

Having built herself up for this, she was a little taken aback when Jack did not address her comment at all.

"Hey, listen, I have a favour to ask of you now."

Jack leaned forward and smiled hopefully at Hayley, who found herself leaning forward towards him.

"Go on."

"Well, you know that I went with you to the Christening at the weekend." Hayley nodded, curious as to where this was going. "Well, by pure coincidence," Jack paused and avoided his aim of not looking guilty, "well, coincident-ish, I have to go to my cousin's wedding a week next Saturday and I'd really like it if you'd come with me, please?"

Hayley was momentarily speechless and was even more shocked when she became acutely aware she was beginning to blush.

This was not lost on Jack either who instinctively, and with an unexpected sense of surprise, felt he should clarify the situation and put his friend at ease straightaway.

"Oh, obviously not as a 'date' or anything like that." He looked a little embarrassed. "Oh, sorry, I didn't mean anything by it."

Hayley now felt even more embarrassed herself, both because she was now beginning to actually light up the corner of the room with her glow and because she felt she had embarrassed Jack.

"Don't be silly Jack, of course I didn't think you meant it as a date!"

"Oh," Jack joined in the awkward fake laugh, "good, sorry. I think it just came out wrong. The thing is we had a great laugh at the weekend and, and please believe me that this isn't the real reason 'cos I know this sounds bad, but if I go with a beautiful woman – and that's you by the way – then my family are not going to try and set me up with anyone there!"

"Ah, so you're using me?" Hayley knew this wasn't the case but wanted to divert some of the heat away from herself.

"No, not at all. In fact," Jack tapped her knee, "if you're lucky perhaps I'll set you up with a date with one of my mates who'll be there."

This was not what Hayley was expecting to hear. Her mind was suddenly crammed with confusion once more. To make matters worse, another wave of pink was rushing through her.

"Oh no, it's alright Jack. Seriously, I'm not looking for any blind dates at the moment. I'm quite happy as I am."

Jack looked warmly at his friend.

"I don't understand it Hayles."

"What?"

"How someone as lovely as you hasn't been snapped up a long time ago."

Hayley returned an awkward smile.

"Ah, I guess I haven't found the right guy yet, and besides," she patted Jack on his knee as she stood up, "hey I don't need a proper boyfriend as I have you."

Jack shrugged as he too started to stand up.

"Great – a platonic boyfriend. All of the grief and none of the sex."

"That's right! Now stop moaning and go and make me a coffee."

"Yes darling."

Jack made his way into the kitchen. Hayley stood and watched him. As soon as she became aware that she was casting her eyes over his frame she averted them and the voice in her head chastised her and sent her back to her desk.

This was a strange feeling for Hayley. She was normally

self-assured and her relationship with Jack was something that was genuinely really good in her life. In the past when she had become friendly with men it had very quickly developed in their eyes into something more than just the friendship that Hayley sought. Jack was different. They had an understanding where they both instinctively knew that they would always be the best of friends. In many ways Hayley almost felt that the depth of her friendship with Jack was something she shouldn't expect from a prospective partner. She couldn't quite understand the logic behind this because surely, if you could have such a good friendship and be lovers at the same time, then that must be as happy as anyone could ever be. Hayley sat at her desk thinking this through and briefly allowed herself to imagine what such a relationship would feel like. Her breath quickened as she pictured her and Jack together.

The voice in her head chastised her once more.

The Bridesmaid

Saturdays in July are never quite as warm and sunny as you would hope. Well, the ones where you are planning to do something aren't like that anyway. Last year Jack had planned a weekend camping down at the coast and had ended up bailing out the water from his tent with a plastic mug whilst cursing profoundly and swearing it would be the last time he went away in July. This promise was broken the following weekend when he and a group of friends went on a paint balling expedition which, as the thunder clouds opened, turned into a fight for survival, running from the cover of one tree to another screaming "Fucking Hell!" as several of the aforementioned trees in close proximity were hit by the violent electric bolts. Despite this the group still decided, against the good advice of the group leaders, not to get out into the open.

"We'll be fucking open targets then lads," was the general consensus, although Jack's team hadn't realised that their opposing team had shown the good common sense to get themselves back to the base camp and agree a refund on the premise that "we're not going to stand under trees and wait to be fried". Had Jack's team realised this then they may not have continued to run from one combusting fern to another for the next three hours in search of a foe who were now happily ensconced in the Beech Arms five miles down the road getting happily bladdered.

Jack had shown the good sense to decline any invitation to go out for the last two weekends of the month, convinced that somehow his own personal movements were responsible for the nation's weather and that therefore the only way to guarantee sunshine would be for him to stay inside. It was a noble and selfless act, if a little psychotic.

So, taking last year's events into consideration, it went some way to explaining Jack's appearance when Hayley opened her door on the morning of the wedding.

"Jack, why are you wearing a rain mac?"

"It's July."

"Yes," Hayley peered up at the beautiful clear azure sky and then back at Jack, "and, if the weather men are to be believed, this is going to be the hottest weekend of the year."

"Ah, but they said that last year, and look what happened."

"Jack, at least put your hood down."

Hayley closed the door behind her and strode past Jack towards his car. She was wearing an airy white summer dress that hugged her curves as it was caught by the light morning breeze.

"That's a beautiful dress Hayles." Jack caught her up and opened the door for her.

"Thankyou," Hayley thought so too but was pleased Jack had noticed, "and that's a beautiful bright red and blue rain mac."

"Ha ha." Jack made his way round to the driver's side and sat himself uncomfortably down as the plastic coat crumpled at his back.

"Seriously Jack," Hayley was sure she would not be able to cope with the constant rustling if he continued to wear the coat, let alone deal with the embarrassment if he actually got out of the car wearing it, "you look ridiculous. It's not going to rain. Just look outside for God's sake. I haven't seen a cloud for three days let alone one that's going to have a secret stash of water which it's earmarked for you. Please take off the coat."

Jack huffed before adhering to the request.

"Do you promise it's not going to rain then?"

"Yes!"

"Good," Jack smiled and unwound the sun roof, "then I can let some air in here, it's bloody baking today."

Hayley laughed as they pulled away.

"I'm getting a bit of déjà-vu," she began, "do you know the way or do you want me to read a map?"

Jack grinned as he pulled out onto a roundabout and headed off to the A road that would take them to the wedding.

"No, I know the way fortunately. And besides, I only have a map for the actual town we're going to and I know you much prefer the challenge of trying to get us somewhere reading a map for a completely different place in the country."

Hayley smacked Jack's arm.

"Woking, Wokingham. It was an easy mistake to make!"

Jack glanced at Hayley and nodded totally unconvincingly at her excuse.

The country house where the wedding was being held was set in the most beautiful grounds. The elegant tall trees that flanked the long drive up to the main house stood suited and booted to attention saluting the guests as they made their way to the gathering.

Hayley stared out of the window lost in her own thoughts. There was something surreal and unquestionably romantic about the day. The setting was sublime, the weather was as perfect as you could ever wish, and the crystal clear skies provided the perfect framing to the perfect scenery. There was a hint of a cooling breeze ready to gently sooth you if you began to feel the heat from the accommodating sun, and the occasion was the happiest of events that was always guaranteed to have women sighing and briefly grasping onto the notion that the perfect world actually did exist.

"Fuck!!"

Hayley's idyllic thoughts were rather rudely disturbed as Jack winced and cursed each small stone that hurled itself in a relentless attack on the defenceless paintwork of his car as he made his way over the potholed gravelled car park.

"Bollocks! Christ you can almost hear the underside of my car crying!" The car dived in and out of another crater. "Shit, did you hear that? That wasn't a stone, that was my car wincing."

"'Fuck, bollocks, shit,' you say the sweetest things Jack."

Jack held off his reply as he carefully pulled the car into the nearest space he could find.

"Sorry," he turned off the engine and turned his ear towards the steering wheel, "listen, I'm sure I can hear a little whimper."

Hayley gathered her skirt and opened her door.

"That's strange, as the only whining I can hear isn't coming from the car, now come on let's go."

Jack looked slightly indignant but did as he was told.

"So," Hayley began, as she cautiously looked to negotiate her way over the treacherous pebbles and rocks that lay between her and the comfort of the softly-barked pathway that led towards the open pavilion where a throng of busy chattering summer-skirted and suited people were sipping from their champagne flutes, "you've kept quite quiet about your family Jack, whoops.." she flung out her hand to grab onto Jack as her balance was momentarily lost.

Jack caught her hand and kicked away the offending rock.

"Well," he scrunched up his nose as he squinted towards the sun reflecting in the large pavilion windows, "there's not a lot to say really. They're all, well, quite normal."

Hayley looked a little disappointed.

"What, so no mad aunties, drunk lecherous uncles, spotty delinquent gothic-clad cousins, senile grandparents, screaming toddlers or interfering overbearing parents trying to marry every other singleton off?"

Jack offered his hand to Hayley once more to help her up the small step out of the car park and on to the path.

"Well, obviously we've got those."

"Ah, so 'quite normal' then."

The two friends exchanged a laugh and made their way towards the crowd.

"Danny!" Jack shouted and waved enthusiastically towards a group of smartly cloned suits, and in doing so almost causing Hayley to jump out of her skin in surprise.

Danny turned around, champagne in hand, and beamed towards his friend.

"Jack!" he strode purposely down the pathway moving his glass into his left hand so he could give his friend a warm and firm handshake.

"Ah, it's great to see you Jack."

Hayley stood next to Jack, waiting patiently to be introduced.

"You only saw me on Wednesday Danny! I take it the nerves have kicked in?"

Danny took a sip from his glass, a deep breath and then announced,

"Yep, this is my fourth glass."

"Christ mate, no more!"

"I'm joking," Danny smiled and turned to Hayley who was still waiting patiently for her introduction.

"Hi," Danny offered his hand, "I'm Danny, but you probably worked that out when Jack called me Danny."

"Ah yes," Hayley smiled and shook his hand, "I had worked that out, but it's nice of you to confirm it for me!"

"Oh, I'm sorry guys," Jack was extremely apologetic, "Danny, this is Hayley. Hayley, this is.."

"Danny?" Hayley completed his sentence.

"Hayley, it's lovely to meet you. Jack has told me all about you."

Hayley was momentarily lost for words.

"He has?"

"Well not 'all' about you I guess, but he does go on a bit I must tell you."

Hayley looked at Jack who shrugged his shoulders,

"What can I say, my life is very dull Hayley and often you are the only thing I can think of to talk about!"

Jack cowered away in anticipation of the thump that duly arrived accompanied by a couple of stifled expletives and a hearty laugh from Danny who then escorted the two down into the pavilion.

The room was alive with laughter and a constant stream of excited conversation, fuelled by several waiters patrolling the room with their trays of champagne, Bucks Fizz and fruit punch. The well drilled staff ensured that there were no empty glasses in hands and as such, and much to the approval of their manager, also ensured that the bill for the wedding increased by the minute.

A wedding where Hayley could remain largely anonymous was basically all her Christmases rolled into one. This was a haven for people watchers. Obviously Hayley was not alone in this pursuit as there were many women there and all were clearly showing a keen interest in everyone else. In the far corner of the room one elderly gentleman made the mistake of saying to his wife,

"Dorothy, don't be so nosey."

At this point it seemed as if every pair of women's eyes descended not upon Dorothy, but upon her husband who stood bewildered wondering why the chorus of 'tutting' was directed at him. He clearly had no idea that he should never draw attention to his wife's voyeurism, or indeed that at family gatherings 'people watching' was actually a pack pursuit. In his defence this was very much a secret society where the unwritten rule was that you never disclosed this fact to any man. Whilst Dorothy's husband was oblivious to what was going on Jack, on the other hand, and no doubt due to his time spent with Hayley, was a little more switched on. He had pondered whether women would actually make notes on what they had observed and, because they could not discuss this in front of men, and in order that they can compare notes, that this is the reason why women always seem to go the toilets in pairs.

"So Jack," Danny grinned at his friend, "have you seen who one of the bridesmaids is?"

Jack stopped his lips just short of his glass and hesitated

whilst his brain tried to hurtle through all the reasons why Danny would have just said what he just said.

Hayley too was briefly distracted from the view of Dorothy shaking her head at her husband and disappearing off to the toilets with one of her new-found friends.

Jack's brain, not quite able to resolve the puzzle, instructed his eyes to dart about the room in search of anyone in a cream dress looking slightly envious of the bride. He spotted a couple and stared at them for a moment.

"Not them Jack!" Danny couldn't help but laugh at Jack's growing panic, "Christ they're only about five! Over there," Danny pointed with his glass to the French doors in the side of the pavilion where, gracefully stepping into the room, was a beautiful young woman, "that's who."

Jack stared over at the lady who was smiling sweetly and looking a little embarrassed at all the compliments that were descending upon her as she made her way through the room.

"Wow, she looks lovely Jack," Hayley felt a tinge of envy, "who is she?"

Jack paused and took a rather large gulp of his wine leaving Danny to answer the question. He leant over to Hayley.

"That's Imogen."

"Imogen?"

"Imogen," Danny seemed a little bemused that the name meant nothing to Hayley, "Jack's ex."

Hayley paused and took a rather large gulp of her wine.

She took another mouthful as Imogen looked over in their direction and waved shyly at Jack. Jack smiled back and acknowledged her by raising his glass and then turning as quickly as he could, without appearing rude, to Danny and Hayley.

"Er, so you were saying Danny, er, something?"

"Yes. I was saying that had you seen who one of the bridesmaids was, but, clearly you have now."

"She's beautiful Jack," Hayley had composed herself after yet another large intake of alcohol, "you've never mentioned her before."

Jack looked a little embarrassed. Seeing Imogen after three years was a little unexpected to say the least.

"No, well," he rolled his shoulders to try and ease some of the anxiety that had suddenly stretched itself over his body, "it was a long time ago and sometimes somethings are better left in the past."

"Oh, sorry, was it a bit of a disaster?" Hayley could sense Jack's unease.

Jack hesitated with his answer, mainly because he was trying to work out if he should admit to why it was a disaster. He needn't have worried, however, as Danny once more replied on his behalf.

"If your definition of a 'disaster' is breaking up with someone – who you've told your mates is the best sex you've ever had – just because you feel things are moving a little too fast, then I think it probably was."

It was Hayley's turn to fall silent.

"It was a long time ago, I guess I got a little scared. But," Jack couldn't help but glance over to Imogen who was now chatting to the father of the bride who had himself just stumbled into the pavilion having already knocked back four glasses of champagne, "you know, sometimes when you meet someone great it's just not the right time to have met them. She deserved better than me back then anyway."

"And anyway," Danny broke the unexpected air of

tension that had suddenly descended on their little corner of the room, "Jack's got you now Hayley!" He nudged her gently.

"Don't you start!" Hayley fell out of her silence, "that's all we got when we went to a Christening a couple of weeks ago."

"So this is your second 'family event' then?" Danny's question was clearly loaded, "ah, and you wonder why people might think you're a couple!"

Jack smiled, "We're just best mates!" He put his arm around Hayley and planted a small kiss on Hayley's cheek with, "aren't we darling!"

"Yes," Hayley wiped her cheek dry, "you big tart."

Danny just looked at them both and started to nod his head knowingly, unable to stop the grin spreading over his face.

"Yes, of course you are."

The banter continued briefly until Hayley noticed that Jack was once again looking a little uneasy.

"Are you okay?"

"Yep," Jack stared past his friend, "but be warned," his stare turned into a slightly forced smile, "here comes my mother."

Hayley instinctively turned around and found herself looking at the scariest, and most enormous of pink hats bounding towards them.

She wasn't sure whether to run for cover or continue to try and conceal her desire to explode into laughter at the ridiculous sight that was now only matter of feet away from her.

As the hat got nearer Hayley could make out that there was indeed a small woman underneath it, and, as the small woman literally shouted her greeting across to Jack, could also work out that this was Jack's mum.

"Jack," his mum cast her eyes excitedly around the room, "isn't it a beautiful place. The perfect setting!"

"Yes mum," Jack was torn between looking apologetically towards Hayley and the fact that, despite the numerous social flaws his mother managed to possess, she was, after all, his mother and he loved her. There was therefore no need to be embarrassed – or so he was trying to convince himself.

Needless to say Jack looked apologetically towards Hayley who once more found herself concealing the pending explosion within.

"Yes, it's a beautiful place. Anyway mum, let me introduce you to my friend Hayley."

The large hat turned towards Hayley.

"Ah, Hilary, I've heard so much about you!" Jack's mum grabbed Hayley's hand fondly.

"It's 'Hayley' mum." Jack leant forward to correct his mother.

"I know that!" His mother gave him a chastening look which swiftly gave way to a wide smile as she addressed Hayley once more,

"Sorry, as I was saying 'Hilary'," she looked over to her son as she emphasised the name, still completely oblivious to the fact that she had got it wrong again, a fact that Jack decided he could overlook on this occasion, "I've heard so much about you. My Jack is always talking about you!"

Hayley looked at Jack who was mouthing the words 'I'm so sorry' and shaking his head.

"Well, Jack is always talking about you as well Mrs Matthews."

Quite why Hayley had said this she had no idea as Jack seldom mentioned his mother and she swiftly found herself regretting it.

"Ah bless him," Jack's mum paused momentarily to afford her son a brief smile before returning her gaze to Hayley, "what sort of things does he say about me?"

Hayley's panicked glance over to Jack was wasted as he was already burying his head in his hands.

"Well, you know," Hayley, the proverbial rabbit caught in the headlights, began to dig herself into the hole that Jack had foreseen prior to burying his head in his hands, "he says how much he misses being at home."

"Really?" his mum looked quite genuinely shocked. "Jack," she looked at her son who had removed his head from his hands on hearing Hayley's last comment as he needed it to shake at Hayley in a desperate attempt to stop her from speaking, "you know you can come back at any time. We've still got your old room. You should have said something to me, not confide in Hilary."

Hayley tried to repair some of the damage.

"Well Mrs Matthews, when he says he misses being at home, what he really means is that it's easier at home as everything is done for him."

"Oh," the stern disappointed tone followed by an equally stern frown that began to wrinkle itself across Jack's mother's face was a fair indication to Hayley that she was again stumbling down the wrong path,

"and, whilst he misses that to a degree," Hayley's well practised bull shitting, developed out of necessity to survive in the bank, kicked into auto pilot, "Jack told me that he wanted to stand on his own two feet because you had done

so much for him in the past." Hayley noted a slight un-
furrowing of the brow in front of her, "and Jack knew that it
was time for you to have some time back for yourself."

"Oh." Jack's mother was momentarily lost for words. She
turned to her son and then back to Hayley and then, as the
tear began to squeeze itself free from the side of her eye, she
fumbled awkwardly in her handbag for a tissue. Hayley
stepped backwards – partly to avoid the large hat that was in
danger of knocking her over as Jack's mother continued her
search in the depths of her bag, but mainly to pick up a
napkin from the table immediately behind her.

"Here you are Mrs Matthews."

This merely served to set the woman off again.

"Oh Jack." She moved over to her son and placed her
hands on his cheeks and leant forward to kiss him.

Obviously she missed in her first attempt, the rim of her
hat bashing into Jack's forehead, prompting Hayley to force a
small cough in order to camouflage her inadvertent giggle
and Danny, who had been enjoying himself observing the
goings on, to partially choke on his wine.

The second attempt, with some delicate manoeuvring,
was successful. His mother turned to Hayley again and
reached for her hand.

"You're a lovely girl Hilary, Jack's very lucky to have
you."

"Mum!" Jack started to interrupt but it was too late. His
mother had released Hayley's hand and was wondering off in
search of a friend to accompany her to the Ladies.

"Wow," Hayley watched her move off into the distance
before turning back to face Jack, "I think you should move
home Jack."

"Hilary's right," Danny couldn't resist joining in, "and look on the bright side – even if your old bedroom wasn't available you could always sleep in her hat."

The wedding ceremony was typical of a country house wedding. The string quartet squeaked out Vivaldi's Four Seasons and a few other standard baroque classics to entertain the guests before the Wedding March had signalled the arrival of the happy couple. Various members of the family had all reached for their tissues and all bar one of the elderly women had commented on how beautiful the bride was as she slowly made her way past them towards the minister. The one who had failed to comment only did so on the grounds that she was snoring loudly and not responding to the gentle prods from her embarrassed immediate family. Fortunately help was on hand in the form of a small child who leant over and screamed, "Wake Up Grandma!" It was hard to say which had prompted more laughs – the small boy shouting or the rasping fart that the old woman had let rip as she awoke somewhat startled from her peaceful slumber.

There were tears from both families, the speeches were a mixture of the good, the bad and the unfunny. The three course meal produced a mixture of a good starter, an indifferent main course and a pudding you either loved or hated.

But, in what seemed like a flickering of an eye, the main event, an event that had been looked forward to and precision planned for months on end, causing as much stress and strain to the newly betrothed couple as it had love and laughter, was over.

With the last scraping of a spoon against china to pick up

the final crumbling morsel of the exotic fruit cheesecake, the well regimented routine which the country house staff had been executing all summer kicked into action. Tablecloths, tables, chairs, plant pots, bowls of sweets, streams of party poppers and elderly dozing relatives were all swiftly cleared away to make room for the dance floor. Heaven knows what sins against rhythm would be committed upon those floorboards during the evening reception as the alcohol levels increase to the point where people would genuinely fall under the grave misconception that, after years of sobriety-led common sense, they had in fact been wrong to shy away from their one true calling – the need to dance.

The country house manager was aware of this and had ensured that several of his staff were well versed in dealing with such instances. The team were on full alert at certain strategic points of the evening, the first of which was code named 'Patrick Swayze'. This related to the point in Dirty Dancing where, towards the end of 'I've Had the Time of My Life' belting out, 'Baby' runs to Patrick Swayze and jumps at him. Patrick's strong muscular arms lift her lithe arched slender body gloriously above his head, completing the difficult lift they had failed to make at their previous public performance. Even the most hardened of chick flick movie goers understands that these actors are in fact trained dancers at the top of their professions, skilfully choreographed and punished into shape by overtly motivated personal trainers. It is therefore to alcohol's credit that many of these normally sane women find themselves moving towards one end of the dance floor where they kick off their heels before turning to face their equally inebriated partners standing at the far end of the dance floor shouting over to their mates to watch the impending doom as he beckons his woman with his finger. She obliges and begins her ill-fated charge – much as a bull would head for an overconfident matador who had mistakenly put on his red sweater in the morning. As she approaches she hits her top speed, which isn't particularly fast as it's hard enough to walk in a straight line when you're pissed, let alone run. She then pauses before making her final death defying (all being well) leap onto her partner who crumbles underneath her, his natural instinct for survival having overridden his alcohol-sodden brain just a fraction too late to take any evasive action like jumping out of the way and bringing her down with a tranquillizer dart, but just a fraction too early so as to enable him to suddenly realize what was about to quite literally hit him.

Other songs that the First Aid team looked out for were 'New York, New York', 'The Can Can' – there are few less appealing sights than watching an 80-year-old incontinent great-grandmother trying to raise her leg above waist height – and finally, 'The Lambada'. One of the even less appealing sights than the 80-year-old great gran showing off her knickers is an 80-year-old man dancing, or more accurately, riding on the leg of a woman young enough to be his granddaughter – and please God may it not actually be his granddaughter. This dance is mercifully short as the old man will inevitably have to sit down feeling faint on the grounds that whatever blood he had left in his body had left his head and made its way down to an area it hadn't visited for many a year.

Fog

Evening receptions are, by common agreement, generally far more entertaining and likely to generate scandal and gossip than their more institutionalised daytime cousins. Short of calling your spouse the wrong name, shagging the best man or bridesmaid just before you take your vows, or breaking down at the speeches declaring you've made a 'terrible mistake', the standard daytime wedding and meal rarely offers any surprises. An evening reception, on the other hand, possesses that delightful air of unpredictability. We have already documented the prospect of some terrifying dance moves which would normally not be allowed at even the most liberal of forward thinking clubs. You can also be sure that there will be one or two irritating children aged between 6 and 8 who will run around for hours on end fuelled by the additives pumped into them courtousy of the numerous glasses of coke they have relentlessly consumed, and the fact that they have been round to all the tables and licked the sugar coatings off all the little almond parcels that had been left out in a bizarre fertility tradition cleverly instigated by the makers of sugared almonds many years ago after they had the good foresight to realise that no-one actually ever buys sugared almonds. Despite all this however, there is still the scope for all manner of madness to evolve once you mix several generations of two families, each secretly suspicious of the other's respective bride or groom's worthiness to join their family, loads of friends/colleagues who you didn't want to be there during the day, and a bar that never seems to close.

It wasn't therefore surprising that the topic of 'Weddings' was on the agenda as Jack, Hayley and Danny sat around a small circular table at the side of the dance floor. The table was chosen by Hayley, well aware that it was a prime vantage point for a dedicated people watcher, a fact confirmed by the occasional comment of "smart girl" from the elderly female family members as they swiftly hustled their way to the other key tables.

"Weddings are weird aren't they," mused Danny as he sat back in his chair and cast his gaze around the large hall that was filling up with all manner of folk.

"Mmnn," Jack hummed his agreement

"Weird?" Hayley wasn't so sure.

"Well," Danny leant forward as he considered his explanation, "they just are aren't they."

Hayley looked at him and furrowed her brow in slight surprise at his particularly appalling justification of his previous comment.

"They just are? Well, ladies and gentlemen of the jury, I must concede that my learned colleague's argument is just too strong for me to contend!"

Danny couldn't help but laugh at Hayley's mocking.

"Well you know!" he started.

Hayley shook her head, "Er, no, again not a good argument Danny!"

"Help me out Jack."

"You're on your own mate, you should know never to question the sanctity of marriage to a woman, least of all when you're actually at a wedding. Seriously, you might as well just throw in that you don't know what all the fuss is about 'periods'."

"Well, what is all the fuss about them anyway?"

Fortunately for Danny, Hayley was quite sure that Danny was not quite as ignorant as he was portraying.

"What I mean is that it's so damn expensive and you have to invite loads of people you wouldn't want to socialise with in a million years."

"We're not talking about 'periods' now are we?" Jack enquired with an air of innocence.

"I hope not," Hayley looked a little indignant. "Danny, why would I want to have a family party to celebrate every time I'm 'on'?"

"Yes Danny," Jack tutted towards his friend, "that would be bloody ridiculous – literally bloody!"

Hayley just shook her head.

"Well people," Danny was not going to rise to their bait, "surprisingly I wasn't actually talking about periods. Hayley," he lowered his head to her in deference, "I am glad you do not feel the need to facilitate family gatherings every time the Arsenal are playing at home. Jack," Danny turned and once more bowed his head, this time in Jack's direction, "you are quite right, it would be bloody ridiculous. Mind you, finding a venue for the parties wouldn't be an issue would it?"

Hayley and Jack weren't quite expecting this and could therefore only give a mumbled response roughly equating to "go on.."

"Well, Hayley could have it at her 'pad'!" Danny sat back in his chair as the groans from Hayley and Jack followed his rather poor pun.

"How do you know Hayley uses pads?" Jack began, "she might be a tampon kinda girl."

"Er, hello," Hayley sounded a little indignant, "I am here boys."

"Well that's good then as you'd know the answer then won't you!"

The smile that sat across Jack's face swiftly stood up and made a mad dash for it when it saw the look that Hayley was hurling over from across the table.

"But, that's clearly your business," Jack began to step back over to the correct side of the mark he had just crossed, "and therefore let us not discuss things any further tonight, nor indeed, ever again come to think of it!"

Hayley smiled and nodded her agreement.

"Absolutely, and if you ever mention it again Jack then, so help me God, I'll ram one of my tampons right up your arse!"

Danny found himself laughing once more and raised his glass to Hayley. Hayley smiled sweetly back and raised her own glass in acknowledgement.

"So," Danny stretched as he stifled a small yawn, "Jack, now that I've failed to convince everyone that marriage is a waste of time, I think it's only fair that you should have the opportunity of offending Hayley as well. So, what do you think of marriage?"

The truth was that Jack didn't think anything about marriage. To be more specific he hadn't given any thought to marriage probably at any stage of his life other than a brief disastrous look into the future a few years ago that prompted the somewhat premature closure on his relationship with Imogen. Little wonder then that he had not given it any thought since.

"I don't really have any thoughts on marriage."

"Really?" Hayley was curious. Her tone had been surprisingly intense, prompting Jack to suddenly give the issue more consideration than he had initially thought was required.

"Well, you know," the fact that he didn't have any real thoughts on the subject should have been reasonably obvious to all present as Jack searched his mind for any sort of opinion. As he did so his attention was caught by a pretty young lady approaching their table. His stare did not go unnoticed by his companions who turned to view the subject of his interest. As they did Jack found himself completing his sentence, "I think it's great if you find the right woman."

Hayley averted her gaze from the approaching Imogen and looked at Jack. She had instinctively expected that he would be staring longingly at Imogen's beautiful frame; however, much to her surprise and slight embarrassment, he was looking at her. The awkward tingling as her cheeks began to turn crimson prompted Hayley to pick up her glass, turn on a big smile, and turn to welcome Imogen who had arrived at their table.

"Hi all," Imogen waved her hand coyly as she spoke.

"Hiya," Danny began, swiftly followed by greetings from Jack and Hayley.

"Your dress looks lovely." Hayley was such a girl.

"Ah thanks. Oh I'm sorry, I'm Imogen." A more formal introduction seemed appropriate

"Don't be sorry," Hayley smiled warmly, "I'm Hayley. Hey, are you going to join us?"

Throughout this brief exchange Jack sat a little nervously on the edge of his chair. His usual confidence had been somewhat suffocated by his feelings of guilt and the fact that he still found Imogen really attractive. This may not normally be a problem to most men but Jack did possess a sense of nobility and he held onto the notion that he had been given his chance with Imogen but had lost the right to be with her after ending their relationship previously. As far as he was concerned he no longer deserved to be given a second chance and Imogen deserved to find someone else. Ironically if it was Danny facing this particular predicament - not that at this moment it was a predicament as Imogen had only just sat down at their table which did not actually constitute re-igniting the flame that existed between her and Jack - but had it been Danny who had dated Imogen then Jack's advice would be for him to 'go for it'. Not in a seedy, 'go for it, it's a wedding, she's wearing a bridesmaid dress and is therefore likely to be more emotionally vulnerable than in normal circumstances and therefore more susceptible to the offer of a meaningless shag with an ex', but a 'go for it, you know you made a mistake, she's a great girl and you're a nice bloke, don't beat yourself up over the past, just take this opportunity that fate has delivered to you to make amends and have a truly amazing relationship'.

But, it wasn't Danny, it was Jack.

"You must be really hot in that dress," Jack found himself saying and then immediately felt self-conscious and even briefly skirted with paranoia as he hoped that she didn't interpret his remark to mean that he wanted her to get out of her dress.

"Well, I'm not taking it off here Jack!"

Okay, so perhaps he wasn't paranoid.

"That's not what I meant, I," Jack was almost bumbling over his words,

"I know!" Imogen interrupted him warmly, "I'm only joking. Anyway, how have you been?"

Her warm smile had a calming effect on Jack who was finally able overcome his brief stint as a tongue-twisted little boy and regain his natural persona once more.

"I'm good Imogen, and how have you been?"

"I've been good."

Hayley and Danny sipped on their drinks in order to be doing something so as not to been drawn into the pile of awkwardness that plonked itself into the middle of their table upon Imogen's arrival.

"So how long have you two been going out?"

Hayley almost choked on her drink. She coughed instinctively, not because she had to, but because she felt she needed to buy a fraction of time to try and evaluate whether the question was friendly fire or otherwise.

"Oh, we're not," she began and coughed again, "we're best mates."

"That's what they say Imogen, but I'm not so sure." Danny enjoyed his stirring.

"What is it with everyone?" Hayley had a defiant look upon her face, "wherever we go people are trying to pair us off!"

"I think you look good together." Imogen's tone was quite genuine.

Jack had remained quiet through this, feeling a little guilty at his surprising enjoyment in watching Hayley squirm.

"What made you think we were together?" He finally broke his silence.

Imogen nodded in the direction of the bar,

"Your mother."

The four of them looked over towards the bar where a big hat was ordering drinks for a gaggle of ageing ladies.

"That's an amazing hat she's got on Jack."

"It's not a hat," Danny corrected Imogen, "it just looks like a hat. She's actually smuggling refugees into the country. She's got eight Poles, three Somalians and a goat herder hiding under that thing."

"That's true," Hayley continued to spin the yarn, "bloody goat herders, it was Jack's mum who brought Chico into the country."

"What did she say to you?" Jack decided to ignore Danny and Hayley's ramblings and ask the question, even if he wasn't sure he wanted to know the answer.

"Well, first she asked how I was, then introduced me to her two friends as the girl her son Jack had a 'fling with'."

"I'm so sorry," Jack felt a little bad at his mother's complete, but it had to be said, consistent tactlessness.

"That's okay, bless her she was always like that, it's kind of endearing. But anyway, she then told me that you were seeing a wonderful girl called Hilary."

Hayley couldn't help but laugh,

"Where has she got Hilary from?"

"I don't know," continued Imogen, "but she was raving about you. The only thing she didn't like was your name. 'Hilary is such an old person's name' is what she said."

Hayley hid her face in her hands and gently shook her head.

"Cheer up Hilary!" Danny was enjoying his evening, even more so as the middle finger on one of Hayley's hands that had been covering her face duly extended in response.

"Ah don't worry about it Hayley, honestly, when I was

seeing Jack she was always trying to marry us off as well. She's just a little, well, a little eccentric I guess."

"Nicely put," Jack agreed, "she's a character all right my mum."

"and," Danny leant back on his chair and turned his head to the bar, "I think it's time you and I got these ladies a drink Jack."

Jack looked back at his friend and then in the direction of the bar.

"That's a good idea Danny. Ladies, what are you drinking?"

Hayley and Imogen placed their orders and watched, a little bemused, as Jack and Danny practically jumped out of their chairs as they swiftly headed for the bar.

It didn't take long to work out why they had made such a hasty retreat. No sooner had they left their seats than they were ducking and swerving to avoid crashing into the hat and its entourage whilst Jack announced, "Can't stop now mum, catch you in a while."

Hayley and Imogen exchanged a glance as they held back the mutual desire to laugh at their impending liaison with the Hat.

"Imogen! Darling, I see you've met Hilary."

Before either Imogen or Hayley could acknowledge Jack's mum she was off again,

"Mary, Olive, Mo, this is the lovely young lady I was telling you all about."

Hayley took a deep breath as she was engulfed by the swarm.

"Ahh, you're a canny girl, picked a good table," Jack's Auntie Mary nodded knowingly at Hayley in acknowledgement from one people watcher to another. Although, to be fair, Auntie Mary wasn't a pure people watcher in Hayley's mould. No, Auntie Mary was just a bloody nosey old woman.

Back at the sanctuary of the bar Jack and Danny placed their orders and agreed that it would be impolite for them to return immediately to their table. Rather they should allow the girls some 'bonding' time.

"I think that's a fine idea Jack." Danny nodded and raised his glass.

"Well, it's only fair isn't it." Jack acknowledged his friend and the two spent a brief moment savouring the silence that accompanies the downing of a good cool welcome pint.

This peaceful moment was suddenly shattered by a screeched "coo-ee" from behind them.

Jack, somewhat startled, turned around to see his cousin Mary leaning in towards him, her cheek readied for the traditional kiss for the Bride.

"Hi Mary," Jack kissed her accordingly and took a step back, "you look great Mary. She looks great doesn't she Danny?"

"You look ravishing Mary." Danny hadn't meant to sound quite so over the top but this was lost on Mary anyway who just giggled like a schoolgirl,

"Oh stop it you two! You're embarrassing me!"

"Ah, but Mary," Jack took her hand, "surely a man must be able to tell his cousin that she looks beautiful."

"And in certain parts of the country that's a prelude to a marriage proposal you know." Danny's comment sailed above Mary's tiara-covered head.

Jack scanned the horizon,

"So where's the lucky man?"

Mary turned around to look and for a moment all three of them were casting their eyes around the room.

Jack looked back at Mary.

"You don't know where he is then?"

Mary stopped scanning the horizon and re-focused on Jack.

"Well, what does he look like?"

Jack and Danny exchanged glances.

"He looks like your husband."

"Really," Mary looked out into the crowds again, "he looks just like my Michael? Wow, that would be an amazing coincidence don't you think?"

Jack and Danny exchanged glances once more and a slight shaking of heads for good measure.

"Mary, he is Michael." Mary looked a little confused as Jack tried to explain. "The 'lucky man' is Michael...because... he has married you."

Jack found himself nodding through this sentence in the hope that if Mary started to nod too then she would have understood his remark.

To his relief, albeit after a brief pause, Mary began to nod and smiled coyly once more,

"Ah, stop it you're embarrassing me again."

Jack couldn't help but smile. True, his cousin was somewhat lacking in the brain department, but she had a heart of gold and was always good value for a few laughs even if invariably they ended up to a greater or lesser degree upon her.

"Hey Mary," Danny decided to bring up the one slightly unusual event from the wedding ceremony, "that was a very interesting ceremony earlier."

"I thought it was beautiful. Did you see my flowers?"

"Yes, they were lovely," Danny continued, "the whole thing was beautiful, obviously, but I found the exchanging of the wedding vows the most interesting."

Mary looked a little embarrassed and playfully smacked Danny.

"The minister said no-one would mention that again!"

"Ah, but it was brilliant Mary, wasn't it Jack?"

Jack hadn't ideally wanted to be brought into this conversation but knew if he had started it he too would have called on Danny for re-inforcements just in case it backfired.

"Mary, it was very memorable and really lovely."

"Ah, stop it you two, you're embarrassing me!" was beginning to become somewhat of a catchphrase.

"No seriously," Jack continued, "I think burping 'I Do' should be made compulsory at Civil wedding ceremonies."

"I agree," Danny confirmed.

"Really?" Mary looked almost grateful that cousin and friend should consider her rather unfortunate nerve-induced belched confirmation of her willingness to abide by her sacred wedding vows to be not only memorable but also lovely.

"Absolutely Mary." Jack held her hand once more.

Danny sucked in the air around him to facilitate a belched confirmation, "I do Too".

"Ah, stop it you two, you're embarrassing me!"

Jack winced slightly as Mary's statement was accompanied by a rather hard thump on his upper arm. Danny managed to swerve backwards and only take a glancing shot himself.

Mary giggled once more before her attention was immediately taken in by a wave from an ageing uncle ensconced on a stool at the other end the bar. He eased himself out of the stool as she approached in order that he could prepare to try and land a rather disgusting squelching kiss on his unsuspecting, but fortunately naïve, favourite niece.

Jack cringed as he looked on and prayed that he would not turn out like that one day. At the same time he nodded his acknowledgement that at least the old guy was making the most of his opportunity.

"I guess we should go and rescue the girls." Jack began to gather up the drinks.

"Imogen's looking hot isn't she?" Danny clearly wasn't quite ready to return and Jack replaced the drinks accordingly.

"Yeah, she's looking fantastic."

"I think you missed a trick there my friend." Danny sipped on his pint.

Jack mirrored his companion's actions and nodded his agreement.

"Yeah, you could be right. But, sometimes things aren't meant to be are they."

Danny leant purposefully against the bar.

"Yeah, I guess you're right. Wrong time, right place as you've said before." He took another sip from his drink, "so what about Hayley?"

Jack was slightly startled by this latest remark.

"What about Hayley?"

"Come on Jack, there's real chemistry there, everyone can see that. So is she wrong time right place as well?"

The startled look that had descended over Jack moments before had now settled in and wasn't planning on immediately vacating his face.

"We're just mates Danny. Best mates."

"Best mates? She's intelligent, funny, drop dead gorgeous and she's already your best mate. You can't tell me it's never crossed your mind."

"What?" Jack clearly knew what his friend was insinuating, however, he was only just beginning to recover from his startled phase.

"'What' my arse! You know 'what'. What it would be like if she was more than just your best mate?"

Jack, in truth hadn't really contemplated this, well certainly not to any significant degree. In the early stages of their relationship he had found himself drawn towards Hayley but he had been kind of seeing someone at the time, which had put paid to any idea of actually asking Hayley out. By the time that particular relationship had fizzled away his friendship with Hayley had taken root and those initial twinges had passed.

"Not really," was his considered approach, "it's just so good to have someone I can talk to, and to flirt with but without any pressure or hidden agenda. It's kind of cool."

"'Kind of cool?' What decade are you living in?"

"You know what I mean." Jack's gaze moved over the girls who were finally saying goodbye to the group of elderly women. Danny's gaze followed. "Sometimes it's great to have found a really close friend who you know will always be able to cheer you up. You," Jack pointed accusingly at Danny, "you are one of my best mates but you can piss me off from time to time." Danny feigned a look of hurt, "Don't try and look upset you tart – you know what I mean. If you're pissed and we're out you can be a complete twat!"

"Ah," Danny felt obliged to defend himself, "but in

fairness I am only a twat when I am drunk and you are not drunk. If you are drunk and I am sober then it is you who acts like a twat. And when we're both hammered, we get on fine and it's just everyone else who thinks we're a couple of twats."

"Absolutely," Jack raised his glass in agreement, "so tonight, as I am only having a couple, you will end up being the twat."

"Absolutely," Danny raised his glass, "I should think so too. Well, it's Best Man duties isn't it?"

"My point was that you're a great mate but you can piss me off. Hayley has never pissed me off, never. She, well she always has a way of making me smile."

"You see, I still don't get it. Why aren't you with her again?"

"You see, you're already beginning to tread the path towards Twatsville. She's my best friend and I would never want to lose that."

Danny knew he needed to turn back up the path.

"Good man."

Danny gathered up the glasses and the two friends headed back to the table where Hayley and Imogen, cronie free, were gassing away.

The evening continued on with the four of them talking and joking until Danny and Imogen, guided by their duties, made their excuses and went off to 'mingle'. Imogen's evening would consist of smiling politely and thanking everyone for their nice comments. She would also find herself deflecting questions of when she would be the Bride and declining several offers from over amorous inebriated old men to make her one, knowing that their true desire was actually just to 'give her one' so to speak. It was pretty torturous as was Danny's evening of firm handshakes, accepting numerous offers of drinks, and deflecting questions as to whether he was going to shag any of the bridesmaids.

"So how's your day been?" Jack looked across at Hayley.

"It's been really nice thank you Mr Matthews. How's yours?"

"It's been good. It's a shame I'm driving, weddings are occasions when it feels that you should be having a good drink."

"Ah, we could have got a taxi. It's not too late if you want. I'm sure we could book one or share someone else's?" Hayley felt a little guilty staring at the four empty wine glasses in front of her.

"Na, don't be silly!" Jack was touched by Hayley's concern, "there's not too long left now and trust me, the last thing you want is to be hanging around outside at kicking out time when all my drunk relations stumble into the open air."

"Ah, your family are great Jack, particularly your mum."

"Mmnn, yes, sorry about mum. She likes you though."

"Well, she likes 'Hilary' actually. If she knew the real me – Hayley – then she might change her mind."

"You realize I will be calling you Hilary all next week don't you."

"Only if you want me to call you Dick." Hayley smiled.

Jack's attention was distracted by the opening bars of Dancing Queen booming out of the speakers and the immediate scraping and banging of chairs and murmurings of "thank God, something decent at last" that accompanied a mass stampede towards the dance floor, a dance floor that had been gradually emptying over the last ten minutes as the DJ had indulged himself and inflicted his collection of obscure hard core drum'n'base upon the gathering.

"Come on then," Hayley pushed her chair back and extended her hand towards Jack, "let's dance."

They joined the heaving mass on the dance floor and danced extravagantly, taking care to avoid clattering into any of the more elderly and frail members of the throng. The hotel staff gathered around the perimeter of the dance floor – their well rehearsed drill kicking into place in the expectancy that a mass surge onto the dance floor by a mixture of the old and young with two things in common – high levels of intoxication and the fact that 'rhythm' was indeed going to get them – was almost certainly going to lead to some kind of minor catastrophe. The more entrepreneurial members of the team would always have a camcorder with them at this point, eager to profit from the £250 'You've Been Framed' had promised them at the end of each episode. This may seem a little callous, however, it is thought that 90% of the wedding clips seen on home video programmes are actually supplied in this manner.

"I love this song!" Hayley was shouting in Jack's ear.

"Everyone loves this song!" Jack leant forward with his hollered response.

Next to them one of Jack's elderly aunties was removing her teeth for safe keeping and putting them into her handbag. She licked her lips slowly and, carefully, ever so carefully, bent forward and deposited the handbag onto the floor.

It was as if a beacon had suddenly illuminated in the middle of the dance floor. From all corners of the room elderly folks charged towards the old lady – although in fairness to say 'charged' may be exaggerating somewhat, 'staggered' or 'limped' or 'were escorted under the weight of their walking sticks/zimmer frames' would be more accurate. After several moments the crowd had reached their destination and had formed an orderly circle around the handbag. As Jack looked on in amusement he couldn't help thinking that this kind of ritual had probably been around since the dawn of Man where our ancient hairy ancestors would dance around a fire. Whether they would have been chanting "watch that scene, digging the dancing Queen" was another matter, of course.

Jack's musings were interrupted by a sound slap on the back. He turned around to see Danny's broad smile – Danny's slightly inebriated broad smile – beaming at him. Holding Danny's hand was a slightly embarrassed looking Imogen who had been dragged away from a group of admiring – okay, nosey – old women.

"I love this song!" Danny was shouting in Jack's ear and, for that matter, any ear that was in close proximity.

"Everyone loves this song!" Hayley shouted back and threw a smile at Jack.

However, no sooner had they all agreed upon the fact that everyone does indeed love that song, it was over. In its place came the brooding swirling saxophone introduction to Careless Whisper. Simultaneously across the dance floor the men took a step back from their partners, contorted their faces in disgust and began to shake their heads. All the women, on the other hand, took a step forward and grabbed their unfortunate prey and whooped with delight that they "love this song as well".

Jack, Hayley, Imogen and Danny were all included in this rather embarrassing display. Jack eventually offered his hand to Hayley and they assumed the positions of a waltz.

Slow dances are a strange beast. Half of the guests – predominately the younger ones or couples – stood face to face, her arms around his neck, his arms in the main perched around the small of her back, their feet making slow pigeon steps as they gradually rotated roughly on the spot. You could spot the more amorous – or drunk – partners quite easily as their hands would, in the case of the females, be gliding up and down their counterpart's neck, and in the case of the males their hands would be spending most of the time exploring the buttock area in between occasional forays up the spinal chord. The remainder of the guests, not wishing to find themselves caught in any potentially awkward or embarrassing situations adopt the waltz position, keeping their respective partners at arm's length. Jack had learnt this rule the hard way. A couple of years ago he had attended a friend's wedding. He, like may of the guests, had drunk his fill through the course of the day and night, little realising that this would leave his reflexes and subsequently his defences somewhat hampered. The slow dances arrived in a similar manner as to how they had done on this particular evening and Jack had been accosted on the dance floor and had found himself with his hands on the small of a lady's back and her arms around his neck.

"You're a handsome young man," the woman had whispered into his ear.

"Thank you," Jack had replied, understandably not thinking that this was the prelude to anything else, "and you are an attractive woman," he had continued with a smile.

"My room's upstairs, number 301, if you meet there in 5 minutes I'll give you the time of your life." This remark and the gentle squeeze on his manhood prior to the lady's swift exit had left Jack frozen to the spot.

After this momentary immobilisation Jack had, in complete contrast, never moved so quickly in his life as he darted for the exit and hid outside in a bush until a taxi arrived thirty minutes later to seal his escape. Somewhat extreme behaviour, it's fair to say, however it would be equally fair to say that at most weddings you don't normally expect to be propositioned by the Groom's mother.

Whilst this episode hadn't actually flashed through Jack's mind today he had automatically assumed the waltz position and was enjoying his gentle flirting with Hayley.

"So, you've enjoyed the day then?"

"Yes, you've already asked me that Jack. It's been really nice thank you."

"Good!" Jack found himself pulling Hayley a little closer towards him. It had been an instinctive move, not one born out of any romantic overtures but more from a genuine feeling of comfort that comes from a true friendship.

"Oi, Oi! We've got our eyes on you two!" Jack and Hayley smiled over at Danny and Imogen who were shouting over and, having got the attention they were looking for, proceeded to mimic Jack's pulling in of Hayley thus drawing Jack and Hayley's attention to the occurrence which they had both taken for granted.

George Michael's final 'whoa whoa's' faded in the background to be replaced by another smooching classic at which point Danny interrupted Jack and Hayley.

"May I?" His hand was offered to Hayley.

"You may," came the reply after a very brief glance at Jack.

Jack found himself standing in the middle of the dance floor face to face with his ex-girlfriend who was looking both a little embarrassed and extremely beautiful.

"Would you care to dance?" Jack bowed slightly as he offered his hand.

"I would love to kind sir!" Imogen curtseyed and the two of them adopted the waltz stance.

"It's been really good to see you again Jack." Imogen had leant forward to ensure Jack could hear her and in doing so the two of them now found themselves dancing closely.

"It's been really good to see you too." Jack was genuine in his reply. He was a also a little confused as he found himself rather enjoying the feeling of Imogen's body pushed up against his, albeit that her bridesmaid's dress somewhat cushioned the sensation. On the plus side however, its low cut front did enable him to have a sneaky glance downwards which briefly ignited a few rather fond memories from the past.

"Hayley's really nice Jack."

"Yeah, she's great."

"Are you two really not an item?" Imogen seemed genuine enough in her questioning although Jack's ego was insisting to his brain that the enquiry was merely a prelude to Imogen blurting out a desire to take Jack right there and then on the dance floor. Jack couldn't help but laugh. His ego regularly talked a load of bollocks.

"Why are you laughing?"

"Oh, no reason," Jack had thought he'd only laughed to himself, "and no, we're not an item. We're just best friends."

Imogen rested her head against Jack's shoulder as they started to make a slow circle in the middle of the dance floor. She slowly released her hands from his and they slid towards his neck. Jack's hands, with, it's true, few alternative options available, moved to the small of her back.

"Were we best friends Jack?" Imogen's head remained on Jack's shoulder as if she didn't want to look him in the eye just in case he didn't give her the answer she really wanted to hear.

Jack hadn't been expecting the question and hadn't even really considered whether there were any parallels in his relationship with Hayley to that of his previous relationship with Imogen.

"Um," this was one of those instances that although Jack knew the question probably deserved some deliberation and thought, he also knew the answer, "Yeah, I think we were."

"So why did we split up?" Again Imogen's head stayed on his shoulder.

Jack hadn't been expecting this question either, although somewhere at the back of his conscience he had realised that one day he would need to give Imogen an honest explanation. At the time of their break he had hidden behind excuses of 'It's not working' and 'I feel we're growing apart', both of which weren't true.

"Truth?"

"Yes."

"I ballsed up basically. Things were moving too fast and I got scared. I guess, rather than deal with that, I panicked."

There was an uncomfortable silence as they continued their pigeon-stepped circle.

"I'm sorry." Jack gave Imogen a small kiss on the top of her head.

Imogen looked up at him and leant forward to return the kiss on his cheek.

"That's okay," she glanced over towards Danny and Hayley who were chatting and laughing a few feet away, "so is it that you've learnt from the past and you're taking it slow this time so you don't make a mistake again?"

Jack, who had followed her eye line to Hayley and Danny, was thrown once again into confusion. His ego, tired of getting things wrong, said nothing. His brain, confused, simply ran around in circles for a while.

"I think Imogen and Jack are staring at us!" Danny waved over to his friends.

"That's because we're such great dancers!" Hayley waved at Jack who, brain back in gear, waved back and continued his dance with Imogen.

"So," Danny began with a deep breath, "be honest then. Are you and Jack going to get together or not?"

"Oh My God!" Hayley smacked Danny on the arm, "why do people keep going on about that to me?"

"Because you behave like a couple, and he obviously is crazy about you."

Hayley took a deep breath. Danny was one of Jack's best friends. Did this mean Danny knew something she didn't? Had Jack been confiding in Danny? Was Danny actually scouting for Jack and checking the coast was clear to make a move without risking their friendship? With so many thoughts crashing through her mind her brain was in a similar state to Jack's at that moment.

"Has Jack actually said that?"

"Well, no," Danny answered honestly, "but there's real chemistry there isn't there?"

Hayley suddenly found herself feeling a little disappointed. A bit of her actually wanted Danny to have said that Jack had been talking about her and that yes, he wanted to be more than friends. Equally, a bit of her was holding back and saying that she didn't want to lose what they had at the same time.

"We're just best mates Danny."

"Okay, cool, but you might just want to check that Jack knows that as well."

It was Danny and Hayley's turn to dance in silence for a short while.

"You've gone quiet," Danny hated awkward silences, "listen, I didn't mean to say anything out of turn."

"You haven't," Hayley interrupted

"I hope I haven't. It's just Jack's a great bloke and I can see why he talks a lot about you. You're funny, intelligent and beautiful. It's a pretty powerful combination," Danny smiled warmly at Hayley as he gave her his honest observations born out of the time they had spent together that day, "and if you and Jack are meant to be then it seems a shame to waste time. I thought when he ended things with Imogen he had made the biggest mistake of his life. But, now I've met you I reckon it could have been fate just giving him a huge break."

Hayley was both flattered and touched by Danny's comments. She wanted to respond but genuinely didn't know what to say so she just smiled, a slightly awkward embarrassed smile, and rested her head on Danny's shoulder.

The muffled "thank you's" from the DJ signalled the end of the main entertainment for the evening. This, and the congregation's en-mass blinking brought on by the sudden flickering and spluttering of the bright fluorescent lights as they were called into action, signified the start of numerous hugs and fond farewells as people began to edge away towards the exits and either their rooms, cars, waiting taxis or, of course, toilets.

The flow into the gents' toilets - if you pardon the expression - was generally fast and functional. The combination of a wedding and alcohol does, however, have a strange effect on the unwritten etiquette of gents' toilet behaviour. Jack, like all men, knew these rules well.

Number One - never stand directly next to someone at the urinal unless there are absolutely no other spaces.

Number Two - never, on any account, even if politely requested to do so, in fact, especially if politely requested to do so, never look at the crotch of the man standing next to you. The exception to this rule may well apply in toilets frequented by the less heterosexual members of the male species.

Number Three - never look at anyone in the toilets.

Number Four - never speak to anyone in the toilets unless you are spoken to. If you are spoken to then firstly, you have the sympathy of every straight man who has found himself in such an unenviable position, and secondly make sure you keep your reply as succinct as possible. Keep your reply friendly enough to avoid any escalating aggression from the fool who is obviously already drunk enough to have broken the Gents Loo Code, but not too friendly to inspire any misunderstanding that you are in fact gagging for some man on man action. Again, Jack's understanding was that this rule is mainly directed at the heterosexual community.

There are other rules as well, for example governing the acceptability of breaking wind loudly. The rule is that this is perfectly appropriate behaviour provided you accompany this with a manly declaration of "Better Out than In". At this point everyone else in the toilets will feel obliged to laugh heartily and may even feel so inclined as to add their own farts into the fray, or more accurately, into the choking atmosphere. A word of warning however, one of Jack's friends had attempted to do this once but clearly he was more inebriated than he thought and, as such, he forced the fart just a little too much. Nothing more embarrassing than spending a night of socialising with a small turd moulding itself to your pants.

Weddings however turn these rules on their heads. That's not to say that everyone at a wedding spends their time admiring each other's private parts, but the combination of several generations, the sense of optimism, lashings of alcohol and the general good humour means that the usual social taboos can be lifted and you can have a good old chat with some seventy-year-old drunk next to you and can even forgive him as he loses control of his little hose and begins to spray everything around him other than the urinal into which he should be aiming.

The flow into the ladies' loos, by contrast to the gents', was extremely slow and a queue had soon formed outside. The ladies had even stopped going in pairs. The end of the evening, whilst a good time to gossip and discuss the evening's events, is also a time when an awful lot of elderly women realise that their bladders are not quite as watertight as they had been in their heyday and the need to alleviate this potentially embarrassing realisation takes priority even over a good old chinwag.

It was in this queue that Imogen and Hayley found themselves standing.

"There must be other loos around here surely?" The

wine Hayley had consumed over the last few hours was beginning to push downwards in search of a way out.

"You'd think so, it is a hotel after all!" Imogen agreed but, with only three people in front of her in the queue and her need not quite so pressing as Hayley's, she wasn't planning on going to investigate this further.

Hayley looked up and down the corridor and watched as a small old lady edged her way towards them, smiled sweetly, slowly moved past them and pushed open the toilet door.

"Excuse me.." began one of the ladies in the queue; however, this fell on the quite literally deaf ears of the old woman who was now in the toilets and trying to push her way into one of the already occupied cubicles.

"Oh, I'm going to have to find another loo," Hayley shook her head, "if I don't see you again tonight Imogen, it's been great to meet you."

"You too." Imogen and Hayley exchanged a small kiss on the cheek and Hayley headed off down the corridor and turned inadvertently into the main hall.

"Hilary!"

Hayley turned to see a small woman waving at her as she made her way over to Hayley's side.

"Hello, how are you?" Hayley recognised the old lady as Jack's grandmother from one of her not so brief introductions from earlier in the evening.

"Oh, I'm very well my dear," came the ever so slightly slurred response, "oh I'm so glad I've managed to see you."

"Really?" Hayley didn't mean to sound so surprised but needn't have worried as Jack's gran was in the process of checking her teeth were still in before continuing,

"I wanted to ask you something."

Hayley tried to force a smile but her impatience at wishing to find a quiet place to relieve the burden within her bladder rather turned it into a grimace. She decided it was best to avoid a prolonged questioning session.

"I know what you're going to ask me."

Jack's gran smiled knowingly back.

"The thing is, Jack and me are just best friends."

"Oh."

"Yes, I know that it may look otherwise to a lot of people, at least that's what I seem to have been hearing all evening, but really there is nothing going on."

"Yes dear but…"

"No, seriously, there are no 'buts' here," Hayley smiled reassuringly at Jack's gran who, Hayley gleaned from her expression, seemed to be taking the news somewhat badly, "but, don't worry, I know Jack will find someone really nice." Hayley was now becoming a little more concerned as the woman in front of her seemed to be getting more upset as Hayley went on, "I'm not saying there's anything wrong with Jack, you understand don't you?"

Jack's gran nodded as Hayley continued, "In fact Jack's amazing. He's kind and he's funny. He always has time for me and he always knows what to say to make me smile when I'm having a bad day. He listens to me when I need to have a good old moan and doesn't try and judge me or tell me I'm wrong – even when we both know I am."

Hayley paused for a moment and took in what she had just said. Everything she had said was true. Jack really was this wonderful person whom she had just described to his gran. Hayley stood motionless as her minor epiphany lifted her out of her body and circled above her.

"Yes, that's all very well dear," Hayley had momentarily forgotten his gran was there and found herself crashing back down to earth as the old girl's words broke the idyllic thoughts that had so lifted her, "but I wasn't going to ask you that. I just wanted to know where the loo was."

"Oh," Hayley was truly embarrassed and extremely apologetic, "I am so sorry, I'm actually looking for one too. There is one down there but there was a bit of a queue."

"Don't worry dear," the old lady leant forward and whispered into Hayley's ear, "I think it's a bit late for me to be honest."

Hayley this time managed to force a smile and watched as Jack's gran slowly walked away, pausing only briefly to pick up an empty wine glass from the floor and slip it discreetly into her handbag.

There's something very peaceful about driving along country roads in the early hours of the morning.

It's probably the silence.

This is all the more prevalent when no-one is talking in the car you're driving.

"You're quiet," Jack observed.

"I'm just tired." Hayley briefly turned to face Jack and then quickly, and for no apparent reason, averted her gaze before they could make eye contact.

"You alright?" Jack sensed a slight unease in Hayley as he glanced towards her before returning his attentions to the winding country lane before him.

"Yeah, I'm fine." Hayley stared ahead. The truth, however, was she wasn't particularly fine. In fact she was anything but particularly fine. Yes, the whole day had been a lot of fun, but as she thought back on the proceedings all she could focus upon was the seemingly numerous references to her and Jack as a couple. As she stared ahead the car lamp lit pathway through the countryside took on a hypnotic aura and she slipped into deep intense thought. It had been a strange few weeks during which time her friendship with Jack, a friendship that had been very personal to them, felt like it had been thrown out into the public domain for analysis and debate. Everyone from her relatives, to Jack's relatives, to her best friends, to Jack's best friends had either already assumed they were a couple or at the very least had the effrontery to ask them why they weren't together. Even when Hayley had found herself talking about her relationship with Jack she had found herself describing her perfect man. So why was she still confused? Why was there this nagging uncertainty in her mind? Why had Jack never mentioned Imogen before – was it because he didn't want to affect his chances of a relationship with her? Why was she holding back from asking Jack how he felt about the whole thing? Why was Jack not slowing down as they approached another set of stubborn red traffic lights?

"Jack!!"

"Oh, whoops!!" Jack and Hayley jerked forward against their seat belts as the car ground to a halt with a slight screech from a distinctly unimpressed set of tyres.

"Sorry about that." Jack was a little embarrassed.

"Are you okay?" Hayley was a little panicked. "Had you fallen asleep?"

"No, no," Jack hadn't, "I was just day dreaming, or night dreaming I guess."

Both stared up at the light which was still showing red and waiting patiently for them to continue their conversation.

"I was miles away as well," Hayley confided.

"I was just thinking," Jack began. Hayley felt her heart beat double in a split second as she prepared for Jack to go on, "your mum's just like mine isn't she."

Hayley opened her mouth to reply but her brain had not quite registered what response she should give so nothing came out. The traffic light immediately, and it seemed with a wry smile, began to make its way to green and show the couple on their way.

"Don't you think?" Jack laughed at his observation.

"Maybe..a little I guess." Hayley wasn't even trying to make a connection but her brain had at least had the courtesy to go into automatic response mode.

"Well, I know your mum is quite a bit taller than mine and hasn't got quite the same liking for hats you can build your own commune in, but they both seem to have the same kind of values and attitudes."

"Maybe."

"I bet they'd either get on like a house on fire or drive each other nuts."

"Why?" Hayley started to make spurious connections in her mind which began to run away from her, painting images of hers and Jack's mums sitting in her flat, sipping their cups of tea, complimenting each other on their hats, and discussing the name of their first grandchild. "When are they going to meet?"

"Oh I don't know, they may not I guess," the image disappeared from Hayley's mind in a puff of smoke, "who knows, maybe at our wedding," the image began to appear again, "well if half the people we spoke to tonight had their way anyway!" the image tutted and disappeared again.

Hayley forced a little laugh and looked out of the window. The roads soon became familiar and in a very short time she found herself staring at the trees that adorned the side of her street as the car slowly came to a halt adjacent to her flat.

Jack pulled on the handbrake and turned to Hayley expecting her to be gathering her bag and reaching for the door handle.

He was therefore a little surprised to see her sitting somewhat uncomfortably and staring directly ahead. She fidgeted in her seat, her discomfort increasing as she realised that Jack was now looking at her.

"Are you alright Hayles?" Jack was genuinely concerned.

Hayley motioned as if to speak but then said nothing, which merely served the purpose of increasing Jack's concern still further.

"Hayley?" Jack instinctively and protectively reached out his hand and placed it on her wrist.

Hayley jumped, the unexpected physical contact seemed to heighten both her senses and her anxiety. Jack started to move his hand away having jumped himself in reaction to Hayley.

"Hayles, you're beginning to worry me. Are you okay?"

Hayley finally managed to compose herself and, taking a deep breath, turned to face Jack. His eyes were full of worry which both touched Hayley and made her feel a little guilty. She forced a smile in a bid to ease the tension which descended from nowhere upon the car.

"Sorry," she placed her hand reassuringly on Jacks, "it's just," she paused as she double checked in her mind that she definitely wanted to throw her thoughts out into the open, "it's just I think we need to have a talk."

Jack looked back at his friend. He was confused and concerned once more.

"Yeah, of course," he began, "what do you, sorry, we need to talk about?"

"Okay," Hayley turned herself in her seat to face Jack. He in turn sat back a little but naturally mirrored Hayley's pose. "Jack, what are we?"

Jack said nothing. He was expecting Hayley to go on and explain what she was talking about. For her part Hayley was chastising herself for making what seemed like a clichéd remark. The silence, which in reality was fleeting, felt as though it hung in the air like a musty fart from an incontinent elderly dog.

"What are we?" Jacks well practised interview technique of repeating a question in order to buy you more time kicked into autopilot. His face, however, betrayed the fact that he really wasn't sure where Hayley was going with this. Hayley sensed this to a degree, although she could not be sure if Jack was just avoiding the issue.

"Me and you." Hayley hoped that this further clue would enable Jack to take the conversation forward and give her the chance to just listen and not make herself vulnerable by saying completely the wrong thing.

"Me and you?" Jack was not stupid. This time he knew that this conversation was going to go somewhere significant. He too, however, did not want to make himself vulnerable to saying the wrong thing and damaging their relationship.

An awkward silence followed as the two friends made, and then broke, eye contact with each other a couple of times, each imploring the other to take the initiative with the conversation.

Jack felt both relieved and a little guilty as Hayley took the responsibility, which in fairness she should have done as she had raised the subject!

"You know what I mean Jack. All I've heard all night is people telling me what a great couple we are. You said it yourself a minute ago! It was the same at the Christening and, well, everyone seems to have their opinions and are only too happy to give them." Hayley had become increasingly frantic as she had opened up.

"Ah, yes, sorry," Jack looked apologetic, "my family do tend to go on a little don't they."

"It's not just your family Jack," Hayley interjected swiftly, somewhat startling Jack, "it's my family, my friends, your friends, distant relatives, compete strangers, any old Tom, Dick or Harry wants to tell me how great we are together and what a great bloke you are."

"Hey, hey," Jack gently raised his open palm to try and calm his friend, "calm down, I'm sure they're just being friendly. Although clearly they have great taste if they've told you I'm a great bloke!"

Jack's instinctive reaction to hide behind a funny remark wasn't particularly appreciated by Hayley who was feeling distinctly out on a limb at this moment.

"Yes I know! But Jack, this isn't about how great a bloke you are, I already know that. What I don't know is if you're feeling what everyone else seems to be implying that you're feeling. Is there something I've missed that everyone else, including you, can see?"

Jack looked back at Hayley. Her face was etched with

The India Shop
Honey Street Mill
Honeystreet Village
Pewsey Vale
Wiltshire   SN9 5PS

Tel:- 01672 85 11 55
Fax:- 01672 851 742
Email : info@ theindiashop.co.uk

apprehension, her eyes pierced deep into his looking for answers, for re-assurance, for something to give her some understanding of where she stood in amongst all this seemingly sudden confusion.

Jack had never seen Hayley looking so vulnerable. His unconscious reaction was to reach out and take Hayley's hand. As he ran his fingers over her hand he gently squeezed it. This action, intended to re-assure Hayley , simply left her more uncertain.

"Jack," she squeezed his hand back and softly released their grip, "seriously, I need to know what you feel about our relationship."

Jack sat back in his seat and moved his gaze away from Hayley and to the road before him. The street lamps, though shining, were hiding amongst the tree branches, peering anxiously towards the car, waiting for Jack's response. A fox that had, moments before, scurried across the road on the trail of a small fieldmouse, dived into the undergrowth and seemed to stare nervously back towards Jack. Even the late night breeze that had been playfully tossing an old newspaper sheet back and forth across the street grew still in anticipation of Jack's next words.

Silence, it seemed, had descended across the entire neighbourhood.

Jack was not entirely sure what Hayley wanted to hear. He wasn't entirely sure what he wanted to say. Previous experience of situations where he had found himself in a state of confusion did not, unfortunately, provide him with a clear route to take. In the past he had tried saying what he thought someone else had wanted to hear and then suffered the consequences when it turned out he had got it wrong and didn't even mean what he said anyway. He had also been down the route of telling the truth on the grounds that 'honesty is the best policy'. This too, however, had also gone wrong – although it has to be said that Jack's judgement in choosing the 'honest' approach was somewhat misguided; after all, admitting to a girl on a first date that you had originally fancied her best mate is a pretty obvious taboo.

Confusion therefore reigned in the mind of the man sitting in the driving seat of the car in the middle of the street, in the middle of the night, in the middle of a potentially relationship changing conversation.

Not a great scenario.

"Jack?" Hayley needed Jack to say something, anything.

Honesty, as it stood at that precise moment in time, felt once more like the best policy.

Jack restored his gaze upon his friend. He also restored his hand into hers.

"Hayles, since I met you my life has been so much better than it was before – not in all aspects granted, I haven't managed to hold down a successful relationship in that time it's true, well, other than our relationship that is." He shuffled a little in his seat to give his thoughts the time they needed to convert into the words he wanted to say. "But generally, I've been happy. And, I've been happy with our relationship as it is." He squeezed her hand once more as he continued, "You mean the world to me and I do, I do love you dearly, but as my absolute best friend. You're always there when I need you and you always make me smile. And it's great to have a best friend who's a girl – I get to flirt with you with no ulterior motive!" Hayley smiled. "And it helps that you're really fit too!" Hayley smiled again and smacked Jack.

Jack took a deep breath,

"The truth is Hayley that your friendship is so special that I wouldn't ever want to mess that up." Jack took a deep intake of air. "Phew, it's getting a bit warm in here!" He leant forward and pressed a button which opened both their windows, enabling the cold night air that had been craning to listen in on their conversation to ease its way into the car and sit patiently waiting for the rest of the night to unfold.

Hayley peered down briefly. Jack's last statement had, until the last couple of weeks, been exactly how she saw their relationship.

"A friend of mine," she began, "asked me what it would be like to have a best friend as your partner. Take that extra risk and potentially have it all."

"Or," it was Jack's turn to look down, "potentially lose it all."

Both sat there in silence for a moment.

The fog that had clouded all in Hayley's mind over the last few weeks slowly started to lift. She began to smile as she recognised everything that Jack had just said was practically the same things she had said to her friends before they had begun to throw her well ordered life and relationship into turmoil. The reality was that Jack was her best friend. Had there been a spark that would have taken the relationship to the next level, then surely they would have discovered this by now themselves. Jack gave her comfort. He gave her stability. He gave her someone she could rely on, someone who accepted her for who she was and did so unconditionally.

Hayley found a smile spreading slowly across her face. How could she have doubted her own thoughts and understanding of their relationship?

The fog had now completely lifted and, seeing the open window, slid outside into the late night air. It swirled around and moved up towards the street lights, which were still hiding in the trees, before swishing higher still to survey the solitude of the night from a distant vantage point. It looked around and huffed. Everything was so quiet and still and, well, to be honest, rather boring. It peered down to the car below and smiled to itself. Swiftly it descended picking up speed as it excitedly neared its target. Its initial route, however, was blocked as Hayley had just instructed Jack to close her window.

The fog looked through the window and huffed once more in frustration. However, staring through the glass it noticed that Jack's window was still open.

Whistling contently to itself the fog skipped around the front of the car, dived headlong through Jack's window and straight into Jack's unsuspecting head.

"Goodnight Jack." Hayley leant over and gave Jack a tender kiss on his cheek. She turned, opened the door, bid farewell again and left the car.

Jack stared out the window and watched her walk towards her flat. His eyes examined her beautiful frame. He had always known she was beautiful but the stillness and anonymity of the night enabled him to take in just how gorgeous this woman walking away from him really was. His eyes focused initially on her calves - her shapely, smooth calves. Having nodded appreciatively at her legs his gaze move upwards towards her equally amazing backside that curved sensually towards her slender hips..

"Oh Fuck!" The fog, settling comfortably in the recesses of Jack's mind, laughed aloud as confusion swept uncontrollably through him.

Jack closed his eyes tightly to try and re-set his brain but, on opening them again, found himself still staring longingly at the woman walking through the gate at the entrance to her home.

'*Hooooooonnnnnnnnnnnnnnnkkkkkkkk!!*'

Jack's head had plunged forward in despair and repeatedly thudded itself against his steering wheel. The collision with the horn section of the wheel was a little unfortunate and had nearly caused Jack to jump out of his seat and bash his head on the roof. Moreover, it had prompted Hayley to turn back and return towards the car believing that perhaps she had forgotten something.

"Oh Shit!" Jack was in panic mode. His coordination, usually very impressive, took on the properties of a blind kitten trying to pick up a ball of string, his fingers, frantically searching for the button to coolly lower the window to enable him to call out to Hayley and let her know it was an accident and that she could turn around and go back to her flat and leave him to sit there and bang his head against a less volatile piece of his car, could only hit the controls for all manner of other accessories.

Hayley halted her approach to the car as she wondered why Jack had turned his windscreen wipers and fog lamps on, and why the stereo was suddenly on full blast.

"Oh Shit!" Inside the car Jack was frantically trying to regain control. He finally managed to do so just as Hayley tapped on the passenger window. Jack flicked the switch and the window slowly opened.

"Are you alright Jack?"

"Yeah,yeah,yeah," Jack rattled, "I'm fine. I was just checking everything was working."

Hayley looked at him and then at their surroundings.

"At 1.30 in the morning?"

"Er, yeah. It seemed like a good idea at the time." Jack winced.

Hayley smiled and blew Jack a kiss, "Night Jack."

"Night Hayley, see you Monday."

Hayley turned and made her way once more towards her gate.

Jack stared once more at her stunning figure before returning to banging his head.

A New Couple at Work

Monday mornings are grim. That is an undeniable fact albeit a sweeping generalisation at the same time. There are times of course when Mondays are right up there amongst the best days ever, primarily if they happen to be Bank Holidays or the culmination of a long weekend. However on the whole they are days viewed with dread and, let's face it, Sir Bob Geldof knows what he's talking about and clearly the somewhat tragic subject of his one classic song was not alone in their disliking of Mondays. Even Karen Carpenter, a woman with the voice of an angel, a voice that could uplift the gloomiest of the glum, confessed that it wasn't just rainy days but another day right at the start of the week that always got her down.

Jack had a theory about good Mondays. That theory was simply that there weren't any and that people who couldn't wait until Bank Holiday Mondays or long weekends were actually missing the point. It wasn't the Monday that was great, it was in fact the Sunday. A Sunday when you don't have to go to work on the Monday is indeed the most wonderful of days. A Sunday when you are going to work on the Monday, even if you are doing something really exciting, fun, exhilarating, unusual, or even technically illegal but pleasurable nonetheless, is always going to be tainted with the knowledge that you are going back to work the following day. Therefore when you have a Monday off all that happens is that Monday becomes the Sunday - a day of treading water pending the inevitable doom of having to go back to work the next day. Tuesday - through no fault of its own - becomes Monday. Either way, Friday and Saturday are laughing as they're great all the time.

These were Jack's musings as he made his way to work on this particular Monday morning. At least they were part of his musings. His thoughts had drifted briefly onto this subject as this particular Monday morning was a most unusual one for Jack Matthews. He had given his normal gloomy stares in the mirror as he shaved and questioned his chosen career path as well as the mournful sighs as he watched the clock tick rapidly towards the time where he had to depart or run the risk of turning up late and incurring the wrath of his punctuality obsessed manager. However, today these depressive thoughts were intermingled with a nervous excitement and confusion that had been clouding his mind since he had starting banging his head against his steering wheel in the early hours of Sunday morning.

Jack had spent the last twenty-four hours since that time trying to recount all the events of the last couple of weeks where he could have somehow missed the obvious signs that Hayley had been brave enough to talk about. He had taken a long walk on the Sunday - he did his best thinking when he was walking - and had gone over most of the details of the previous day's wedding in his head. He had thought about the closeness of his dancing with Hayley, the constant references by his friends, relatives, and heavens, even his Ex, to the fact that he and Hayley were seemingly a couple.

Most significantly for Jack, however, were the words Hayley had said to him in the car after he had tried to say that they were the best of friends. He had re-played the image of that moment over and over again in his mind – "A friend of mine asked me what it would be like to have a best friend as your partner. Take that extra risk and potentially have it all."

Jack had, at the time, come back quite quickly with a line about 'potentially losing it all' but the more he had allowed himself to immerse his thoughts around his relationship with Hayley the more he had found himself agreeing with her logic. The fact was that Hayley was perfect.

Jack smiled and nodded to himself as he came around the corner and into the market square. How had it taken so long for him to see what was so obvious to everyone else?

"Morning Jack!"

Jack looked up to see Ken striding purposefully from the other direction.

"What are you smiling about Jack," Ken drew up alongside his colleague, "did you get lucky last night? Did your hand not reject you?"

"Ah, I see you're on form today Ken. Always good to see you starting a Monday morning with a reference to your favourite pastime."

"Not mine Jack," Ken smiled the kind of smile that was screaming out for someone to ask him why he was smiling, "I don't need to resort to that kind of behaviour," he looked at Jack and raised his eyebrows imploring Jack to show the interest Ken was convinced his private life merited, "not me, not anymore," his voice grew a little more desperate as Jack continued to refuse to rise to the bait, "not now I don't need to," and another ignored raising of his eyebrows followed, "not now!"

Jack, fully aware that he was expected to show an interest

but too engrossed in his own situation to really care, finally decided it was best to acknowledge Ken lest he proceeded to start re-enacting from Monty Python's 'nudge nudge wink wink' sketch. Ken had a habit of misquoting comedy classics. This was a habit that really infuriated Jack who was always compelled to correct Ken's errors which in turn always resulted in heated debates that really served little purpose other than to show them both up as a couple of sad losers (as Hayley had rather accurately put it).

Jack let out a loud sigh.

"OK Ken," he turned to look at the beaming smile and self-satisfied smug look on Ken's face, "why do you no longer have the need to wank yourself silly every night? Have you purchased a doll?"

"No!" the previous self-righteous look had momentarily dropped off his face.

"You know shagging your pillow doesn't count don't you Ken."

"Ha ha, Jack you're so amusing, or is it jealousy perhaps?" The look was returning to Ken's face. Even Jack's put downs could not destroy Ken's spirit today. A shag is a wonderful thing for the confidence.

"OK, who is he?" Jack wasn't prepared to give up just yet however.

"She! She! A woman Jack," Ken was practically drooling, "you remember what one of those is don't you Jack?"

"Absolutely, I'm just amazed that you do. So this is a real woman – as in a human?"

"Yes!" Ken's broad smile was almost falling off the side of his face.

"And she was alive?"

The smile was still there.

"And she wasn't drugged or of questionable intellect? Actually, scrub that last remark, clearly she is of questionable intellect."

"You can try and take the piss as much as you like my friend, the fact is, I shagged a woman last night and you didn't." Ken patted, well, thumped Jack's back in triumph and strode off towards the bank doors.

"She was blind wasn't she?" Jack called after Ken and smiled as Ken's reply was delivered in the form of a solitary finger.

Before he knew it Jack found himself striding through the banking hall, through the open security door and towards the stairs.

"Morning Ladies" his customary call to the cashiers was met with the customary mixture of replies. Some would call out 'Morning Jack', some would say nothing at all but just stare blankly into space, and others, well, Sharon, would make a smutty innuendo.

Jack smiled as he went up the stairs. For once Sharon had said nothing. It was so nice to come into work on a Monday morning and not have an ageing sex obsessed cashier ask him to show her his cock. Jack had grown used to this over the years and was still amazed that Sharon had been able to get away with this behaviour. When it first started, apart from going bright red, Jack had found himself looking frantically around for witnesses or a manager to put her in her place, however no-one ever seemed to hear or care. Jack had also decided quite early on that the last thing he really wanted to do was to go and speak to his manager and grass up a colleague for asking to see his penis. Sexual harassment was a strange beast, as indeed was Sharon.

"Why don't you just show her your cock and be done with it?" had been Hayley's tongue-in-cheek solution to Jack's predicament

"You ARE joking," had been Jack's immediate response, "what if she tries to grab it?"

"Or stamp it with her till stamp?" Hayley had found it all rather amusing, "it would be like having your own tattoo on your nob, only it would be a little different from your average tattoo as it would just be the date and the word 'PAID'. At least you'd never forget when it was done I guess!"

Jack smiled to himself as his mind wandered back in time to that event. He hadn't necessarily found it amusing at the time, well maybe a little, but this morning, as he walked purposefully towards his desk he used this as further acknowledgement of just how great Hayley really was.

"Why are you smiling?" Ken was making his way to his desk with a mug of coffee, "I thought we'd already established that you hadn't had sex last night and that I had."

"Okay Ken. If this is really a woman and, importantly, if she isn't a corpse, paid by the hour, or deaf, dumb and blind, then who is she?"

Ken tapped his finger on his nose.

"Jack, a true gentleman doesn't kiss and tell about his conquests."

"Conquests! Ken I need to check, firstly for your own sake that you do know it's not meant to be a battle don't you – I mean if you have to actually fight them into submission it's not the best way to secure a long term commitment from a woman, and secondly, for the sake of my stomach, can I just check whether you're going to go on about this all day? It's just I need to know whether I need to completely switch off from anything you say earlier than I normally do."

Ken laughed and sat down in his chair with an air of confidence and authority he seldom possessed.

"Ah Jack, you are funny mate. Jealousy really doesn't suit you."

"Unless you were with Mylene Klass last night – and I mean literally and not in your head or watching an old Hearsay video – then I'm really not jealous."

Ken shook his head almost in pity at his colleague and flicked on his computer.

Jack did the same and looked over at Hayley's empty desk.

The sound of footsteps prompted him instinctively to quickly turn around in anticipation of seeing Hayley's smiling face beaming towards him. His own smile had already formed on his face which was a little embarrassing as the footsteps belonged to Sharon.

"Morning Sharon." Jack covered this embarrassment and removed the smile from his face as quickly as he could and returned his gaze to his computer. He braced himself for a whispered request to view his genitalia but today was his lucky day and Sharon merely returned his greeting as she scuttled past the gents' desks and towards the kitchen.

"Do you want a coffee Jack?"

Jack removed his gaze from his screen and turned it in slight amazement towards Ken.

"Erm, blimey you are in a good mood!" Jack smiled at Ken who returned a somewhat embarrassed smile himself. "Haven't you just got one for yourself though?"

Ken looked down at his cup, the steam still rising from its lip.

"Er yes, but what the heck.." his hesitancy was a little surprising.

"I guess you are celebrating," Jack helped him out and, besides, he didn't want to miss out on this rarest of occasions - Ken getting the drinks in, "so if you don't mind, yeah, I'd love a coffee please Ken, white with one," Jack paused to briefly contemplate how he felt about his body shape this morning, "actually make it two sugars."

"No problem mate," Ken swiftly stood up from his chair, "and how does Hayley take it?"

"What!" Jack's neurological pathways collided in one almighty crash.

"How does Hayley take it?" Ken repeated his simple request.

The twisted wreckage in Jack's brain began to untwine itself and send messages to its relevant lobes advising on all possible meanings of Ken's comments and the likelihood of them being anything other than a perfectly innocent enquiry as to how their mutual colleague liked her coffee.

Did Ken really mean how does she take her coffee?

Or, did Ken in actual fact mean how does she take 'it' as in her sexual preferences?

If the latter was right then did Ken mean how did she take 'it' specifically from Jack?

If this was the case then what had Jack done to betray this potential scenario?

Paranoia, much like sexual harassment, was a strange beast.

All these thoughts had passed through Jack's brain in an

instant, which was a shame, as had they taken a little longer he may have replied to Ken in a slightly different and far more coherent manner than he did.

"How do I know how she takes it, it's not as if we're married, er, or seeing each other or anything like that is it?"

Ken stared back at Jack, a slightly bemused stare it has to be said.

"You get her a coffee every day Jack."

Jack stared back at Ken, a slightly embarrassed stare it has to be said.

"White no sugar please Ken. Thanks."

"Righto…freak." Ken made his swift exit towards the kitchen leaving Jack to bury his head in his hands.

"Morning!"

A hand gently, and briefly, lay on Jack's shoulder before Hayley continued on her route to her desk.

"Morning!" Jack called out his greeting and smiled broadly as Hayley took her seat opposite him. He found himself holding the smile for an unnaturally long time as he waited for Hayley to settle in and return his gaze. Hayley, meanwhile, was paying no attention at all to the Cheshire cat on the other side of the desk but instead was rooting around in her drawer searching for her diary and pen.

The smile was now actually beginning to physically hurt Jack's cheekbones to the extent that he seemingly had little alternative other than to briefly massage his face and gyrate his jaw before returning to the rather inane grin.

Hayley started to raise her head from the depths of her drawer which enabled her to catch a glimpse of the weird facial contortions on the other side of the desk. A glimpse was all it was, however, as she returned back to the quest for her pen.

Jack sank in his seat as the prospect of having to hold the smile for even longer loomed large.

"Are you alright Jack?" came a voice from the drawer.

"Er, yeah, I'm fine," Jack sat up smartly, "and you?"

"I'm fine too, it's just you had a weird look on your face."

Jack looked a little taken aback and the 'smile' was finally relieved of its duties.

"Oh?"

"Yep," Hayley had now arisen triumphantly grasping her pen and was smiling at Jack, "I wasn't sure if you were having some kind of mental breakdown or were just constipated."

Jack forced an embarrassed, but this time genuine, smile.

"Oh, no, I was just pleased to see you." Jack wasn't sure how that sentence had come out. Had he sounded like friend pleased to see a friend? Had he come across as a love-sick puppy desperately trying to send not so subtle subliminal messages to the woman of his dreams across the table? Had he lost his mind?

Jack shook his head as he tried to shake all these thoughts out of his confused mind.

Hayley looked back at Jack with a slightly bewildered stare.

"Are you really alright Jack?"

"Yeah, yeah, yeah," came the eager reply.

"It's just you've told me you're pleased to see me and then shook your head."

Jack opened his mouth to reply but his brain had clogged up again and, as an emergency measure, had sent out an SOS to his voice box temporarily suspending it from duties to avoid any further unnecessary damage.

"Now you look like a goldfish."

Jack shut his mouth.

Hayley giggled and shook her own head affectionately at her friend.

"Hey, thanks for Saturday Jack," Hayley paused to turn on her computer before continuing, "it was a really great day. Your family are completely mad."

Jack opened his mouth and waited for his response to eventually form.

"Thanks."

He shut his mouth and inwardly chastised himself for not being able to come up with anything more than a simple acknowledgement.

"Oh My God, have you heard by the way?" Jack was slightly taken aback by how quickly Hayley had changed the subject.

"Heard what?"

"About Ken!" Hayley's face was alive with excitement as she realised she might be the bearer of great gossip.

"Oh has he got to you already?" Jack tutted. "All I've heard this morning is the fact that he had a shag last night."

"Did he tell you with who?"

"No," Jack sighed and stared at the information loading onto his computer. He, in truth, was sulking slightly. He didn't want to talk about Ken. He wanted to talk about the weekend, about their chat, about all the things Hayley had said.

"Ken won't divulge the name of the poor unfortunate beast he mounted. He assures me a true gentleman doesn't kiss and tell."

Hayley beamed excitedly at Jack, drawing his gaze away

from the computer. Jack found his mood lifting. Hayley was almost bobbing up and down in her chair with the excitement of a child about to open her Christmas presents knowing that they've got the big one that their parents had told them they can't afford and couldn't find anywhere in the shops. In reality, of course, the parents weren't lying as they couldn't really afford it and the shops didn't have them, thus leaving the only option to find the one remaining gift on some arsehole's EBay site and enter a bidding war with the poor unfortunate parents of other ungrateful spoilt brats. Ah, the magic of Christmas!

"What do you know?" the rather inane grin had returned to Jack's face. What with Jack's contorted face and Hayley bursting with the desire to tell her secret, but at the same time wishing to keep the suspense going for just a fraction longer, the two of them looked like a couple of naughty school kids about to share some priceless knowledge such as who had left a small turd on Sir's desk.

"Let's just say that your dick is now safe for a while!"

A fleeting moment was all it took for Jack's brain to gather and sort all the relevant information from his sub-conscious and conversations of the morning.

"You are joking!"

"Nope," Hayley was nodding furiously, "you know what she's like, she can't keep her mouth shut – which is ironic really as from what she was just telling all the other cashiers downstairs her mouth spent a lot of time open last night!"

Jack's facial muscles, which had already seen a lot of action in the brief time he had been at work today, recoiled as the rather disturbing image painted by Hayley's previous remark tried to force its way into his mind.

"Oh My God, really?"

"Yep!" Hayley nodded furiously, "How funny is that!"

Jack was mirroring Hayley's nods when it occurred to him that Ken and Sharon were obviously in the kitchen together.

"Hey," Jack got up and beckoned Hayley, "follow me."

Hayley did as she was asked and followed Jack who crept up to the kitchen. He raised his finger to his lips and whispered "ssshh" before slowly, ever so slowly turning the door handle and then bursting through the door as loudly as he could manage.

Ken almost dropped the mug of coffee he was holding and Sharon, in a bizarre attempt to avoid looking suspicious, opened the fridge door and muttered,

"Now where's the coffee?"

"I don't think it will be in the fridge Sharon." Jack pointed to the big jar of coffee on the work surface. "I think it's there in that big jar of coffee with the huge sticker with the word 'Coffee' printed on it!"

"Oh yeah, thanks." Sharon was too flustered to pick up on the gentle hint of sarcasm in Jack's tone.

"I was just finishing your coffees." Ken's voice and posture leaked guilt.

"You've made me a coffee?" Hayley sounded stunned, "what's with you, did you get lucky last night or something?"

For the briefest of moments there was complete silence in the room as each of them pondered how to react to this last remark.

The fact was that Ken would have loved to start bragging about how he had indeed got lucky the night before but clearly felt this was completely inappropriate as the woman with whom he had 'got lucky' was standing right there. For her part, Sharon would have also liked to start bragging, as indeed she had already done to the rest of the cashiers this particular morning, and as indeed she would continue to do so for the rest of the day. However, as the person with whom she had done all the things that, during the course of the day, would turn the stomachs of most of the unfortunate people whom she would subject to her tales, was standing there, Sharon decided not to comment. The fact that she had also promised Ken that they would keep things quiet also bore some influence on her decision.

Jack, however, had no vested interest in keeping things quiet.

"Too right he did!" Jack slapped his colleague on the back. "I tell you, when Ken came in this morning all I heard about was the fact that he got some action last night."

Ken squirmed in the corner.

"Ken!" Hayley beamed, "Congratulations! Who is he?"

"It wasn't a 'he'." Ken, despite his embarrassment, stood proudly to defend the honour of the woman standing by the fridge, "It was a woman, a beautiful woman." Ken couldn't help but glance over to Sharon who was both immediately touched by this comment and laden with guilt over her perhaps less than flattering comments to her colleagues downstairs over Ken's performance and, another twinge of guilt set in, over his size.

"Wow," Hayley was also a little touched by Ken's romantic gesture, "I'm amazed. I was convinced you were gay." Okay, she was touched, but she still liked to see him squirm from time to time.

"Ken's not gay!" Sharon splurted out her comment

before she could realise that this would turn the focus onto herself.

It was Ken's turn to feel touched.

"Thanks Sharon."

Jack looked at the both of them. His temptation was to twist the knife in a little more and really milk this opportunity. Heaven knows that both Sharon and Ken had wound him up enough over the years to warrant some high quality revenge; however, the genuineness in Ken's voice had rather thrown Jack. Whether this was due to his own present circumstances and accompanying confusion he wasn't sure, but he was sure that at this precise moment the right thing to do, if not the most enjoyable, was to leave Ken and Sharon in peace.

"Sharon, you had some action last night as well didn't you. I heard you telling some of the girls downstairs." Hayley, on the other hand, thought it would be fun to continue for just a little longer.

"Er, well, you know.." Sharon was completely flustered and started to open the fridge again.

"Who were you with? Anyone we know?" Hayley smiled innocently.

"Ah, that's a question you shouldn't ask a lady?" Ken interjected.

"Or Sharon." Jack pinched himself. He wanted to leave the two of them in peace but the joke was just too obvious and his instincts had taken over.

"Hey - Sharon is a lady." Ken puffed out his chest as he leapt to the defence of his woman's honour. The fact that Sharon really wasn't a lady and had absolutely no honour at all was neither here nor there.

"Oh Ken!" Sharon almost gushed. No-one had referred

to her as lady before - well no-one who wasn't trying to get her into bed or to perform various acts upon them anyway.

Jack and Hayley looked on a little bemused.

"Jack, Hayley, I don't want you to talk about Sharon in that way. If you must know," he looked over to Sharon for some sign of approval which was given in the form of Sharon rather over-dramatically clutching her hands to her heart, "the woman, or rather the lady, I was with last night was Sharon."

Ken offered out his hand and Sharon sped forward, ignored his hand completely and instead attached herself to him in a wild embrace.

Jack and Hayley looked on, once more a little bemused.

"Christ, this is like a soap opera," Hayley observed, "but with really bad acting."

"I'm a bit concerned it might turn into a porno," Jack started to avert his eyes, "but with really bad actors."

With a quick nod Jack and Hayley made a swift exit and returned to their respective desks.

Hayley headed straight for her diary to check out how the rest of her day would unfold. Jack stared around at the various items on his desk - his last post-it pad, the small blu tac model of an elephant he had meticulously crafted the previous month during a moment of extreme boredom, his desk-top daily calendar - yesterday's page of which he had yet to rip off and thus he had not yet had the opportunity of reading the supposed gem of wisdom or witty thought for the day that would almost certainly cause him to spend the briefest of moments contemplating why he bothered to waste his time and energy removing the sheet, and why he didn't just pick the whole thing up and place it in the bin under his desk. He would normally then spend a second briefest of moments convincing himself that out of the 365 'gems' he would subject himself to there would surely be the occasional one which would make the whole process worthwhile after all.

Jack would then spend one final briefest of moments chastising himself for wasting the briefest of moments each day contemplating this most irrelevant of 'problems'.

Jack, today, had got as far as the first briefest of moments as his gaze had fixed itself on the previous Friday's offering:

"Where there's a will – there's almost certainly some lawyers making some money out of someone's bereavement."

Jack stared blankly and, in his mind, uttered "What a load of crap."

"What?"

Jack was a little startled as Hayley interrupted his chain of thought.

"What?" Jack replied.

"What's a load of crap?"

Perhaps he hadn't uttered this just in his head as he had thought. The alternative, of course, was that Hayley could in fact hear his thoughts. A truly nonsensical and shocking prospect but netherthless one Jack just checked out by uttering in his mind, "I bet you look good naked."

Jack wasn't sure what was worse: the fact that he was actually trying to see if his friend could hear his thoughts, or the fact that, in the unlikely event that she could, that he was telling her that he thought she would look good naked. The honest truth was that Jack, whilst always having admired

Hayley's rather gorgeous frame and having paid rather more attention to it than normal over the weekend, had, out of respect and his friendship, not even started to ponder what she would look like naked. He certainly hadn't started to think what it would be like to then move on to the next stage. Well, not until this moment when suddenly images started to flood into his mind quite uninvited and unwanted.

"Are you alright Jack?" Hayley was a little perturbed by the strange blank expression across the table that accompanied the panic crashing around in Jack's head, "You're acting really weird today."

Jack shook his head, not so much as to let Hayley know he wasn't alright but rather to try and shake all the rather bizarre images out of his brain.

"Um, yeah, I'm fine," Jack pushed back in his chair and started to stand up, "I, er, just have to go somewhere."

Jack turned and walked away from their desks and made his way downstairs, past the cashiers who were still reeling from Sharon's torrid tales of her seduction of poor Ken, out through the banking hall and into the Market Square. There he took in a couple of huge breaths and allowed himself to close his eyes and compose himself.

It had been a most confusing morning so far for Jack and, as his eyes were closed, he frantically tried to make sense of it all. This, however, wasn't easy but suddenly, and to his great relief, a calming voice took control of him. He opened his eyes and moved himself to a small bench not too far away from the entrance to the bank.

The voice in his head instructed him to close his eyes once more and just relax, count to ten, and take in all the sounds and smells from the early morning hustle and bustle around the square. All the other voices that had tormented and confused him through the course of the day so far, and latter part of the weekend, fell silent.

Jack felt the tenseness slide out of his shoulders. The tightening of the back of his neck, which Jack hadn't even been aware of until he felt it melt away, did just that and Jack slowly rotated his head gently on its axis feeling the slight crunch as the last segments of stress were squeezed away.

The calming voice that had moved into his mind at his time of need offered no answers or explanations. It merely offered him some peace and a sense of perspective.

As Jack opened his eyes into the bright sunlight he found himself re-energized and momentarily almost spiritually awoken.

"Fucking weirdo!"

Jack's karma was somewhat shattered by a couple of gothic-clad and piercing-holed teenagers shuffling past him on the way to buy a couple of milkshakes and to no doubt discuss this year's must have fashions - basically anything black.

Jack didn't care however. 'Fucking weird', he thought to himself as he headed purposefully through the banking hall, was actually a very good summary of the morning's events.

Quickly he found himself back at his desk. Ken, who had returned from the kitchen moments after Jack's exit, looked up at Jack as he sat himself down.

"It might be a little cold," Ken waved a finger at the cup of coffee he had put on Jack's desk a few minutes earlier, "where have you been?"

"Er, just here and there, you know." This seemed the best answer. "Where's Hayley?"

"She's got an appointment and, oh," Ken checked the scribbled note on the scrap of paper on his desk, "you missed Sarah Michaels. She called and wanted to speak to you."

"Ah that's a shame. Does she need me to give a call back?"

"Nah, I don't think so. I've booked her in to see you next Monday."

"But I'm in not in next Monday."

Ken smiled.

"Oh well, I'll have to see her this time!"

"Ken you're a married man. What if Sharon finds out?"

Ken gave a nonchalant shrug of his shoulders and thrust out his chest like some kind of parading peacock.

"Hey, I am but flesh alone and if Sarah finds me irresistible, as have many other women, then who am I do refuse her her chance?"

Jack tilted his head just so he could look at Ken from a slightly different angle, just so he could be sure that it was actually Ken sitting there and not a brilliantly constructed clone from Bullshitters-R-Us.

"Ken," Jack waited until he had obtained some rather sheepish eye contact, "what would Sharon do to your bollocks if you cheated on her, actually, scrub that, if you even looked at another woman?"

Ken stared back and after much careful consideration concluded,

"She'd remove them with her bare hands and feed them to her dog."

Both men nodded in agreement that this indeed was the most likely outcome and proceeded to get on with their work.

For his part, Jack was a little distracted but his general mood was now one of a calm resolve. He knew he needed to speak to Hayley but he now knew that this was not the time and that work was certainly not the place. He would engineer a scenario where they could spend some quality time together, alone, outside work.

Happy Hour?

Lloyds Bar, Happy Hour, Tuesday night – a haven for Karaoke lovers everywhere.

It was only a quarter to seven but the inebriated squalling of a bedraggled middle-aged woman, ironically proclaiming 'Stand by your Man' as she herself struggled to stand up having spent the last few hours drinking herself into a stupor in an attempt to find some tenuous excuse to justify her own recent infidelity, filled the pub and sent half the occupants dashing to the bar to place their last cheap orders. The other half of the occupants simultaneously raised their hands over their ears in an instinctive reaction born out of the need to prevent any further irrevocable mental damage.

"Has anyone got a gun?" Danny shouted over the noise and looked hopefully at his friends around the table.

Jack shook his head, carefully ensuring that in doing so his hands maintained their tight protective grip around his ears.

Chris, one of Danny's work colleagues whom Jack had known for a couple of years but hadn't seen since they had all been out some four months previously, also shook his head and motioned that he was going to go to the bar.

Aiden, a mutual friend of them all and who had gone to college with Jack several years previously, didn't reply. His gaze was upon the bedraggled woman and his head was rocking slowly in time to the lilting country beat.

"Aiden...Aiden!" Danny tried to get his friend's attention,

"Aiden…" a sharp poke to his ribcage finally did the trick.

"What?" his redirected gaze and attention were only fleeting as they returned to the woman at the mike who, mercifully for all in the room, save Aiden so it would seem, had finally reached the last slaughtering of the line 'Stand by your Man'. Everyone in the place sighed in genuine relief, everyone except Aiden who applauded enthusiastically and ensured he caught the eye of the tone deaf woman as she staggered gingerly off the small stage and back to the table where a couple of her equally hammered friends were glugging intently on their alco-pops.

Aiden, eye contact and smile exchanged, finally returned his gaze and attention back to Jack and Danny who, in turn, were staring back at him shaking their heads.

"What?" Aiden protested. "She's got talent."

"She's got breasts you mean." Danny's gaze had turned into a frown, the sort of frown a disapproving teacher would give you as a warning that if you carried on doing what you were doing then there would be trouble.

"And she's completely rat-arsed." Jack continued the observations.

"And she's emotionally vulnerable," Danny added.

"And she's walking this way." Jack's voice tailed off and he buried his head in his folded arms on the table hoping not to have to watch whatever was going to happen next.

Aiden, on the other hand, positively lit up. A broad, well, in all honesty a well practised and irritatingly smarmy, smile spread across his face as he turned to greet the woman.

"Hi." He oozed confidence.

"Hi," the woman stood by the table ensuring that she gripped its edge tightly so as to maintain her balance, "my friends said I should come over here and see you."

"Did they now," Aiden peered round her frame and waved at her giggling friends, "well I'm glad they did."

The woman blushed but, in truth, was so pissed she wasn't quite sure what to do or say next.

"You were fantastic," Aiden nodded throughout his stream of compliments in a well-rehearsed routine meticulously constructed with the sole purpose of conveying sincerity. "Seriously, you had me transfixed. I've been here many a time and I don't think I've ever seen such a combination of voice and stunning," Aiden paused to look the woman up and down ensuring that she was aware of his body check, "stunning beauty. You were amazing. Where do you normally sing?"

Danny had now joined Jack in hiding on the table.

"I'm not actually a professional singer," slurred the woman as she found herself falling under the hypnotic charms of Aiden's penetrating eyes.

"Really?" Aiden turned and poked his two hiding friends who reluctantly looked up, "Guys, can you believe she's not a professional singer?"

Jack and Danny decided it best to play dead, say nothing and avoid any movements lest they give their friend any encouragement to try and engage them in the conversation.

"Are your friends okay?" The woman was a little confused why two men were apparently hiding their heads on a table.

"They're fine, they just can't handle their drink."

"Oh, well, to be honest," the woman crouched down and whispered into Aiden's ear, "I'm a little tipsy too." She giggled as she stood up.

"Well, you hide it well if you are." Aiden really was completely full of shit.

"I tell you what," Aiden took hold of her hand resting on

the table - a usually good ploy but one which on this occasion nearly back-fired as the poor woman almost lost her balance and toppled over onto Jack who, fortunately, had a nose for impending doom, and was able to catch her before she completely collapsed and return her to her almost upright position. Aiden, in mid bull-shit, chose to ignore this and carried on, "After I've finished my drink with my colleagues why don't we pick up? I have a couple of really good contacts in the music business who I think might be interested in someone like you."

Before the woman could reply Aiden had kissed her hand and subtly pushed it back in the direction of whence she came.

"Great, really? Wow!"

"You are really hot, you know that don't you?" Aiden threw in one last comment to hopefully seal the deal and smiled as the woman staggered back to her friends.

There was momentary silence at the table.

"You are a complete shit." Jack summarised the situation quite nicely.

"Who's a complete shit?" Chris had returned to the table with the drinks, having mercifully been spared Aiden's pre-mating ritual.

"Aiden." Danny answered and looked over at Aiden who just smiled smugly and shrugged his shoulders as if to indicate he had no idea what they were talking about.

"Who was it this time?" Chris handed out the pints and, following the line from Jack's pointed finger, stared over at a small table on the other side of the bar.

"Not the singer!"

Aiden smiled and raised his glass, "Cheers!"

"Fucking hell Aiden, she was practically paralytic."

"He used the music connection line again." Danny shook his head in quite genuine disparagement, something which was completely lost on Aiden, and sipped at his pint.

Jack picked up his own pint and, after a brief pause, took a short sip that then turned into a long drawn slug which, by the time he had returned the glass to the table, had left it half empty.

"Bloody hell, thirsty are we?" Aiden observed.

"Aye, but don't worry," Jack began, "I'm not going to risk getting pissed, not with you around."

"What?" Aiden protested his innocence but clearly revelled in his reputation.

"Seriously?" Danny, who in the past had found Aiden's techniques amusing, and at times very useful, had, over the years, got a little tired and more recently increasingly embarrassed by his friend's behaviour. "You are an absolute nightmare. You're like a ruthless predator seeking out the desperate and vulnerable in order to see if they have a spare orifice you can get your dick into."

"Hey, I wouldn't shag Jack, even if he was pissed. I'm strictly hetero." Aiden momentarily looked a little indignant. "And in reply to your last comment I don't just go for the desperate and vulnerable, they have to be good looking as well you know. I have my standards."

His three friends stared across at him trying to work out if he was being serious. Aiden stared back at them trying to work out the same thing.

The last time the four of them had met up they had been through a similar conversation. Aiden had cracked onto some poor unsuspecting soul who had succumbed to his charms and, as a result, had found herself pressed up against the graffiti-clad wall of the local chippy at 3 o'clock in the morning. This was due to the somewhat misguided impression that this would help her pursue her career in modelling on account of the various contacts Aiden had assured her he possessed. The other three guys had scorned him at the time; however, at least one of them shared that shame as they had knocked off one of the girl's friends at the same time. Such was their shame, however, that they decided not to share this with the group and their identity therefore remained anonymous.

They hadn't seen each other as a group for some months thereafter which was due to a combination of factors. Firstly, they did have reasonably busy jobs but that in itself isn't really an excuse. Secondly, some of them had hobbies like going to the gym, reading (FHM, Nuts or similar publications) or playing with sticks and masks ("it's called 'Tai Kwando'" as Chris had vociferously protested) but these, again, in themselves aren't really an excuse. Thirdly, some of them were getting a little older (well all of them were technically a little older) but some were also a little wiser. Whilst this in itself was not a great excuse it did lead to perhaps the real reason behind the increasing periods of time between their get-togethers.

People change.

Jack had mulled this over many times in his head over the years and, whilst he was only in his mid to late twenties himself, he had realised that he wasn't the same person now that he was even two to three years ago, let alone five or ten. He had clear evidence to back that up just by recalling how he had dealt with his relationship with Imogen. He was convinced that he would not make the same naïve mistakes the next time he got seriously involved with a woman.

In the same way that his attitudes had been moulded and influenced by his own experiences, and the experiences of those people closest to him, so had the attitudes of Aiden, Danny and Chris. Common bondings that had held their friendship together for the last eight or nine years had in some cases, over the fullness of time, gradually been stretched as they had each meandered down their separate paths to the point where for some of them the only tenuous common bond they now shared was the fact that they knew each other and would meet up from time to time.

It is true that, as we all wander down our own separate paths, many of these paths can cross each other, join for a while and even run parallel to one another. It is when these paths are in some form of reasonably close harmony that those travelling along them are most likely to remain friends. Often the paths are heading in roughly the same way and even if you are not on someone's specific path you can momentarily allow yourself to lean over and peer down it and nod approvingly at the familiarity of the direction in which it is going. Of course, conversely, sometimes the destination of the path may be somewhat alien to you. In these cases we may often find ourselves looking a little more closely at the person heading down that track. If they are well equipped for the journey and their purpose is clear and works for them and, importantly, if they are willing to understand that the road taken by yourself is equally as valid then that mutual respect enables both parties to go their separate ways, safe in the knowledge that their friendship is secure.

The difficulty comes when a friend starts off down a track that, for you, is not a track to be trusted. If you were facing that particular fork in the road you would see that the side they have opted to skip merrily down has a big black sign with a skull on it, the words "Keep Out" etched in blood on the barbed-wire-garlanded walls that align one side of the cracked and potted rocky pavings, and, rather more worryingly, the squirrels in the trees that align the other side would be armed with flick knives and small hand guns.

Aiden, it would seem, had been following one such highway for a while now.

Jack had tried to think back to the time when they had reached the junction at which point three of the friends had turned right and the other had turned left. It wasn't a particularly nice thought process for Jack to have undertaken as it had forced him to admit that often the roads down which he had trodden had their fair share of ninja squirrels hiding in the bushes as well. Nethertheless Jack had sought some comfort from the knowledge that 'People Change' and that it was far from uncommon for young men in their twenties to be brainwashed by their penises. After all, the odds are stacked heavily in favour of their dicks - they have two brains in a sack directly behind them directing operations whereas the rest of the body only has one and that's about as far away from their dicks as is physically possible. Jack could also, with justification, console himself that his 'shag at all costs' period had been reasonably fleeting. Where Jack had found himself in unplanned impromptu sexual encounters – such as the monster-breasted New Years Eve woman – he had invariably had the best intentions at heart and had not set out to take advantage of anyone.

Aiden, the man sitting across the table from Jack with a pint in one hand, a twirling beer mat in the other and a cocky grin taking centre stage on his innocent-looking face, could not claim any such redemption and indeed wasn't seeking to. Aiden had convinced himself that he was quite happy to carry on counting up the notches on the bedpost, or in his case more specifically counting the names and dates he maintained in an old diary to ensure he could accurately provide the accumulated total of his conquests to anyone who asked. A more interesting statistic would have been if he had added a column to indicate how many of his conquests were attributable to his genuine personality as opposed to excessive alcohol, false promises or extreme desperation and vulnerability. Not a column that Aiden had considered.

As Jack stared back at the face opposite him he mulled over a few of these brief thoughts. He came to the conclusion that Aiden's path was so far removed from his that the signposts thereon were almost certainly in a different language and those who travelled this path were doing so on the other side of the road.

"Guys, c'mon, she'll be up for it," Aiden pleaded his case and motioned towards the table in the corner, winking at the giggling ladies as he did, "and look, her mates seem up for it as well."

"Jesus Aiden," Jack's reaction was honest if not necessarily the kind of reaction you give to a supposed mate who you haven't seen for a fair while, "what the hell's up with you. It's not even seven o'clock and you've already picked out the most vulnerable girl in the bar, told her some blatant lies, and are now trying to get us involved just to ensure you can get a shag at the end of the evening."

Chris and Danny nodded their agreement, if only perhaps with a little more reticence than Jack's outburst, an outburst which hadn't quite finished yet.

"Aiden, I can't believe what a complete wanker you are sometimes."

There was a stunned silence around the table.

This was one of those times when Jack's brain had quite specifically requested that these words had remained as thoughts, uttered in the privacy of his own head; however, rather unfortunately these instructions had somehow been misinterpreted with the result that the words had inadvertently hurled themselves out of his now somewhat embarrassed mouth.

The silence was, fortunately, sufficiently brief not to turn the whole evening on its head. It was broken by Danny forcing a huge and infectious laugh that spread around the group finishing with Jack, who was grateful for his friend's intervention.

"Jack's right," Danny concurred as the four of them cracked up around the table, "you've got to admit Aiden, you are a complete wanker!"

"To Aiden," Chris joined in and raised his pint in a toast, "a complete wanker!"

"To Aiden," all four raised their glasses, "a complete wanker."

"Thankyou my friends," Aiden acknowledged each of the three around him, "it's good to know that you can all be relied on to tell it as it is. And," he raised his glass aloft, "it takes one to know one. So, a toast if you please, to Us," all glasses were raised once more, "a bunch of wankers!"

"Bunch of wankers!" chorused the group.

"Good to see a bit of honesty," the barmaid had made her way over to their table to collect the empty glasses just at the moment of this declaration, "every man I've ever known has been a wanker but none of them would admit it."

"Ah, you see Tracey," Aiden leant forward in an attempt to catch the barmaid's eye, "that's why you should take me up on my offer and let me take you out one evening."

"I don't think so." The glasses were now efficiently gathered and stacked and Tracey nonchantly moved on towards the adjacent table.

"Ah come on, why not?" Aiden called after her, having seemingly already forgotten the Karaoke princess.

Tracey turned round and, whilst raising her eye-brows, made a small circle between her thumb and index finger, and shook her hand violently for a brief moment, just enough for Chris, Jack and Danny to break into a round of applause.

"I don't know why you're all clapping," the wind was temporarily absent from Aiden's sails, "we've all just told her we're wankers."

"Yes, but we're not looking to shag her are we?" Danny had a point.

"I dunno," Chris had hooked onto Tracey's hips as she walked from table to table and was struggling to pull away his gaze, "I wouldn't say 'no'."

"Thankyou." Aiden saw this as some kind of endorsement of his behaviour.

"I meant I wouldn't say 'no' to her, not you." Chris had got a little confused.

"I know that." Aiden tutted. "I bet you would if you were a gay though?"

"What!" Chris was getting even more confused.

"Bloody Hell, not the 'if you were a gay' conversation again Aide." Jack shook his head in anticipation of the onset of a conversation that it felt like they always had at some part of their evenings out. "And why do you always say it like that?"

"Like what?"

"Like, 'if you were *a* gay', why do you always prefix 'gay' with '*a*'. You make it sound so impersonal."

"Well how do you want me to say it?" Aiden didn't see what the fuss was about.

"Can't you just say, 'if you were gay', and leave the '*a*' out of it?"

Aiden looked a little perplexed. "Does it matter? I'm sure if you were a gay you wouldn't care."

"You've done it again!" Jack didn't mean to get frustrated, in part because he knew that Aiden was kind of right and it didn't really matter, but also because, in part, he knew that he was right and that the way Aiden referred to gay people did come across as condescending.

"What!" Aiden was getting a little flustered himself now.

"You said 'I'm sure if you were '*A*' gay'. You make it sound like they are another race or species or something."

"Alright, keep your hair on Jack. Where's your Gay Rights banner?"

"Guys, guys.." Danny felt the need to intervene, "every bloody time we have this conversation and every bloody time it ends the same way. So let's cut out the next five minutes of confusion and picking apart of how Aiden constructs his sentences and what possible hidden contexts lie beneath them, and just agree now that the only reason Aiden thinks

Chris would shag him if he was gay is because Aiden is so vain he thinks anyone would want to shag him."

Aiden nodded. "Thank you Danny."

"You're welcome."

A couple of uneventful hours followed where the conversations were mercifully non-confrontational and the humour, like the alcohol, flowed.

Jack checked his watch. It was only a quarter past nine but he had kind of had enough for the evening – early drinking didn't always agree with him. It seemed like a good time to consider calling it a night and to get home before he began to run the risk of incurring one almighty hangover that he would certainly regret when his alarm clock shouted abuse at him early the following morning. Besides, Aiden was getting a little restless at the thought that he had left the Karaoke Princess alone for too long and, unless he slimed his way over to see her now, there was a serious risk that he would not be able to add to the list in his diary.

"Right chaps," Jack sat up straight and addressed his friends, "it's only Tuesday so the prospect of staying here to closing time and having to subject my liver to even more abuse, let alone my ears to any more drunken Karaoke, is not a good one."

"Me too I'm afraid guys." Danny finished up the last couple of mouthfuls of beer from his glass and set it firmly down on the table.

He and Jack grabbed their jackets and started to stand up.

"Are you two coming?"

Aiden peered over to the table where the Karaoke girl was still sitting with her friends.

Jack and Danny laughed.

Aiden raised his glass, "Wish me luck."

Chris sheepishly sipped his pint. Yes it was only Tuesday but a few pints already downed had left the beer goggles firmly attached to his face and he was hoping, not for the first time, to quite literally ride on the back of Aiden's success.

Jack and Danny wished them both luck again and made their way out into the fading light of the late evening.

"It was weird seeing Imogen again wasn't it?" Danny observed.

"Yeah," Jack hadn't given it a huge amount of thought since the actual wedding, his mind being otherwise distracted, "I guess it was a bit."

"She still looks hot doesn't she?" Danny smiled, confident that his friend wouldn't mind him referring to Jack's ex in this manner.

"She certainly still looks hot," Jack had to agree as the picture of Imogen in her bridesmaid's dress flitted into his mind.

"Weren't you a little tempted?"

"Eh?"

"Ah, come on, you must have been a little tempted surely?" Danny was beaming as he tried to encourage his friend.

"No, not really," was the honest and considered response, "it was great to see her and it gave me a chance to say sorry for being a twat I guess."

"Well, I suppose that's true," Danny nodded, "you were a bit of a twat to let that one go."

Both men carried on a few steps nodding silently in agreement.

"Hey, your friend Hayley," Danny broke the silence, "she's great."

"Yeah," Jack felt his heartbeat suddenly start to pound in his chest at the mention of her name, "she's, well, she's amazing."

"I was sure there was something going on between you two initially."

"Initially?" Jack didn't mean his tone to be quite so defensive.

"Well, yeah, you know," Danny was a little surprised by the nature of Jack's response, "I think everyone assumed that, as you brought a beautiful woman to the wedding she was your date. I think they would have carried on thinking that if you both hadn't been so quick to point out that you weren't together."

Jack felt a tinge of embarrassment. Why would anyone think they were together after the efforts both of them had made to contradict that assumption?

"The thing is," Jack paused as he considered whether to open up to his friend, "the thing is," he paused again just to make sure, "I have kind of realised that I do, well, really like her."

Danny was silent, a little stunned by Jack admission.

"What happened to 'we're just friends'?" was the eventual question after a few more steps.

"Well we kind of got talking in the car on the way home and she, well, she brought up the subject of our relationship."

"She told you she wanted more?"

"Not exactly," Jack's mind was racing as he tried to recall the events of that evening and conduct his conversation with Danny at the same time.

"How 'not exactly'?"

"Well she kind of talked around it and we both kind of said we were just friends, I think."

Danny had stopped walking.

"You 'think'?"

"Well, yes, I think so. I'm not sure to be honest." Jack shook his head in the vain hope that this would shake yet another bout of confusion out of it. "I think that's what we agreed but since then I've been seeing her in a different light and I think she sees me differently as well. I'm just not entirely sure what to do next."

"Have you tried talking to her?"

"Well yes," Jack bit on his lip as he reflected that in actual fact he hadn't really tried as yet, "and no. I've kind of decided that to talk to her at work isn't really the best plan. I think I'm going to ask her out for a drink and chat to her there."

"Oh right," Danny looked a little thoughtful, "are you sure she feels the same?"

"I don't know." Jack didn't.

"I'm just a bit worried that if you talk to her and she doesn't, it might be awkward for you."

"Why wouldn't she feel the same?" Jack had asked himself this question many times over the last few days and still hadn't been able to answer it so why not ask someone else!

"Well, it's just that when I was chatting to her at the wedding she," Danny slowed down his sentence as he realised that Jack was setting so much store by it, "she seemed quite adamant that you were just friends, best friends mind." Danny suddenly felt very guilty as he watched his friend take in this new piece of information.

"I dunno," Jack shrugged his shoulders, "she seemed a little less certain when we were talking later. I guess the only way to find out is to talk to her again."

"Yeah, I guess so," Danny nodded his tentative agreement, "just," he paused as he considered whether to carry on.

"Just what?"

"Just don't bank everything on it Jack. She is amazing but it sounds like you really are just best friends. That might have to be enough."

Jack had hoped for a little more support from Danny. The last thing he really wanted was to hear someone relaying back the very fears that Jack was trying to overcome by speaking of them in the first place. He shrugged his shoulders again and the two of them, largely in silence, continued their journey home.

Date

Jack sat at his desk, twirling his pen in his fingers and staring out of the window. He had been in this semi - comatose state for what had felt like several minutes but what, in reality, had probably only been one or two at the most. The rest of his section was empty, the result of appointments, coffee breaks and off-site training.

Jack had contemplated that the silence and consequent lack of interruptions presented an excellent opportunity to really crack on with some of the tasks he would otherwise leave to one side. This contemplation had, however, been somewhat short before another option had barged its way past these work-orientated issues.

That option was to daydream. In fairness to Jack he hadn't really made a conscious decision to follow that route, it had just crept up upon him unexpectedly. The issue Jack faced was one that everyone no doubt faces on a frequent basis, simply that life isn't simple, it's as simple as that. There are far too many worries, concerns, trials and tribulations running manically around our minds to be contained in good order. It's only natural that from time to time you're going to relax and they are all going to come bundling out of the recesses of your subconscious and start pogoing around in your semi-conscious mind whilst whacking you with sticks. Each issue vies for your attention with the result that your daydreams take on all manner of bizarre and surreal lives often resulting in minor panic attacks as you briefly consider that they might be true and not just figments of your troubled imagination.

It had been a week since Jack's night out with his friends. He had heard little from them since that time other than a text from Aiden confirming that his mission, or rather his missionary, with the Karaoke drunk had been successful.

Jack had spent most of the remaining days of the previous week thinking about Danny's words of caution. As a result he had managed to keep himself reasonably sane around Hayley and consequently their relationship had actually seemed – on the outside – much as it had always been. This had been reasonably easy to sustain for the last three days of the week; however, the same could not be said for the ensuing weekend which had presented Jack with ample opportunity to dwell on the predicament into which he had somehow managed to manoeuvre himself. Fortunately the weekend had eventually passed but the days had ticked slowly over to Wednesday and, to make matters worse, Hayley had been out of the office for the last two days on a training course. Jack's productivity had, as a result, rather nose-dived as he allowed himself to drift off at every chance in an attempt to find a resolution in his own mind as to what he should do, if anything, next.

Jack banged his head on his desk.

"Bollocks," he confided to himself.

He stood up and cast his eyes over the empty desks around him, finally resting them upon Hayley's desk. He, for reasons of which he wasn't entirely sure, found himself walking around the desk and sinking into her chair. He surveyed the office from Hayley's viewpoint – initially her literal view point as opposed to her mental one. However, he couldn't help but wonder how she saw him as she would look across the office.

As he sat back into the seat further he started to open her drawer. He suddenly felt, with some degree of justification, like some kind of stalker. He picked up her pen and ran his fingers across it, as if by holding something Hayley held he, in some mystical way, would be holding her. Jack knew this was of course bollocks and uttered this to himself quietly under his breath once more.

"What are you doing?"

Jack dropped the pen and scrambled to pick it up whilst praying desperately that by the time he had done so he would have both lost the dark red patches that had immediately adorned his cheeks and that he would have found some kind of appropriate answer to give Sharon as she passed through to the kitchen.

"My pen had run out," was as good as Jack could have done, to be fair.

"Oh right," Sharon shook her head, "weirdo," she moved on past him before turning back, "do you want me to get you a coffee?" Her smile re-assured Jack that she had in fact fallen for his explanation.

"Ah, okay, yeah that would be great thanks." He smiled back and made his way back to his desk.

"Aren't you going to take the pen?" Sharon pointed at Hayley's pen which Jack had put back on her desk.

"Oh yeah," Jack returned to pick up the pen, "that would help wouldn't it!"

Sharon shook her head and made her way to the kitchen.

Jack shook his head and made his way further into despair.

His despair, however, was short-lived as it was disturbed by the sudden interruption of his phone ringing impatiently for attention.

"Good afternoon, you're through to Jack Matthews, how can I help?"

"Wow, you do sound hot on the phone!"

Jack's face lit up, it felt like it always did when Hayley rang him.

"Well hello gorgeous!" Jack didn't mean to gush as much as he did but it was one of those times when he really had just needed to hear her voice, "how's the course going?"

"Ah, you know, nothing really new but the food's great." Hayley had managed to sum up every course Jack had ever been on in one very succinct sentence. "I'm just finishing off a rather nice prawn vol-au-vent at the moment. We've got to head back in a few minutes but I thought I'd just give you a buzz to catch up. So, how's it going this week, are you missing me?" Hayley's tone was upbeat and flirtatious. The course had, in fact, been extremely tedious and right now she needed to speak to a friend and feel good about herself. Whenever she felt like that Jack was the one person she could always rely on to tick both of those boxes.

"Hey, of course I'm missing you," the warmth of Jack's smile resonated through his reassuring tone, "it's been so boring and, of course, I've had no one attractive to look at either."

"Ah, you say all the right things Mr Matthews."

"One tries," the smile across Jack's face was now actually beginning to hurt, "anyway," the words came out of Jack's mouth before he could realise what he was saying – a victory for his sub-conscious which began to dance around in his head giving itself hi-fives, "do you fancy meeting up for a drink one evening after work this week?"

The beam that had lit up his face moments before was suddenly replaced by a look of complete panic.

"Yeah, that sounds great, I wanted to speak to you about something anyway." Hayley, whilst seeming very matter-of-fact, had just a brief hint of mischief in her voice.

"Oh really?" Jack was intrigued, taken aback, concerned, excited and a whole further stream of emotions which were clogging up his ability to think straight.

"Yep," Hayley paused to take another quick bite of her vol-au-vent, "anyway, look I've got to go, everyone's piling back into the training room. I'm back to work on Friday but do you want to go out on Thursday night?"

"Yeah, absolutely, that sounds great."

"Cool, listen, got to go. Do you want to come round for me at 7.30-ish?"

"Yeah, no problem, it's a date."

With a swift 'bye' Hayley had gone. Jack began to replace the handset slowly as he started to obsess over his final words, 'it's a date'. Was it a date? Did Hayley think it was a date? Was that just an over-used expression? Had he meant it as a throwaway line or had he, deep down, hoped that by saying 'it's a date' Hayley would pick up on this and her own secret desires for it to, in fact, be a date would be awoken and she, in turn, would now see it as a date?

"Here's your coffee."

His rambling stream of thought was mercifully cut short by Sharon plonking down his mug of coffee.

"Ah, thanks Sharon."

Sharon took this as an invitation to talk and promptly eased some of Jack's paperwork to one side and perched herself on the end of his desk.

"So how's it going Jack?"

Jack was suspicious.

"Er, good thanks Sharon. How about you?"

Sharon nodded enthusiastically.

"Yeah, great thanks."

"Good!" Jack smiled in the hope that this would signal the end of the conversation and that he could get back to obsessing about Hayley or at the very least try and do some of the work that had began to pile up and just been moved to make space for Sharon's backside.

"Jack," his hopes were swiftly quashed, "I wanted to talk to you about something."

Jack's head was now full of dread. If Sharon was about to talk him through her latest sexual shenanigans with Ken then Jack may have to stab her with Hayley's pen.

"What's that then Sharon?" He tried to sound as businesslike as possible.

"Well, as you know, me and Ken have been seeing each other for a little while now," Jack began to reach for the pen, "and I wanted to check that you're alright with that?"

Jack stopped in his tracks and looked to Sharon with a rather puzzled expression that cried out for an explanation.

Sharon misinterpreted this look for one of affirmation that she was right to bring up the subject.

"Jack, I am a woman." Sharon's low-cut top was testament to this, a fact that Jack was trying to ignore, which was not easy as her breasts were at his eye level and barely a foot away from him. "You've been acting a little strange in the last week or so since you've found out about me and Kenny. Even Kenny has noticed it."

Jack looked even more bemused now.

Sharon reached out and gently and reassuringly placed her hand on his.

"Listen, I'm sorry I haven't paid you much attention recently."

Jack began to grasp where this poor misguided woman was heading and foolishly tried to stop her flow,

"Oh, no no no.."

His protestations were cut short by two of her fingers pushing against his rather startled lips.

"Jack, Jack. We have to face facts. I can't ask you to show me your cock any more. It's just not right."

The two fingers pressed firmly against his lips prevented Jack from letting Sharon know that it had never, and would never be right. Besides, he was too scared that if he opened his mouth she might put her fingers in it!

"What we had Jack," Jack's eyebrows raised at the terrifying thought that he had had something with Sharon, "was just something on a spiritual plane. Do you know what I mean?"

Sharon removed her fingers to enable Jack to speak. Jack didn't quite know what to say, with the result that a series of non committal half words fell out of his open jaw.

"Jack, look. I think if we had turned our relationship into something more physical then it would have been incredible. Seriously, I am very open minded and extremely flexible," Jack winced at the sincerity of Sharon's analysis, "but the fact is that we missed that opportunity. I'm with Kenny now. It would be wrong for us to carry on as we did. I may be a real woman, a real sexual woman, but I'm also a faithful woman. I can't cheat on Ken. Is that okay Jack?"

It was obviously very okay for Jack. All he had to do was

to work out how to say it was okay without encouraging Sharon to jump on him there and then.

"That's fine Sharon. And to be honest, I don't think we ever actually got to the stage where a physical relationship was on the cards."

Sharon looked a little shocked. However, calm swiftly returned to her as she allowed herself to re-interpret Jack's sentence.

"Perhaps you're right Jack. Perhaps we needed to wait a little longer. Sometimes when I've been out with people, and we've waited before having sex, the sex has always been that much better. I remember one time when I waited to the third date before screwing this guy and it was truly amazing."

"As indeed you are," Jack felt the impulsion to interrupt and curtail this discussion as soon as he could lest Sharon start to go into even more detail and, heaven forbid, work herself up into a frenzy whilst perched on his desk, "and on that note Sharon I really must get on. But thank you for taking the time to set things straight between us."

"You're welcome." Sharon kissed her two fingers and planted them on Jack's cheek before easing herself off the side of the desk and heading back to the rest of the cashiers who had themselves been enjoying a break from the numerous graphic stories of Sharon's last holiday.

Jack smiled to himself and shook his head. How could one person so misunderstand a situation?

Cupid

The clock on Jack's microwave glowed its way to seven o'clock inducing within him a mild stream of panic. He had just finished shaving and had wasted the last thirty seconds alternating between picking up and putting down a rather nice shirt as he tried to reach a decision as to whether it needed an iron and, if it did, would he have time to iron it or should he pick out something else. Picking out something else would involve him having to return to his wardrobe to thumb through his selection of equally creased shirts which would eat up yet more time and inevitably leave him having to make exactly the same decision with which he was presently pre-occupied. To iron the shirt would also clearly impact on his time as well and this task, so as not to feel left out, came with its own set of mini dilemmas – should he use the ironing board? Would a tea-towel on his kitchen worktop suffice? Did it need more water?

The neon winked onto 7.01.

"Alright, alright!" Jack didn't appreciate the microwave's impatience.

With that, the decision was made. Jack slipped the shirt on and stumbled back towards his bedroom – stumbling on account of the fact that he was trying to button up his shirt as he went. Such a task would not normally warrant stumbling – or swearing – however, the makers of this particular shirt had elected to provide the wearers with the most microscopic of buttonholes in which to try and manoeuvre the unusually large rectangle buttons that adorned its central seam – as if the challenge of having to decide to iron the bloody thing was not enough already.

"Oh fuck!" Jack began to make growling noises as his frustration grew.

A little voice in his head began to tell him to calm down, that rushing wasn't really going to help him at all.

"Oh Fuck Off!" Jack knew all this and didn't need the self-righteous voice in his head to tell him again. The little voice folded its arms, stuck up its nose, uttered 'fine then, arsehole' and sulked off back into his subconscious.

The face staring back at Jack from the mirror was etched with tension. He slapped it with some aftershave in the hope that it would help him come to his senses.

He stopped.

His eyes closed and he allowed himself to take in a huge breath, sucking up the air initially through his open mouth and then through his nose as he felt his lungs and chest expand.

At the point the felt he couldn't take any more he held his pose for a second before allowing the air to explode out of his mouth and with it, hopefully, all the anxieties that had been gathering in the pit of his stomach for the last few hours.

It didn't entirely work so he tried it again. And again.

By the fourth time he had found himself in an altogether calmer place and the little voice in his head had returned triumphantly, reassuring Jack that everything was going to be okay whilst smugly congratulating itself that it had managed to influence its master from its sulking place in his subconscious.

Jack stared closely into the mirror checking for any stray nasal hair or sticky out terror eyebrow strands. Fortunately no such horrors were to be found. Therefore, after one final quick check and straightening of his shoulders, Jack strode purposefully out of the bedroom and through to the kitchen. He picked up his wallet and mobile from the small kitchen table and, after a brief acknowledgement to the microwave, who had confirmed that the time was now six minutes past seven, Jack made his way to his front door.

The evening was still quite warm and with the long summer evening light betraying the true passing of time Jack suddenly felt the pressure of his seven-thirty deadline lift. Long summer evenings have this calming effect on people. It's almost as if we're so pleasantly surprised to be experiencing warmth and light for anything longer than a brief parting of the clouds that something inside us allows us to find some kind of inner karma and we become so laid back that, not only are we practically horizontal but, for some inexplicable reason, we find ourselves nodding a lot and declaring "Yeah'man" at every opportunity, particularly if we happen to be sitting in a pub garden holding a pint of cider on the rocks. Bizarre.

Jack had decided to walk to Hayley's flat tonight. She herself was within walking distance of a rather pleasant pub and Jack felt that a couple of drinks would be necessary in order to summon up some Dutch courage.

As he made his way along his route the inner peace that the initial evening air had afforded Jack began to slip away.

The truth was that Jack wasn't sure what he wanted to say, let alone how to say it. To a degree he felt they had some unfinished business that they needed to tie up. Hayley had thrown him into turmoil and opened up a can so full of worms that his mind had been riddled with them since. Their conversation earlier in the week had re-assured him a little that there still was the spark he had previously detected in the car that night of the wedding.

However, like any of us, when faced with the prospect of putting your heart on the line, Jack was understandably nervous.

Jack became aware of himself mumbling as he walked along and began to play out potential scenarios in his head – what he would say, what she would say, the occasional knowing smile, the lingering eye contact, the shared private joke, the 'accidental' touch.

Jack was normally quite self-aware and this stood him in good stead on this occasion.

"Calm down you bloody idiot!"

Okay so he was self aware but he was also occasionally a little harsh on himself.

"She's your best friend. That's all it might be – don't fuck it up."

The little voice in his head was, not for the first time, now the little voice coming out of his mouth. But Jack knew that sometimes this little voice was the one voice he could truly trust. It was often the one voice that spoke without its own agenda, the one voice who spoke it how it actually was.

Jack drew some comfort from this, and chose to pay particular attention to the word 'might'. The reliable little voice had not actually ruled out the possibility that something great was going to happen – it had merely drawn Jack's attention to the fact that this was indeed his best friend over whom he was obsessing and that if that's all it was going to be then provided Jack accepted that, all would be well.

"I won't fuck it up"

"Good. Don't."

Jack smiled. He didn't mind having a conversation with himself. He did, however, just quickly glance around to check that no-one was actually watching him. Jack's own self-awareness meant that he didn't mind acknowledging his own occasional apparent madness but his own vanity meant he didn't really want anyone else to acknowledge it as well.

The rest of the walk passed in what felt like a blinking of an eye. It was one of those times when you may well notice something on your way to a destination – a tree, a person, a bird flitting around and so on – but, once you have actually reached your destination, you can recall nothing more and have no idea how you actually got there. Such was the sensation that suddenly hit Jack as he walked up to Hayley's front door. This had the effect of momentarily throwing him as all the carefully laid plans of what he was going to say both then and later scattered for cover, leaving his mind worryingly blank.

The door opened.

Jack wasn't even aware of the fact that he had rung the bell.

"Hiya, come in, I'm almost ready." Hayley was heading back through her hall and into her bathroom.

Jack hesitated briefly as he found himself watching Hayley as she walked away from him.

"You coming in then?" Hayley had popped her head round the bathroom door after sensing that she hadn't actually heard anything from Jack since opening the door. Indeed she had suddenly found herself questioning whether it was actually Jack at the door. What if she had just opened the door to some psychotic madman and had given him an open invitation to come in whilst advising him she was almost ready. The man who lived three doors down was often propositioning her in what, until this exact moment, she had always taken to be a harmless and affectionate manner. She had always politely turned down his requests for dinner – and breakfast – in the past, and had also told him she didn't think he should carry his binoculars around with him so much either. What if the man at the door was him?

All this had led to the sudden compulsion to check and, check completed and correct, Jack noted standing in the doorway, she had been happy to repeat her offer for him to actually step inside her flat.

"Yeah, yeah, sorry, miles away." Although Jack wasn't a psychotic madman as such, he was feeling a little out of control. The little voice in his head cracked an order for him to calm down and act natural. Jack straightened his posture in an effort to regain some composure.

"How are you?" he called out, aware that he shouldn't just walk into the bathroom.

"Yeah, good," a voice called back, "you?"

"Yeah, great thanks." Jack had walked into the kitchen to wait. He found himself casting his eyes around the room. He had been in there several times before but this time he had a keener interest in everything around him than he had in the past. Previously the room had simply been a kitchen. Now, it was Hayley's kitchen. A small picture of Hayley in sunglasses and a tan set against the background of a beautiful sunny beach grabbed Jack's attention. It was held against her fridge by a fluorescent magnet in the shape of a large smiley face. It made Jack smile too. He slipped the photograph from under the magnet and examined it closely. Hayley looked happy. The smile that Jack had been drawn to on the first day they met was staring back at him now. He smiled again and carefully replaced the picture back in its spot looking over the rest of the kitchen.

"Hi," Hayley appeared at the door, adjusting an earring, "sorry about that. Running a bit behind. My mum rang – she says hello by the way."

Jack was touched.

"Ah, bless her. Tell her 'Hi' from me next time you speak to her."

Hayley smiled.

"Will do. So," she straightened herself up, "where are we off to tonight then?"

"Ah, I thought we could take a stroll down to the Wheatsheaf. Have you eaten?"

"Only a little bit. Wouldn't mind grabbing something small there."

"Will you stop referring to me as small please?" Jack was pleased that his natural instincts to flirt had returned.

"Come on then, let's go." Hayley shook her head and gave Jack's a quick slap as he passed her.

A gentle breeze had joined the warm summer evening in the few minutes that Jack had been inside Hayley's flat.

"I love the summer," Hayley stated as they walked slowly towards their destination.

Jack looked over to her and smiled as they made brief eye contact.

"What?" Hayley smacked Jack on his arm, "what are you smiling at? I like summer!"

Jack laughed and looked at her again.

"I know," he looked ahead, suddenly conscious of not wishing to betray any ulterior motives by maintaining eye contact for too long – that wasn't in his plans until much later in the evening, "Summer's great. I love the summer too."

Hayley squinted at him, waiting expectantly for some kind of punch line.

"I love the summer too…?"

Jack squinted playfully back at her.

"Yes, I ..love…the..summer..too…!"

"And?" Hayley was still waiting for the witty remark.

Jack, on the other hand, was yet again waiting for the blind panic that had suddenly bundled its way into his mind to lift. Was Hayley waiting for him to say that he loved her too?

He tilted his head in the hope it might knock these thoughts off their feet, in order that when he shook his head moments later they would all fall out. Amazingly it worked. Of course Hayley wasn't expecting him to announce his undying love for her, particularly on the back of a statement 'I love the summer'.

"What? No witty remark Jack? You must be slipping!" Hayley confirmed Jack's summation.

Public Houses in town locations take on many different guises and attract many a different demographic as a result. Within the town centre location there were many pubs that, quite frankly, appealed to a generation so flush with the excitement of having recently gone through puberty that even Jack at his comparatively tender age felt woefully out of place and ancient within their four throbbing walls. Equally there were a few establishments where upon stepping across their thresholds you find yourself actually stepping back in time with the only indication that you are still in this, or indeed the previous, century being the exorbitant prices charged in order to support the fact that the pub only has three regulars. These poor strays are only regulars because they can't remember where they live. Somewhere out in the surrounding town are three old women pondering where their husbands went when they left home all those years ago.

The Wheatsheaf, mercifully, sat somewhere between the two extremes and as a result attracted a good mix of people all sharing the same purpose when going out for an evening, that of actually being able to hold a sane conversation with either the friends with whom they had ventured into the pub, or with whom they would meet up once there. Yes there was the obligatory music, however, it was where it was supposed to be – in the background. Jack had always felt that a sign of a really good pub is where you suddenly find yourself saying to the person standing next to you, "I really like this song," having been totally oblivious to the songs that both preceded and would subsequently follow it. It was 'music for the subconscious' – which Jack had always felt sounded like a good title for an album. This was in stark contrast to some of the post-pubescent drinking establishments where by ten-thirty of an evening the sounds emanating from the bass-ridden tone-deaf 30-inch sub-woofers were very much from the album 'Music for the Barely Conscious'.

Jack was therefore rather pleased that the sounds that accompanied their entrance into the pub were from one of his favourite bands.

"I love this song!"

"You and your U2!"

Hayley had spent many a conversation in the past with Jack, listening to him wax lyrical over U2's own rather wonderful lyrics.

"What can I say," Jack began with a slight shrugging of his shoulders.

"Normally quite a lot," Hayley felt she should nip this conversation in the bud early on as there was only so much of Bono worship a girl could be subjected to in an evening, "so let's just agree that U2 are indeed a great band, and that Bonio should be knighted even though he's got the same name as a dog biscuit."

"That's Bono, not bloomin' Bonio!" Jack couldn't believe he had risen to the bait, but there are some things that are sacrilege after all.

Hayley laughed, also not believing Jack had risen to the bait.

"Come on," she grabbed his arm, "I'm going to the bar, 'With or Without you'!"

Jack appreciated the song reference.

"Ah, a classic my friend, you should not mock!"

Hayley leant over the bar and studied the selection of bottled temptations that stood eagerly in the refrigerated cabinets.

"What can I get you?" a young lady appeared seemingly from nowhere and presented Hayley and Jack with a large warm smile.

"Er, pint of cider for me please." Jack was thirsty, hence his eagerness.

"Pint of cider." repeated the bargirl enthusiastically. "And for you?"

Hayley narrowed her eyes as she in turn looked to narrow down her alternatives. She cast her eyes, with a hint of mischief, to Jack.

"Oh, 'I still haven't found what I'm looking for.'"

The joke was obviously somewhat lost on the poor girl behind the bar and not just because she didn't hear the start of Jack and Hayley's conversation; the reality was that she wouldn't even have been born when Bono and his fellow band mates had been walking around Las Vegas in their ponytails presumably berating the fact that the thing they still hadn't found was actually a decent hairdresser. In all honesty Jack had been reasonably young at the time himself but having adopted the great band as his own the least he could do was to familiarise himself with their entire back catalogue.

"What about a Mary, Bloody Mary?" Jack's play on words with one of U2's most famous of early songs was also, sadly, lost on Hayley.

"What?"

"Never mind," Jack looked at Hayley and then at the equally perplexed barmaid, "how about a cider for you as well?"

Hayley considered this for a moment before delivering her verdict to the barmaid.

"I'll just have a glass of wine please."

"Large or small?" came the enquiry from across the smooth wooden bar.

"Large!" came the blurted reply from Jack which took him by as much surprise as it did Hayley.

"Hey, what the heck, I'm paying!" Jack recovered his composure and thrust a ten pound note towards the barmaid.

"I'll just get the drink first." She smiled sweetly and, after clarifying that it was indeed a medium white wine that was required, opened a fresh bottle and completed the order before graciously accepting the note that had resided awkwardly in Jack's hand since first making its appearance a minute or so earlier.

"You're not trying to get me drunk are you Jack?" quipped Hayley as they made their way through the bar and towards the early evening air in the garden.

"Oh no, no, of course not." Jack was thrown a little by the comment and quickly chastised himself. The little voice in his head was getting a little frustrated with Jack's seeming complete inability to interpret anything Hayley said to him in any way other than jumping to all manner of bizarre and monumentally misguided conclusions.

Their walk through the crowded pub gave him sufficient excuse not to say anything more other than the occasional 'excuse me' or 'sorry, can I just squeeze past there' and re-gather the numerous marbles that he felt he was beginning to lose all too rapidly.

The cool summer breeze greeted them as they made it into the garden. For a town pub The Wheatsheaf had a surprisingly good garden that to all intents and purposes would not look out of place in a quiet country village. Granted it was a quiet neighbourhood but nevertheless the garden was a beautiful hidden treasure and the perfect place to hold the intimate personal conversation that Jack had rehearsed over in his head so many times over the last few days that he was now beginning to confuse fantasy with reality and was starting to have minor attacks of déjà vue as the two worlds collided.

"Hayley!!!"

The screech from an excited girl on a table on the far side of the garden shattered not only the gentle sophisticated ambience that had rested comfortably over the grounds but also the best laid plans of mice and men, or more accurately in this case, of Jack and his inner voice which, unusually and terrifyingly for Jack, was speechless.

It was one of those fantastically catastrophic moments that, even though Jack had considered several different outcomes to the evening, and consequently had constructed Plans B, C, D, E, he hadn't actually planned into any of those running into Hayley's friends and, the now very real prospect, of spending the evening with them as he watched Hayley make a bee-line towards the table.

The evening could not have gotten any worse.

"Jack, come on, look it's Jackie!"

It took a couple of seconds for the name to register with Jack, but as he caught sight of the short blond hair sitting prettily on the head of the girl waving their way, register it did and as his mind darted back to the last blind date which Hayley had inflicted on him he realised that he should never, ever, again, consider that an evening could not get any worse.

"Oh good, it's Jackie." The words squeezed reluctantly out between his gritted teeth.

Jack, as he followed a few feet behind Hayley, bowed his head hoping to avoid eye contact with any of the women who were sitting at the expectant table, in particular the blond-haired one whom he was convinced hadn't as yet realised that he was with Hayley.

"Hi Jackie," Hayley leant forward to embrace her friend before stepping back, "you remember Jack don't you."

Jack stood and waved rather pathetically.

"Oh God, yes, hi Jack." Jack was delighted to see the embarrassment spread over Jackie's face.

"Hi Jackie, it's good to see you again."

"Er, Hayley, Jack this is Claire," Jackie started to introduce the three other women sitting around the table, all of whom were work colleagues, "Sandra, and Debbie."

Jack and Hayley waved and politely acknowledged the group.

"Why don't you join us?"

Jack had been dreading hearing those words and had initially felt that there was a chance they could be avoided, having realised that Hayley only knew one of the ladies sitting there.

"Ah you don't want us butting in on your evening."

Jack was impressed with Hayley's response.

"Ah, don't be daft," Jackie turned to her friends, "you don't mind if these two join us do you!?"

Claire, Sandra and Debbie all shook their heads and seemed genuinely happy to extend their foursome to a six-some. Accordingly they all squeezed up along the benches enabling Jack and Hayley to perch themselves on the end.

Jack felt a little awkward, a little bewildered, and a little lost as he tried to devise a Plan F. The impressive collection of empty bottles congregating in the middle of the table raised further alarm. Any chance of Jackie or the other girls picking up on the vibes that perhaps Jack wanted to spend some time alone with Hayley were well and truly gone. Alcohol has many effects, some which can be quite pleasant. The first sip of a cold pint on a hot summer's day and even the first few drinks that it takes to get into that relaxed comfortable state where all is right in the world are such examples of the impact of alcohol consumption at its most radiant. Once past these initial steps the ability to listen, as in truly listen, to anyone else's opinions, let alone pick up on any subtle body language or hidden agendas, are so far off the radar they might as well not exist at all.

With this depressing mindset locked in Jack prepared himself for a miserable frustrating evening. It couldn't get any worse.

"So, girls, you'll never guess how me and Jack first met."

Jack pinched himself, not just metaphorically but literally. The little voice in his head apologised for making the same mistake and vowed that this was definitely the last time tonight it would make such a misguided assumption. Of course things could get worse!

Jackie beckoned everyone closer as she proceeded to tell the tale of the fateful evening where she was 'stood up' by Jack. Jack, though reluctant to partake in the conversation, found himself inevitably having to butt in from time to time to correct what he felt were woeful inaccuracies and embellishing on Jackie's behalf.

"I did not eye you up and down and wink at you!" was one such defence.

"Ah, but you wanted to, I could tell," was the rather weak retort, "and I bet you did anyway!"

Jack considered whether he should give his own interpretation of the evening's events, possibly even walking his fingers off the table as Jackie had done on the bar before ultimately suggesting to Jack that he should 'Fuck off'. However, as he looked up he caught Hayley's eye.

She mouthed 'I'm sorry'.

At that moment the frustration and bitterness dropped out of Jack's mind and body. Who gave a monkey's what

Jackie, or any of her work friends, thought – the fact was that it didn't matter? Nor did it matter the fact that none of them could pick up on Jack's unease. None of this mattered as none of them were Hayley.

With this newly-found inner peace and comfort supporting him, Jack found the confidence to be himself. He had found Plan F – a subtle counter offensive.

"Ah, I must admit it was the weirdest blind date I've ever been on." Jack sat back in his chair, shook his head and allowed himself a little laugh.

It had the effect of momentarily silencing Jackie's tale.

"Weird? You were like some kind of stalker!" Jackie clearly hadn't finished her story.

"Stalker? I think you're confusing me with that weird bloke who was sitting in the corner. Do you remember?"

Jackie paused as she tried, initially unsuccessfully, to recall the man.

"Oh yeah," Jackie felt that a small white lie would do no harm and clearly she didn't want to detract any credence from her tale, "I remember."

"Did you end up going home with him?" Jack asked the question with a smile.

"No!! You cheeky bugger!" Jackie was initially offended but, noticing that everyone else around the table was laughing, played along. "I thought you were with him!"

Jack admired her response, not bad for someone of whom Jack's impressions from their first meeting were as low as they could have possibly been.

"No, he wasn't my type. The whole lack of breasts and having a cock thing was a bit of a deal breaker."

"Was that all?" Jackie continued, "you mean that if he

had breasts and no dick you would have been interested?"

"Jackie! How could I have been interested in a hairy she-male when you were the other option in the bar?" Jack's combination of sarcasm and natural charm was difficult to read for someone partially inebriated, however, his warm smile edged Jackie's interpretation towards the charm.

"So why weren't you this smooth when we first met?"

"Why weren't you this merry?" Jack followed this comment up with another warm smile as well.

"You cheeky bugger!"

"Anyway, I think that's enough of the story of the day we met, I'm sure there's more important things to discuss such as," Jack picked up a menu from the table, "which basket meal should I order tonight?"

"Ooh, I had the scampi earlier," Claire, who had found herself drawn to Jack's charms as well, was eager to offer her advice, "it was.." the four bottles of vodka-based alco-pops downed in the last hour and a half had impacted her ability to pick out adjectives,

"Fishy?" Jack tried to help.

"No!" Claire smacked him on his arm. Jack was always, always getting smacked.

"It didn't taste like chicken did it?" Jack tried again.

"No!" Jack just managed to avoid another clout by sitting back. The salt container and vinegar pot who'd been cowering behind another menu weren't so lucky and were sent clattering into the empty bottles.

"The scampi was," Claire paused briefly before delivering her verdict, "nice."

"Nice?" Jack sat back again, "wow, well you've sold me on the scampi then!"

"Ah, you're going to have the scampi!" Claire was touched.

"Actually, I'm going to have the chicken," he leant forward to console Claire who had suddenly looked somewhat deflated, "it's okay, it tastes like scampi." His accompanying wink caused a small flutter within Claire's heart.

"What about you Hayley?" Jack handed the menu across the table.

"Oh, I think I might just have a baguette or something healthy." Those, at least, were Hayley's initial thoughts, however, on examining the menu a little closer, her attentions were drawn towards the half-rack of ribs.

"Are you salivating?" Jack was convinced he saw Hayley's pupils widen as her good intentions evaporated, much like the milk in the banoffee pie pictured alluringly on the back of the menu.

"No!" Hayley lied.

"So you're still having a baguette?"

"Yes," Hayley affirmed, "just not today."

"It's the ribs isn't it?" Jack had almost fallen for them himself and indeed it was only the thought of having to bite every last slither of meat from the bones – as he would have to do – in front of all these strangers that had prevented him from taking this preferred option.

Hayley hadn't thought this through as much as Jack, although in fairness she always ate ribs with a knife and fork anyway so the possible social faux pas of holding conversations with strangers whilst pieces of marinated pork dangle from your teeth was far less likely to occur for her than it would for Jack. Jack knew that every time he ate ribs he felt like he walked around with a pig in his mouth for several days afterwards.

"Yes, it's the ribs for me please!" Hayley confirmed her wickedness and Jack nodded and made his way to the bar to order.

"He's lovely!" Hayley wasn't sure which of her three new 'friends' spoke first.

"Ladies," Jackie interjected, "he's already taken, isn't he Hayley?"

Hayley looked a little shocked. Who was with Jack?

"Oh come on, it's obvious!" Jackie nudged her friend.

It had been a while since the two girls had spoken back at Lloyds bar. The reality was that it had only been a few weeks although it felt like a lot longer. Hayley, like Jack, had been on a bit of a journey during that time.

"What's obvious?" Hayley's mind was already there but she wanted some time for her mouth to catch up.

"I thought you two had been dating?" Jackie was suddenly a little unsure of herself.

"No!" Hayley sounded a little indignant.

However, she wasn't.

The small doubt-ridden piece of her that had lain dormant for a while had seemingly re-awoken.

"Well, if he's not taken, do you think.." Claire began.

"Oh, oh, when I say I've not been dating Jack it doesn't mean he hasn't been dating someone else." Hayley instinctively found herself cutting Claire's sentence short.

"Oh, that's not fair," Claire sulked back on the bench and took a slug from her bottle, "all the cute ones are always taken!"

Hayley nodded. She wasn't sure why she was nodding.

"Is it anyone we know?" was the reasonable enquiry from Jackie.

"I don't think so," began Hayley before realising that she would have to be far more specific in order to avoid digging herself down a hole for which she didn't have a ladder to make her exit, "actually definitely not."

Hayley shook her head as she tried to work out why she had so eagerly blocked Claire's attempt to see if Jack was available.

"What's her name?" Claire, it seemed, wasn't going to give up so easily.

Hayley opened her mouth to give a response and, distracted by the sudden awareness that all eyes around the table were fixed upon her, briefly lost the connection between her brain and her vocal chords.

"Imogen," the words had already gone before she could grab them.

"Imogen? That's a nice name," the girls around the table reluctantly conceded this fact, "where did he meet her?"

"She's an ex, they met again at a wedding reception we went to a couple of weeks back."

Hayley was just waiting for the ground to open and swallow her up.

"He's kept that quiet, we'll give him a grilling when he gets back!" Claire picked up a bottle and tutted as she realised it was empty.

"Na,na,na,No," Hayley understandably wasn't too keen on this idea, "don't mention it to him please."

"Why not?" was the reasoned comment from Sandra who had previously been reasonably quiet.

"Because," again Hayley felt the full force of the stares around the table, "he gets a little funny about it." It was the best she could do.

"Funny about it?" Sandra had suddenly, and rather irritatingly for Hayley, found her voice.

"Yeah, you know," Hayley nodded hoping that the alcohol induced state the girls presently inhabited would take this as a fair enough explanation, as if the words 'you know' were some unwritten code that all women understood even if they actually 'didn't know.'

"No." Sandra was clearly not party to this code.

"It's early stages, he doesn't want to talk about it in case it goes wrong again."

Hayley hoped this would be the end of the matter.

"What went wrong last time?" Hayley felt her eyes narrowing at the annoyingly persistent Sandra.

"Oh, you know," Hayley tried the code again, although with far less optimism than last time.

"No." Sandra's reply was honest and therefore possibly didn't warrant Hayley's desire to take the large bulbous ketchup bottle that sat proudly in the middle of the selection of condiments on the table and thrust it into her mouth.

"Did he beat her?" Claire was shocked at this possibility which had suddenly occurred to her.

"No!" Hayley's response was swift and intended to be decisive.

"What if he did?" Jackie's mind began to put two and two together and make fifty, a brief summary of her logic being that Jack was too good to be true and didn't seem to fancy her so clearly he must have some kind of major personality flaw. Domestic violence falls into the 'major personality flaw' category hence the real possibility that Jack was some kind of serial woman-beating monster began to grow in Jackie's mind.

"Jack doesn't beat anyone! He's a really sweet guy who just doesn't want to talk about his new relationship until he's confident it is going to go somewhere. Come on girls, you know what it's like when you fire up something with an ex don't you?"

A couple of knowing looks responded from around the table.

"Exactly, so please don't mention it to Jack."

"Don't mention what to me?" Jack had just returned into earshot.

"Nothing!" Hayley tried to force a smile but was struggling and couldn't quite remember how she'd managed to get herself into this predicament in the first place.

"Okay." Jack sat himself down and immediately felt the chill, as if the atmosphere was waiting to be cut by the knife with which he had returned from the bar. The knife, however, was for Hayley's barbeque ribs and therefore could not be used for this purpose.

"Did you order the chicken?" Claire broke the awkward silence, having convinced herself that Jack wasn't going to punch her.

"I did indeed, and they've confirmed they can do me a scampi flavoured one."

Claire forced a small laugh – she did find Jack attractive, irrespective of his potential flaws.

The cooled atmosphere remained for a few more minutes. Hayley felt uneasy and wished she'd kept her mouth shut. Jack felt uneasy and wished they hadn't ordered food. The fact was, however, that they had and were therefore stuck on Table 24 for the foreseeable future.

Fortunately another round of drinks seemed to help everyone relax and the conversation picked up once more. The subsequent arrival of the food and the extra bowls of chips Jack had ordered for the ladies around the table further enhanced the ambience and helped convince the girls of Jack's innocence.

Jack, aware that the evening was pressing on and was unlikely to take the direction of any of his pre-laid plans, decided he could play one of his trump cards at the table and set himself up for another proper attempt to talk to Hayley at a later stage.

"Hayley, there was something I meant to ask you."

Hayley looked up from her food prompting a smile from Jack and an indication for Hayley to remove some of the rib from between her teeth. This prompted a rather smutty joke from Jackie around Hayley always at her happiest when she had some meat in her mouth. Hayley looked rather embarrassed, Jack also found himself going a little red.

"Sorry about that," Hayley pulled the offending morsel from her teeth and set it down in a napkin where it could do no harm, "what were you saying Jack?"

"I've managed to get two tickets to see Eddie Izzard at the end of the month!"

Hayley's face lit up. Both she and Jack were huge Eddie Izzard fans.

"You're joking! How did you manage that? I thought they were sold out ages ago!"

"I have my sources! So, you up for it?"

"God, you bet! That's made my day, my week even!"

"Excellent!" Jack had assumed Hayley would be delighted but a broad beam had moved across his face as his assumption proved correct. "That's a date then!"

"Definitely!"

"Won't Imogen want to go?"

Jack and Hayley had completely shut off from the rest of the table as they had got caught up in their mutual excitement. They had therefore not seen the look of slight confusion that had etched itself over Sandra's face. Sandra was clearly one of those people who, when under the influence, turned into an interfering pain in the arse. Hayley's dislike for the woman, which had been building earlier with Sandra's apparent inability to pick up on the 'You Know' code, now blossomed into a full blown vengeful hatred, prompting her to reach for the ketchup bottle.

"Imogen?" Jack could be forgiven for looking slightly bewildered. He couldn't recall Imogen coming into the conversation that night.

"Imogen." Sandra kindly repeated the name. "You know, your girl friend!"

"My what?"

"Okay, okay, thank you ladies," Hayley offered an aggressive frown towards Sandra in particular and started to stand up and grab Jack, "I told you not so say anything! Jack, come with me!"

Jack did as he was told and was led to a corner of the garden. Back at the table the talk was around the fact that clearly Jack wasn't a woman beater, he was just a two timing bastard.

The walk to the corner had been in silence, a necessity for Hayley who was trying to think what on earth to say next.

"What was all that about?" Jack was still a little confused.

"It was nothing." Clearly the walk hadn't helped Hayley too much.

"Where did Imogen come into it? And why," Jack had peered back over to the table, "is Sandra making the 'wanker' signal at me?"

"Well, the thing is that the girls were looking to ask you out so I.."

"So you thought you should say something to stop them because you .." Jack thought his chest was going to explode. Was Hayley jealous? Did she want to protect him because of her own feelings?

"I thought I should say something to stop them because I…" Hayley felt her chest was going to explode. Was she really jealous? Did she want to protect Jack because of her own feelings? Was this simply that her best friend was too good for the women around that table? Whatever the reason was this was the last thing she had expected to be thinking about tonight. Her fog had lifted a few weeks earlier and she was not expecting to have it descend upon her once again. She finished her sentence, "I had to because I've arranged a blind date for you."

Both fell silent for a moment.

"You've arranged a blind date for me?"

"Yes."

"With who?"

"Imogen."

"Imogen?"

"Imogen." It had been bad enough when she had said Imogen the first time but it sounded so much worse the second. It was almost as though by saying it for a second time she had sealed the contract and it was therefore too late to retract the statement and make up something different instead.

"Why, w-w-why would you do that?" For his part Jack

was completely confused. The excitement and hope of the Eddie Izzard moment seemed a dim and distant memory now.

"Well, you seemed such a lovely couple," Hayley was speaking on her wits now, which is always a dangerous thing to do for anything other than the briefest of moments, "so I thought perhaps you should go out and see if there's anything there."

Jack looked confused, shell-shocked even.

"I didn't want to tell you but I didn't want the girls coming onto you in the meantime and risk you agreeing to go out on a date with one of them."

"Why would I want to go out on a date with one of them when.." Jack cut off his sentence before he could let the words "I want you" slip through.

"I don't know, I panicked!" this was certainly true, "so I told them you were already seeing her, but it was early days and you didn't want to talk about it. I'm sorry Jack."

Jack didn't know where to look. He certainly couldn't bring himself to look Hayley in the eyes lest he betrayed his disappointment. Another glance in the direction of the table was met with a further scowl from the rather irritating Sandra.

"So when is this date set for?"

This was a very good question. When was this imaginary date set for?

"Next Tuesday night, I think, but I'll just need to firm that up."

"I'll just give her a call."

"No, no, no, don't do that," Hayley really wasn't enjoying the evening, "it's a blind date as far as she's concerned. I only told you because of that bitch queen Sandra."

"Fine. But I don't really think it's a good idea Hayley."

"Why not?"

"Just," Jack afforded himself a moment's eye contact with Hayley, "just because." He shook his head in an attempt to clear it.

"I'm sorry Jack, I thought it would be good for you and besides I haven't set you up on a blind date for ages, well at least a few weeks now anyway." Hayley forced an apologetic smile.

"Yep, well other than with Jackie and look where that's ended us!" Jack waved over at the table with a look of defiance.

Hayley laughed.

"I tell you what," she grabbed his arm, "let's go back and join the bitches and just really ham it up. You can tell them you are taking it really slow with Imogen because you think she could be the one. It'll turn them to putty."

"Fine, come on then." Jack allowed himself to be led back to the table where he would, after a few moments, launch into a complete charm offensive that would, by the end of the evening, have all the ladies wishing once more that they could be with him.

Hayley now had to work out how she could convince Imogen to go on a blind date next Tuesday. Before she could do that she also had to work out how to contact Imogen in the first place. She had no telephone number, no address, not even a surname.

Re-light the Fire

"So what do I do?" Jack waited a little impatiently for the answer.

"Just go." Danny's response was a little crackly.

"This is a really crap line. Is that your best advice then?"

"Absolutely. She's a great girl. You'll have fun. Go for it."

"I know all that but I'm not sure it's what I want to do. I've still got feelings for.."

"Jack!" Danny interrupted his friend before Hayley's name was mentioned, "she's set you up on a date with your ex, your drop dead gorgeous ex."

"I know, I know."

"Well then. Doesn't that tell you all you need to know?"

There was silence on the end of the line. Jack hated it when someone else was talking sense. It was normally Jack who was the one who gave the good advice. Jack was the one who could take a step back from a problem or issue and see it for what it truly was. The truth was, however, that he didn't practise what he preached. The logical left-hand side of his brain was nodding in agreement with his friend but the other side of his brain was hanging onto any shred of hope to which it could desperately cling.

"Jack, you've gone all quiet."

"Sorry mate, I'm just," Jack paused and took a deep sigh as his logical self finally eased away the fingertips of its romantic counterpart, "a bit confused I guess. But, hey, you're right."

"I am. And look on the bright side my man, you have a great female best friend and, if tonight goes well, potentially a hot hot new girlfriend. Well nearly new anyway!"

"Yeah, you're right. Cheers Danny."

"No worries mate. Have a good one and let me know how it goes."

"Will do."

"Especially the dirty bits."

"Danny?"

"Yes mate."

"Piss off! I'll speak to you tomorrow!" Jack put the phone down with a smile finally across his face. His 'kiss and tell' days were well and truly behind him but it didn't stop his mates angling for details after any dates. Some of his friends were not quite so discreet which did occasionally make for some very entertaining, if sometimes rather stomach-churning, conversations around a few pints. Jack, however, had always had far too much respect for Imogen and he had never divulged the actual specific details of their intimate exchanges in the past. With these thoughts hanging in the air he turned his attention to the evening ahead. He was due to meet Imogen in a bar in town in approximately an hour and a half. This gave him just enough time to face another 'which shirt to wear' dilemma, have a shave and make a hasty exit as the minutes raced by.

The setting for his latest 'blind date' was better than on his previous outing where he not only had to suffer a few minutes of unnecessary abuse from Jackie the fiery pint of Guinness, but also had to endure the delights of the Hogshead, or as it had felt like at the time, kindergarten with alcohol and drum'n'bass.

As Jack entered into this particular bar tonight he stepped out of the busy bustling early evening crowds and noise and into the smooth sophisticated ambience of a classy establishment. There were no cackling inebriated teenagers, with their breasts hanging out and their skirts set above their panty lines, to be seen anywhere. They had all been drawn towards the booming bases that resonated through the walls of the more appropriate drinking holes for the younger and more desperate members of the community.

There she was.

Imogen was sitting down at a small table in the corner of the bar. She was looking a little nervous and was fidgeting in her handbag looking for nothing in particular other than to keep herself occupied whilst waiting for her date to turn up.

Jack found himself staring over at her for a while. She was as beautiful now as she was when they first met a few years ago. As he stood there his mind started to drift off into details of their past; however, his paralysis was only temporary as he became aware of Imogen smiling and waving in his direction. He waved back and made his way over to the table.

"Hi." He leant over and gave her a small kiss on her cheek.

"Hi, how are you?" She looked a little embarrassed.

"I'm good. How are you?"

"Great, great thanks." Jack sat himself down.

"Oh, I'm waiting for someone." Imogen raised her hand as if to try and stop Jack from taking his seat. This completely threw Jack who started to edge his chair back in preparation to stand back up.

"Oh, oh, sorry, I assumed.."

"What?"

"I, I'm here for a blind date?"

"Oh, alright. That's nice for you. Shouldn't you go and find her then?" Imogen's tone was one of genuine concern rather than sarcasm.

"Er, yes," Jack was hesitating as he tried to work out what to say next, "I guess I should, but," he now found himself actually standing up, "what if she doesn't turn up? Who are you here with?"

"Oh, I'm on a blind date as well."

Jack suddenly felt a little more comfortable.

"Oh right, so what if your blind date doesn't turn up and my blind date doesn't turn up?" Jack smiled knowingly towards Imogen.

"Then," Imogen looked a little perplexed, "I guess we go home, ring whoever set us each up, and have a moan at them."

This was proving a little more difficult than Jack had planned.

"Why don't I wait here until either of our dates turn up?" was his latest suggestion.

"Won't that put them off a little bit – turning up and seeing their date sitting with someone else?"

"Not necessarily," Jack really didn't think he'd have to work this hard, "we can say we are brother and sister."

Imogen's raising of her eyebrow confirmed what Jack already knew, that this was a crap idea.

"Okay, well, we could just tell them the truth. We are old friends who just happened to bump into each other."

"Old friends?"

"Yes," Jack was aware that there was a bit of weight behind Imogen's request for clarity, "old friends. Good friends."

"Former lovers?" Jack couldn't quite work out whether Imogen had thrown this in playfully just to make him squirm or whether she meant this as a serious option.

"I'm not sure that would work for them!"

"Nah, you're probably right."

"Shall I sit back down while we think about it?" Jack was already pulling his seat back and beginning to re-take his seat.

"I'm not sure," Jack stopped in his tracks as Imogen raised her hand again, "I didn't think we'd decided whether it's a good idea yet."

"Really? Wouldn't you like some company in the meantime? I mean, what if they don't show up? What if you're here all alone for the rest of the evening? Think of the sad, weird lonely old perverts who'll be making a bee-line for your table and the woeful chat up lines you'll need to endure?"

"Jack."

"Yes?"

"Shut up and sit down."

Jack did as he was told.

"Are you not drinking then?" Imogen looked at the empty space on the table in front of Jack.

"Oh, good point. Would you like another?"

"Yes please," Imogen turned her bottle to show Jack the label, "and Jack."

"Yep?" Jack was halfway through standing up.

"Nothing, I just wanted to see how many more times I could get you to stand up and sit down." She smiled mischievously and nodded in the direction of the bar.

Jack acted accordingly and went to get a couple of drinks. He couldn't help but smile to himself. He and Imogen had always flirted well together.

"So, what do you know about this blind date then?" Jack asked on his return to the table.

"Not much." Imogen poured the bottled drink carefully into her glass. "What about you?"

Jack had two options. Either he could play ignorant and pretend that he knew nothing or he could tell the truth and get it out in the open that it was indeed himself with whom Imogen had been set up.

"Well, I hear she's very beautiful and intelligent, obviously."

"She sounds nice."

"Apparently so." Jack nodded.

"What else?" Imogen stared across into Jack's eyes. It was a strangely intense stare that threw Jack to a degree as he couldn't quite work out whether she was toying with him or just being a little nosey.

"Um, well, I think she is probably sophisticated, funny, sexy - hopefully! - and good company."

"Wow, she sounds great!"

She did didn't she.

"Yeah, she does doesn't she?"

"Why on earth would you have split up with her in the first place then?!" Jack's initial panic was eased by the comforting wink that proceeded Imogen's last comment.

"Ah, you knew then!" Jack sat back in his chair and reflected the broad smile from across the table.

"Of course I knew you plonker! Do you think I'd agree to go on a blind date without knowing a bit about the person I'm due to be seeing?"

Jack muttered something along the lines of "of course not, that would be crazy," whilst at the same time thinking of

233

all the awful nights he could have avoided if he'd have taken such a commonsense approach in the past.

"You do make me laugh," Imogen's tone was affectionate, "the way you came in here and didn't say you were my date."

Jack realised this was a bit strange but in fairness Imogen hadn't given any clues to the fact that she knew he was her date, indeed, she had played him very well for the last couple of minutes.

"Well I suddenly panicked when you started questioning whether our dates would appreciate us talking to one another."

"Don't you think that I might have thought it was a bit of a coincidence us both turning up here on blind dates?" It was a fair question and one which warranted the accepting shrug of Jack's shoulders and raising of his glass.

Jack's relationship with Imogen had been really good when they originally started dating. In fact it would be fair to say that it had been really good right up until the point when Jack's feet suddenly turned cold and he abruptly ended their courtship.

They had met four years ago when they were introduced to one another at one of Jack's relative's family barbeques. The attraction had been pretty much instantaneous. Jack's first words to Imogen, following the initial "Hellos", were "Nice baps!" This was of course in reference to the burgers that were on her plate and not actually to her rather eyecatching chest that had transfixed Jack and no doubt led to the Freudian comment. Jack had found himself turning red, much like the inside of the hotdog that resided on his plate. His embarrassment however was short lived as Imogen responded with a reference to the contents of his plate with, "thankyou, and you have a magnificent sausage!"

It had been one of those fantastic days that seemingly only come around once every few years. Jack had gone to the barbeque with little expectation other than to be well fed, well oiled and reacquainted with several members of his family whom he hadn't seen since their last annual summer get together. To therefore find himself talking to a beautiful woman with a wicked sense of humour was a completely unexpected and extremely welcome surprise.

They spent most of the afternoon together chatting and when they did acknowledge that they really should mingle they always found themselves bumping back into one another within a few minutes.

Jack hadn't felt the kind of chemistry he experienced that day with anyone else before. He wasn't the sort of man who rushed into relationships, notwithstanding the occasional misjudged and alcohol-induced moments of regret which in fairness didn't really justify the title of 'relationship' anyway. However by the end of that day four years ago Jack knew he had to see Imogen again. What was more was the fact that he instinctively knew that she felt the same. This was another first for Jack who in the past, like many of us, always had that nagging doubt, that fear of rejection that threatens to take away all your confidence and turn you into a jibbering wreck at the very moment you need it most in order to appear eloquent, smooth and sophisticated as you coolly ask someone out. For the only time in his life Jack didn't have those fears on that day. The result was a perfect ending to a perfect day. He and Imogen agreed to meet the next week and had gone out for a wonderful meal followed by a slow walk home and the tenderest of goodnight kisses on her doorstep. Jack said goodnight, told her he would call the next day and walked slowly away as she went inside. Imogen had stood motionless behind her closed door savouring the moment, convinced she could still feel the tingle of her lips against his.

Jack had carried on with his slow walk. The slowness was out of necessity due to a trapped pubic hair that had been caught as his privates got a little ahead of themselves at the moment of the perfect kiss. Whilst his genitals had now got the message that there was to be no extra-curricular activity that night and had reluctantly returned to flaccid resting state, the poor pube had remained strangled and now, with every step, was trying to desperately tug itself free. Jack, conscious of the potential negative impact on any poor soul observing him thrusting his hand down his pants whilst crying out "Oh God yes!" albeit just in relief, decided to carry on with his painfully slow hobble, hoping that Imogen wasn't looking out of her window and praying that he would soon be out of sight and could find a small alleyway in which he could release the unfortunately distressed hair. Once there he also prayed that no members of her majesty's constabulary would suddenly appear as he was sure there were likely to be laws against standing in alleyways late at night with your manhood in hand.

After that first successful date they started to see each other regularly and his privates didn't have to wait too long before given their own successful first date.

Jack had, in a moment of weakness, broken his code of disclosure and confided to Danny that Imogen was indeed the best sex he had ever had. Jack's code of confidence was important to him and therefore, for him to break it, it meant that there had to be a very good reason. Whether it was their natural spark, the incredible chemistry they had seemingly instantly possessed or the fact that, let's face it, they were two horny people in their early to mid twenties, didn't really matter as whatever it was meant that they had a passionate and uninhibited sex life.

Great sex , of course, doesn't automatically equate to a long and lasting relationship. It does equate to a lot of panting, washing of towels, great memories and improved creative thinking skills. Granted, most of the creative thinking is based primarily around the sex – where to have it, when to have it, how to have it, how often can you have it in a single day etc. But great sex isn't necessarily a pathway to a long and lasting future together. That said, it's undoubtedly an important part within such a relationship, it's just not the only thing that has to be thrown into that particular pot in order to come up with a winning recipe.

The strange thing about Jack and Imogen's original relationship however, was that they had loads of other really good things floating around in their casserole dish. Both were considerate and generous people – there was no one person dictating the relationship and having things all their own way. Both had a great sense of humour and genuinely made each other laugh. Both seemed well grounded people, confident in who they were and who they wanted to be. In many ways they appeared as the perfect couple, certainly to their family and friends and certainly to Imogen. Certainly also, until a moment of indecision and a far too premature mid-life crisis, for Jack.

This point of crisis was reached on the eve of his 25th birthday. He had been seeing Imogen for a year and they spent most nights at one or other of their homes.

On this particular night however he was seeing his friends

for a pre-birthday drink. The following night Imogen was taking him out for a meal.

So there he sat, three years ago, around a small table in the middle of a bustling pub.

"Twenty-five mate! Jeez' you are getting old man." Danny knew how to make Jack feel good.

"I know, I know."

"And tomorrow, there you'll be, sitting in a romantic restaurant, the candle flickering suggestively in the middle of your table," Aidan had taken up the story, "when all of a sudden your pretty lady will look deep into your eyes and say 'Oh Jack, there's something I've been meaning to ask you for some time now…'"

Jack looked across at his friend and the other two chaps sitting around who were all seemingly egging Aidan on to continue.

"and then she'll reach into her blouse – and boy you are so lucky to be able to look down that by the way Jack – and pull out a little box."

"Ha ha," interrupted Jack, "very funny. We've only being going out for a year or so."

"That doesn't matter my friend," Danny was back on the story now, "we've all seen it in your eyes, both of you. It's a leap year you know?"

Jack just frowned.

"Yep," Aiden's turn, "and I don't know how to break it to you Jack, me old mucker, but I saw her going into that jewellery shop in town at the weekend." Aiden nodded his confirmation of this fact.

"So," protested Jack, "what does that mean? She's a woman. She likes jewellery."

"She was looking at engagement rings in the window my friend, I'm sure of it."

"Nah, sod off, you're just winding me up now you gits." Jack started to laugh and was a little taken aback when his friends didn't join in.

There then followed a long drawn out conversation regarding the virtues of remaining single, free and keeping your options open versus the merits of committing to a life-long relationship and all the pressures that such a commitment naturally involves. Jack tried coming back with "but we're both really happy as we are, why would we want to change that?" but this was met with a counter argument of "you can't just tread water, eventually things have to change and a woman always wants that change sooner rather than later – it's their biological clocks ticking away."

Now three years later Jack realises that these words of so-called wisdom from Aidan were a sweeping generalisation and totally irrelevant to a twenty-three-year-old woman for whom the patter of tiny feet were a dim and distant thought that to this day hadn't made their way into the part of her mind that wished to pay any attention to it. The mere fact that the words were uttered by Aidan also rendered them complete bollocks by default.

However, at the time, fuelled by three pints of Worthington's, these words clattered into Jack like an express train. He allowed himself to be painted a picture of domestic terror where he was married off within the year and spent the next few producing a steady stream of demanding and expensive offspring, leaving him little energy for anything else other than to curl himself up on his sofa of an evening whilst watching Sky Sports whilst, at the same time, watching his belly gradually spread, dousing his vital organs in layers of fat culminating in a coronary episode by his late thirties.

Suffice it to say, Jack's panic, together with a helping of feeling old having hit his quarter century, led him to make a complete arse of himself at the meal the following night. Imogen had no intention of asking him to marry her and had she had a chance to get a word in edgeways to this effect prior to Jack spouting off about "it's all moving too quickly" and "I'm not just some kind of giant semen factory you know," then maybe things would have been quite different. As things were, however, the evening ended with a separation. A separation that left Imogen heart-broken and Jack devastated.

Just less than three years had passed before they had seen each other again at the recent wedding and now they were sitting around a pub table chatting and flirting away as if the clock had been turned back to the good old days. It was a surreal situation Jack found himself in. All thoughts of Hayley had temporarily disappeared from his mind. This was quite a major achievement for Jack as Hayley had occupied a large proportion of his thinking time for a fair while recently and in particular with regards to why she had set him up on a blind date.

For now, however, as he sat and continued his pleasant evening, these thoughts and questions resided peacefully at the back of his mind.

A sign of a good night out is the rapid passing of the time. This was one such evening where the clanging of the bell behind the bar came all too suddenly. Neither Jack nor Imogen had discussed the end of the evening so the bell provided a fork in their particular journey.

"I can't believe how quickly it's gone tonight," acknowledged Imogen as she began to gather up her bag and jacket.

"I know, it's crazy, it feels like we've just got here," Jack felt himself starting to stand up in unison with Imogen, "can I walk you home?"

Imogen's smile suggested that this was very much what she wanted.

"Yep, that would be nice."

The couple made their way from their seats and out, exchanging a polite 'goodnight' with the barmaid who was busy collecting empty glasses, into the cool night air.

Imogen's flat was a fifteen minute walk from the pub. This extended up to twenty five minutes with a brief stop off at a local Chinese for a satisfying hot portion of chips.

These minutes, like those that had passed earlier in the evening, did so seemingly in a blinking of an eye and before the last chip could be savoured from the paper bag, Jack and Imogen found themselves walking down her road. Both instinctively threw their minds back to that evening four years ago when they made this identical walk. Both knew that that walk had ended up with the perfect kiss that had signalled the start of a seemingly perfect relationship. Both knew that in a matter of moments they would be standing outside Imogen's door.

"Chip?" Jack nervously thrust the bag in front of Imogen.

Thankful for the distraction, Imogen peered into the paper.

"There's only one left," she peered back up at Jack who nodded his approval, "ah, bless you. You let me have the last chip – that's like giving me your last Rolo!"

"You're welcome!" Jack hadn't actually intended the offer of the last chip to take on such significance and he rather hoped that Imogen had meant this as a joke.

"You know I'm joking right?" Imogen's reassurance was in response to Jack's face clearly failing to conceal the momentary mild panic he had experienced at the Rolo comparison.

"Yeah, obviously!" lied Jack.

"Giving me your last chip carries much more significance than a Rolo after all." Imogen had thrown this last comment out playfully just to see if it induced any further involuntary facial spasms in her date.

Jack, fortunately, had reminded himself of his partner's sense of humour and normal comfort was resumed.

"I know. Anyone can give away a last Rolo. They're only 40p a pack. Chips, well they're pushing a couple of quid."

"Absolutely. That's nearly five times the love."

"That's a whole lotta love."

In truth Jack hadn't really wanted to keep flirting. The trouble was that he couldn't help himself. He was good at it! Imogen was also skilled in this art and therefore it's little wonder that the two of them should indulge in some full on flirting. Their history, combined with the cool late night air and reawakening of memories from the past, had fuelled their playful conversation and taken it to the next level. Indeed it was fast approaching the level where they were surely shortly to be faced with yet another fork in their journey this evening.

Both Jack and Imogen know that you can only push the flirt button so much before you either have to back off or put out. They had both seemingly been bashing away at this button all evening and were about to reach the penultimate floor where they either bid each other a fond farewell or zoomed up to the penthouse suite and shagged each other's brains out.

Decisions, decisions!

As these thoughts mulled themselves over in Jack's head he found himself climbing up the steps towards Imogen's front door. Before he could gather his thoughts on this sudden realisation he was already there. In front of him stood Imogen.

Both stood momentarily in silence, nervously avoiding eye contact and fidgeting as each waited for the other to make the first move, whatever that first move was going to be.

"So." was Jack's move.

"So." Imogen wasn't going to be tricked into directing the conversation from here, that was the man's job in her eyes.

"So." Jack was aware that he sounded like a bit of a twit but he had suddenly found himself lost for words.

"So?" Imogen was a little cooler.

"S.."

"Don't say 'So' again!" Imogen got in quickly before the 'O' had managed to escape from Jack's mouth for a third time.

"Sorry." Jack screwed up his face in an apology.

"You know 'sorry' begins with 'so' don't you. So, technically, you said 'so' again." Imogen smiled, rather pleased with herself at her literary observation.

"I hadn't realised that." Jack returned the smile. "You always were really smart weren't you."

"And you were always really charming."

"Well thank you," Jack gave a slight bow, "it was hard not to be when I was with you."

Their eyes, which had managed to somehow continue to nervously avoid each other as this conversation had unfolded, finally locked onto one another. In moments such as these if you don't pull away immediately then you have already stepped too far to turn back. Their eyes drew each other in as they realised they had passed the point of no return and in a fraction of a second their lips were embroiled in the tenderest of kisses that re-ignited the flames that had burned so passionately on the night four years ago when they first stood on these very steps. Jack raised his hands to gently support her head as she stretched to continue their embrace.

Neither wanted to stop the kiss.

This wasn't just because it was a great kiss and hey, savour those whenever you can, but because both knew that this kiss would be a prelude. They just didn't know a prelude to quite what.

Such a kiss, however, cannot go on forever. Jack had, in his dim and distant teenage years, experienced lengthy kisses. He had referred to them as 'kisses' but in truth they were more akin to expeditions where his, and his poor unfortunate partners' tongues would seek out the darkest parts of each other's mouths presumably in a quest to find each other's tonsils - a fruitless exercise in the case of any of his partners as Jack had had his tonsils removed many years earlier. Such 'kisses' were not pleasant experiences and invariably led to all manner of minor ailments from jaw aches to mouth ulcers to heavy colds and cold sores. Jack, in his latter years, had often wondered why no-one had told the young about the follies of tonsil tennis. People often refer to 'tennis elbow', however, Jack was convinced that 'tennis tonsils' was a far more rampant illness particularly amongst the fourteen to nineteen age group. He was all for passion and acknowledged that the occasional momentary eating of a prospective mate's face can be a prelude to some extremely hot action; however, spending twenty minutes on this meal kind of leaves you full up and can ruin your appetite.

Fortunately the kiss Jack had just shared with Imogen had not been in any way invasive nor indeed likely to result in either party choking to death. Nevertheless the kiss had run its natural, and rather lovely, course and now both Jack and Imogen found themselves once again avoiding eye contact in the awkwardness of the aftermath.

"Would you like to come in?" Imogen allowed herself to look up at Jack.

"Er, yeah, that'll," Jack returned the brief gaze, "that'll be nice, I could murder a coffee."

"Wouldn't you rather just drink one?" Imogen smiled as she turned her key in the lock.

"Yeah, that's how I was going to kill it."

Jack surveyed the inside of the flat. He had spent many an evening there previously and had got to know the interior very well. However, very little of the décor remained from that which had been present on his last visit.

"Blimey, this placed has changed."

"Ah, you know," Imogen called out her answer from the kitchen as she filled her kettle and scanned the worktops in search of a couple of mugs, "I had a bit of a spring clean a while back now."

"A bit of a spring clean?" Jack's question was only audible to himself. He cast his eyes once more over the living-room and then followed the sound of clattering cups.

"The place looks great."

"Thanks," Imogen smiled and nodded towards one of the cupboards adjacent to Jack's head, "can you pass me out the sugar? You still take sugar?"

"Absolutely, but only one now." Jack seemed very proud of his reduction in sugar intake.

"Blimey, is that to offset the prospect of your belly spreading as you approach middle age?"

"Middle age? You cheeky mare!"

"Well you can't be too far off thirty now Jack, can you?" The tiniest of smiles momentarily broke through Imogen's attempt to hold a serious expression on her face. She did enjoy winding Jack up.

"Ah, but don't they say life begins at thirty?"

"No," Imogen picked up the kettle and began to pour out the boiling water into the two mugs neatly lined up in front of her, "they say life begins at forty. And they only say that because life actually begins to end at forty, they just miss out the 'end' bit as it's a wee bit depressing."

"Well there's a lovely thought, thank you for that one. So what do they say about thirty?"

"I don't know. Isn't that the time when you're due a mid-life crisis, when you start to discover the joys of grey pubes and your metabolism grinds to a halt with the result that you start to get really fat and out of breath at the first sign of any form of exercise?"

Imogen had stirred the drinks throughout her bleak summary.

"Wow, look at you Miss 'My glass is half empty'!"

"I'm only kidding and besides," she handed him his coffee, "you've got a couple of years yet before all that happens. Mind you," she cast a critical eye at his stomach, prompting a sharp intake of breath from Jack, "I think the old metabolism may have kicked in early in your case."

"I see you haven't lost your appetite to rip the piss out of me then?" Jack raised up his mug.

"Ah, you love it!" Imogen acknowledged Jack with a slight tilt of her mug before taking a wary sip and sucking in some air to cool her lips down.

"You always try and drink your coffee too hot!"

"I don't like it cold."

"It's not going to be cold is it? You've only just boiled it."

"Are you going to stand there and nag me or are you going to come and sit down?" Imogen walked past Jack and gently tapped him on his breast bone as she did so.

Jack turned to follow and took the opportunity to cast his eyes up and down Imogen's practically perfect frame. Transfixed, he followed her to a large sofa that took up most of the living-room and eased himself down into its extremely comfortable cushions.

"Wow, I love this sofa." he started to bounce up and down on it.

"Steady Skippy!" Imogen leant forward to swiftly put her mug down onto the small coffee table set a foot or so from where they were sitting.

"When did you get this?" Jack was still bouncing but not quite as boisterously now.

"A while back. I had a bit of a clear out after we separated."

Jack stopped bouncing.

"Ah." He looked around the room. He knew the place looked different but now he looked more closely he realised that he could hardly see anything that he had seen before. It was swiftly dawning upon him that Imogen's 'spring clean' had involved a complete overhaul of her home and possessions. Had the impact of his folly three years ago been so great as to prompt this beautiful and lovely person sitting next to him to look to remove all trace of anything shared with Jack from her house and life?

As these thoughts passed through Jack's mind the room sat in silence.

"I'm sorry." The silence was broken by Jack's sincere apology.

"For what?" Imogen turned to face him.

"For making you want to change your entire house."

"What?" Imogen looked a bit bemused, "Jack, I wanted to change my flat around because I was bored with it, not because of you, you big wally!!"

"Oh, right, I see, I just thought.."

"You just thought that I'd been so devastated by our separation that I'd have to strip my flat clean to remove anything from it that reminded me of you!"

Jack realised that he may have been a little off the mark with his previous assumption.

"No, no,no, obviously not!" He tried to wriggle out of the situation, "I thought.. I thought.." Jack was actually thinking 'I don't know what to say and was kind of hoping you'd jump in here and finish off my sentence for me,' however, Imogen was far too interested in what Jack was going to say next than to help him out right now. Accordingly she just sat there, stared at him, tilted her head slightly and raised her eyebrows expectantly.

"Oh. Bollocks! I admit it, I'm an arrogant arsehole!" blurted Jack.

Imogen burst out laughing and instinctively put her hand on his knee.

"I'm just winding you up, you plonker!"

Jack wanted to look cross but in truth he was so relieved that he didn't have to continue to squirm and try and dig himself out of any further holes that he was sure were going to spring up around him that he could instead only manage a warm smile.

"I did change things around after you left." Imogen's tone had changed. The hint of playfulness that had accompanied her last few comments had been replaced by a quiet fragile honesty. "Not everything at once obviously. But I did feel the need to start a new chapter in my life, make a clean start, you know."

Jack felt his heart sink. He had loved Imogen. He had been absolutely devastated when they separated and for the first real time he was suddenly fully aware of the magnitude of how his foolish actions had equally devastated her.

He sat there, motionless, as this realisation continued to dawn upon him. After what felt like an eternity, but in reality were only a few comparatively brief moments he spoke.

"I'm so sorry Imogen."

"That's okay." Neither could look at each other at the moment.

"It's not okay," Jack took a deep breath, "it's not okay at all. I was an absolute tit. You mentioned a midlife crisis before, well I reckon I hit that three years ago. I just panicked. You were the best thing that had ever happened to me and I just got spooked listening to my twats for friends and screwed it right up."

"Jack, it's fine."

"No it's not fine. It's not fine at all. And what's not even finer is that I know how devastated I was after we split up and yet it's only now that I've even really begun to understand just how much my cock-for-brains actions affected you."

Jack looked Imogen in the eyes. It was a deep penetrating stare intended to convey the absolute honesty of what he wanted to say next.

"I am truly, truly sorry."

His words were simple. His words were concise. His words said all that they needed to say. His eyes told Imogen all she needed to hear. In that briefest of sentences whatever form of closure they had both needed from the events of three years ago was obtained.

Imogen leant forward and slowly, tenderly their lips once more touched. Jack instinctively slid his hands around her waist and pulled her tightly into his body and the intensity of their kiss began to irresistibly build. As Jack closed his eyes he felt the passions from the past re-ignite and steam through his body.

He pulled himself back from the embrace to open his eyes to look upon the beautiful woman in front of him.

"Fuck!" Jack almost jumped out of his skin.

"What!!" Imogen responded with similar alarm and started to frantically pull at her hair convinced that a spider was about to jump down onto her startled face.

"Imogen!" Jack called out in relief.

"What!! What is it?" Imogen was now flapping wildly around her, "is it a spider? Get it off me!"

Jack jumped into action, "Er, yeah, stay still." He started to flick away at her hair before elaborately cupping his hand close to her forehead.

"Got it," he stated manfully.

"Was it big?"

"Huge. I can feel it wriggling around in my hand." "Urrgh," Imogen looked a more than a little scared at this thought but, nevertheless continued, "can I see it?"

Jack wasn't expecting this request.

Had he been expecting such a request he probably would have decided not to pretend to have a spider in his hand in the first place.

However, his gut instinct was to go with the lead Imogen had given him. If she thought that she had a spider on her head, and more importantly, that this was the reason why Jack had recoiled in shock as he opened his eyes, then why would Jack want to persuade her that the truth was anything other than that. After all, he was reasonably convinced that the last thing Imogen probably wanted to hear was the truth. Why would Imogen, after such a wonderful, shake you to the bones kiss, want the man she considered to be the love of her life to date, tell her that at the moment he opened his eyes it wasn't her face he saw, but the face of the woman who had set them up on their blind date.

"Well? Show me then." Imogen had suddenly gone all brave.

"Er, no."

"No?" Imogen smiled curiously at Jack.

"You don't want to see this spider." Jack shook his head in the rather vain hope that this would help convince Imogen that this was the best course of action to take.

"Why not, it's only a spider."

"Only a spider!" Jack cupped a second hand around the imaginary arachnid.

"I don't think he's going to be offended. There's no need to cover his ears."

"How do you know it's a he?" It was a pointless question.

"What?" Imogen was becoming slightly confused.

"It might be a 'she'."

"And?"

"She might be premenstrual. You don't want to upset her."

"Pre-menstrual? You do realise you're beginning to talk bollocks don't you Jack?"

"Yes," Jack carried on talking as he made a swift sideways dash to a window to let the invisible eight legged figment of his imagination jump out into the cool night air, "I know. It's a rare condition. The doctors have told me they think it's curable but only if I never open my mouth again."

"Well I'm glad I haven't got that then." Imogen's tone had changed once more. It had changed to a tone Jack hadn't heard for over three years now. "I'd be devastated if I couldn't open my mouth ever again."

There then followed a brief period of silent embarrassment as Imogen contemplated how Jack may have chosen to interpret her last sentence and as Jack, indeed, did the same.

During this moment of quiet reflection they had carefully managed to avoid eye contact. However, this proved difficult to sustain and it was to both their considerable relief when their eyes met, prompting both to laugh in recognition of Imogen's apparent faux-pas.

"That would indeed be tragic!"

"Absolutely, I wouldn't be able to eat anything!"

"Absolutely, think of all those things you couldn't eat; ice cream, yoghurts,"

"Chocolates, profiteroles.."

"Ribs!!"

"Yeah, ribs, any Chinese food at all," Imogen continued with the list.

"Sausage," Jack had meant to put that into the plural but, for what he could only consider was down to some kind of Freudian slip, he spoke it in its singular form before belatedly adding in "esss. Sausagesss, not just a sausage, obviously. Why would you just have one sausage?"

Imogen folded her arms and looked on, rather enjoying Jack digging himself a hole and running around the bottom of it clawing at the walls as he tried to find a way out.

"Sausage?"

"Eh?" Jack thought it was time to change the subject.

"What if it was a jumbo sausage?" Imogen clearly didn't, "how big is the sausage you were thinking of Jack?"

"Er, just, just an ordinary, average sized sausage, made of sausage meat, from a pig, or a cow, or some kind of animal. Essentially a 'sausage' as in," Jack was aware his sentence was tailing off badly as he tried to get each word right, "as in…a sausage."

"Well obviously." Imogen squeezed Jack's hands tightly thinking that this would make him squirm a little, but not too tightly as to harm the spider within their cup. She turned and moved towards the sofa, "well if you're not going to show me the spider you might as well go and throw it out."

Jack, who amid the whole 'sausage' confusion had

completely forgotten he was pretending to hold a spider, smiled in relief and went to Imogen's front door.

"I'm opening your front door," he felt the need to let Imogen know what he was doing, "and I'm now throwing…"

Jack cut off in mid sentence.

"Hayley?"

"You're throwing Hayley?" came a rather confused call from the living-room.

"No,no,no," Jack shouted back, "I'm throwing out the spider. I just thought I saw Hayley walking past."

Jack took a step outside to double take against the young woman who was walking up the road. On a second, less neurotic look it was clear that the woman was not Hayley. She was Asian for a start.

Jack took a step back into the hallway and shut the door behind him. He took a sharp breath and shook his head.

"Was it Hayley?" came another call from the living room.

"No,no, just someone who looked like her," lied Jack as he made his way over to Imogen and sank into her rather comfortable sofa.

"That would have been weird," Imogen turned her body in towards Jack a little, "the woman who set us up, walking past my house. It would be like she was some kind of stalker or something!"

"Yeah," Jack forced a little laugh. The truth was Hayley was kind of stalking him only she wasn't outside, she was in his head. "That would be strange, but I don't think Hayley's really like that."

"Nah, she's lovely."

"Yeah." Jack knew she was.

"Anyway," Imogen placed her hand on Jack's knee,

drawing his attention away from the distractions of his thoughts, "thanks for a lovely evening."

"You're welcome, and thank you," Jack was aware of Imogen's hand beginning to make some steady progress northwards from his knee, "thank you for a lovely evening…"

Her kiss stalled his sentence before it could be completed. Her hand had made still more progress and Jack's hands, not to be outdone, had followed suit and were frantically unbuttoning her blouse.

The tender kisses from earlier had been replaced by a frenzied all-devouring passion. Within a few awkward fumbling moments Jack had removed Imogen's blouse and was now struggling to prise apart the clip on the back of her stunningly sexy underwired bra in order to free her equally stunning breasts that were seemingly bursting with anticipation and excitement at the thought of being released into the open.

Imogen had not been idle during this period and had already unbuckled Jack's belt and eased open the three buttons on his jeans that had taken the place of a zip.

As her hand slipped into the gap left by this manoeuvre she sat up. Her breasts groaned as Jack's efforts to release them failed, her movement back taking his fingers just out of reach of their clasp. Jack's initial disappointment was short-lived however, as the bra presented her breasts so beautifully it almost seemed wrong to take it off. It was a bit like when someone gives you a birthday present but the wrapping is so exquisite that it seems a crime to actually unwrap it, even though the present itself is likely to be just as amazing. This isn't always the case of course although, in the case of Imogen's breasts, Jack knew that the contents were indeed amazing and could brings hours of enjoyment to anyone who was lucky enough to play with them.

"Wow," was the extent of Jack's vocabulary at that precise moment.

"So," Imogen had a sparkle in her eyes. Jack looked deep into them and watched them widen as she gave him a little squeeze below the freed buttons.

"So?"

"Sausage." She raised her eyebrows.

"Sausage?" Jack raised his eyebrows. Something else of Jack's raised at the same time.

"I'm a little hungry." Before the last word had left her lips she had leant forward and was planting a kiss on Jack's neck as she seductively pulled his shirt buttons apart clearing away a route for her stream of tender kisses to follow.

Jack leant back and stared at the ceiling.

He closed his eyes and cast his mind back to the first time Imogen had demonstrated her considerable oral skills upon him. It was one of those memories that stays with you for life, a moment where when you close your eyes you can almost feel the sensations again, such were their original intensity. He pictured that scene as he sat there, remembering feeling her kisses as they moved ever nearer their destination. In his mind he saw her beautiful eyes staring up at him and then the top of her head slowly nodding up and down. After a few moments he pictured her looking back up at him.

"Fuck!"

"What, what, are you alright?"

Imogen had only reached as far as his belly button and was therefore more than a little shocked to hear Jack swear -

it's not as if she could have caught her teeth on anything, well not yet anyway.

"Ah, na, na, nothing," Jack had hit another panic moment, "I just got a little cramp in my leg, but it's gone now."

"Okay." Imogen smiled and put her head down to carry on her journey.

Jack put his head back towards the ceiling again, but this time didn't close his eyes. This was on account of the fact that when he had closed his eyes a few moments earlier to recall his first such experience with Imogen, the woman he visualised staring back up at him in his mind wasn't Imogen.

Even with his eyes open Jack couldn't quite get the image out of his head. Imogen sensed his distraction and halted her journey once more.

"Are you alright?" She peered up at him.

"Yeah, yeah," Jack tried to sound convincing.

"Hey," Imogen raised her eyebrows once more, "I think you need to say thank you to Hayley tomorrow."

"Wh,wh,what?" Jack was already trying desperately to get Hayley out of his head and could really do without Imogen thinking about her as well.

"Well, just think. If Hayley hadn't called me on Saturday, then we wouldn't have gone out tonight, and I wouldn't be about to do this." Imogen smiled the kind of smile that every man longs to see and then continued her journey south.

Saturday?

Saturday?

Jack's head had become used to being jumbled with all manner of confusion and paranoia of late, however, the significance of 'Saturday' was initially struggling to get through to him. Significant, however, he knew it was.

Then it hit him.

He had been out with Hayley on Thursday.

She had told him she had arranged the blind date already.

Hayley only rang Imogen on the Saturday.

Why?

"Did you say Hayley called you on Saturday, as in this Saturday just gone?"

A mumbled acknowledgement came from below where Imogen had moments before reached her destination.

The Morning After

The early morning sun lit up the streets and with it the day of all those fortunate enough to be walking to work, or indeed to wherever they needed or wanted to go. It was one of those mornings where you look up to the clear blue sky, feel the warmth of the rays against your skin and you know that, without question, it's going to be a great day.

Everyone is smiling – the postman, the shopkeeper, the bin-men, the mothers with their children walking to school, the paper boys, the delivery drivers, the Lollipop men, all of them, without exception, have been drugged by the glorious light descending from the star in the middle of our universe. People who had previously walked along, blinkered by their own thoughts and social taboos, suddenly were looking up and saying 'Hello' to the person they had passed by for the last year, and whom, during which time, they had actively taken the decision not to acknowledge.

To be caught up in such a morning is a rare and wonderful thing and it is a travesty that not everyone is there to share in the experience. Some are already stuck in offices, some are stuck in their beds, some are stuck in front of the early morning offerings provided by our television executives who have cleverly worked out that a seemingly large cross section of our population are genuinely intrigued to find out why a grotesquely overweight tattoo ridden lard taster thinks that her boyfriend has been shagging an equally hideous monosyllabic tub of folded flab, and, what's more, that they decide the best place to sort this out is in front of a crowd of people who are there with the sole intention of feeding their egos by establishing that at least there are some people in our world with even sadder lives than themselves.

Jack was neither in his office, in his bed nor in front of the television this Tuesday morning. He was one of the lucky ones pacing through the glorious morn.

However.

Jack was oblivious to his surroundings. His head was down, his ears failing to pick up on the several cheery 'good mornings' that were thrown his way by happy strangers. His feet drove on with purpose, his own automatic navigation system taking him safely past unseen obstacles, across busy bustling roads, under precariously placed scaffolding and over chipboard covered manholes adorned by brightly coloured safety bollards.

His steadfast pace and flooded mind was interrupted by the vibration of his mobile phone.

Jack stopped and visibly sank as he saw the instigator of the new text message awaiting his attention.

'What happened Jack? I'm confused. Please call me. Imogen x'

"Oh Fuck!!" Jack looked up to the sky as he let out a huge sigh, desperately trying to exhale some of the bad karma that was seemingly spreading through his body like some horrendous malignant force.

He continued his path towards the bank maintaining his pace despite feeling the additional weight of guilt stirred by Imogen's plea for understanding.

Even the broad 'Hellos' from the assembled cashiers as

they neatly arranged their tills prior to the early morning rush failed to illicit a response from Jack as he strode onwards, past them, and then up the stairs, two steps at a time, towards his final destination - his desk and an impossible conversation with Hayley. Impossible, because he didn't even know where to begin. Ever since pulling himself away from Imogen's most intimate of attentions last night and trying to make the least hurtful exit he could possibly do in such circumstances, Jack had been running a continuous stream of thoughts through his battered mind.

He had finally come to a conclusion.

His conclusion was that he was a 'bit fucked up'.

Such a conclusion, whilst accurate, was not a great deal of comfort to Jack who was used to knowing what to do and what to say. He was a man who could step back from a problem and look at it logically and find the sense in most given situations. Sure, such questions as "Why are we here?" "Is there a God?" and "Why is there a pube in the butter?" have stumped Jack in the past; however, in knowing that this is the case, Jack has been quite happy to move on and find answers to questions that are far more relevant to day-to-day existence.

He had got as far as breaking his latest problem down into key points, and indeed he had even taken to writing these down at 4 o'clock in the morning in the hope that his semi-conscious state would provide him with answers when the morning finally arrived. His note read as follows:

1. Hayley is my best friend.

2. I think she really likes me but I think I may have inadvertently put her off by telling her we're just friends.

3. I think I really like Hayley but I, as per point 2, think I may have inadvertently put her off by telling her we're just friends.

4. I thought that I needed to check with Hayley what the score was particularly when I thought she was getting jealous of the attentions some of her friends were paying me when we were out. But..

5. Hayley then tells me she has set me up on a blind date.

6. I assume that's it and that I've got the wrong end of the stick.

7. I go out with Imogen and find myself having strong feelings for her. But..

8. I kept thinking about Hayley.

9. I still kiss Imogen and let her start to go down on me – shit, feeling very bad about that – but was distracted as thinking about Hayley at the time – shit – that's not good – must ensure never tell Imogen that.

10. Imogen tells me that Hayley only called her on Saturday which means Hayley hadn't told the truth when we were out last week. Therefore surely she did that to stop the other girls asking me out. Therefore surely she was jealous. Therefore, surely she really likes me.

11. Hayley is my best friend.

12. What if I'm wrong?

13. I'm fucked.

14. Shit.

15. I must get to sleep now as I can't read my writing.

16. Hope this makes sense in the morning.

It may have technically made sense but it didn't help. Jack had re-read the note a few times; when he awoke, after his shower, whilst eating his toast, after brushing his teeth and just before putting it in the bin.

Not used to not having a plan, Jack knew that he would just have to 'wing it' unless some divine intervention would strike and somehow show him the way. Jack felt this was unlikely on account of his own lack of belief in anything divine.

Jack's feeling on this subject was upheld as he turned the corner. Hayley's desk was empty.

"Alright Jack?" the enquiry came from Ken who was walking back to his own desk after preparing himself a large mug of sweet strong coffee.

Jack heard him, and in his head answered, but his stare was focused on Hayley's clear clean desk.

"Hello!" called Ken as he waved his arm in a large arc to try and awaken Jack from his seeming hypnotic state, "is anyone there? Earth to Jack, do you read me?"

Jack, his peripheral vision aware of some large unusual movements to his left, moved his stare away from the desk and over to Ken who, frustrated at the lack of response from his colleague, was now making wildly offensive gestures involving his fingers, hands and posturing at his backside.

"What are you doing Ken?"

"Ah, you're alive. I thought you had turned into a Zombie or were sleep walking or something like that." Ken had swiftly run out of any potentially amusing adjectives.

"What?" Jack was still distracted. Hayley would normally be in the office by now.

"You look lost my friend." Ken found Jack's demeanour quite amusing – it was nice for Jack not to be armed with any sharp banter or clever put-downs. "Do you want a coffee? I've got a nice strong one here, on account of the extreme lack of sleep I had last night."

Ken's clear desire for Jack to express some interest in the reasons behind his lack of sleep was falling somewhat flat.

"Has Hayley been in yet?"

"What?" Ken wasn't interested in this, he wanted to talk about his night, "No, she's on that course for the rest of the week."

Shit!

Jack had completely forgotten about the course.

"Fucking mortgages!"

"You alright mate?" Ken was beginning to worry about the rather strange behaviour of his fellow worker.

"Oh, yeah, yeah, of course." Jack was a little embarrassed firstly on account that he had made his last comment in earshot of Ken, and secondly, that he had made the comment so loudly! "I wanted to talk to Hayley about one of my customers, that's all. Nothing else. Nothing else. At all."

"Okay mate, I was just asking. Anyway, do you want a coffee?"

"Yeah, cool, that would be good thanks." Jack took off his jacket and slumped it over his chair. He sat down at his desk and let out yet another long audible sigh as he stared at the dark sombre reflection in his flat-screen monitor. 'Flat' was extremely appropriate as it described nicely how Jack was feeling at the precise moment.

Jack was still in the same position when Ken returned with a large mug of coffee and perched it, and himself, on the side of Jack's desk.

"Get that down you mate, it'll wake you up."

"Cheers Ken." Jack picked up the mug and reluctantly pushed the power button of his PC.

Ken let out a huge, overstated yawn in the hope that this might elicit a response from Jack.

"You tired Ken?"

Ken beamed! At last, there was the tag line to let him legitimately talk about the night before.

"Ah, God mate yeah. What a night! What – a – night!!"

Jack realised the error of his ways and was about to tell Ken to go and sit down when he had a change of heart. He needed some distraction.

"Dare I ask Ken. Dare I really ask, why was your night so good?"

Ken beamed again.

"Really?" Ken wanted to check that he was being given the green light to go ahead. His beam widened still further when Jack nodded. Jack also found himself smiling at this, partly because he could see how happy Ken was to be given the chance to talk about his nocturnal habits and partly because he realised that there was suddenly life outside his own apparent present train wreck of a one.

"Right, well, me and Sharon.."

Jack somehow had forgotten that Ken was seeing Sharon. It was therefore with a sense of dread that he listened to the rest of Ken's tale.

"We bought this book, you know," Ken started to raise his eyebrows and tap his nose, "a book. You know what I mean?"

Jack had a terrible feeling that he had a fair idea upon which subject the book was likely to be written but, nevertheless, thought he would throw another option out into the open in the faint hope he had got it all wrong.

"Was it the Bible?"

"The Bible?"

"I take it that it wasn't the Bible then?"

"Why would we buy the Bible?"

"I don't know," Jack was beginning to wish he had just shut up and let Ken get on with his story, "perhaps you both have found God or something."

"Oh, I don't think God would have approved of this book, if you know what I mean?" Ken started to raise his eyebrows and tap his nose once more. This brought a reluctant smile to Jack's recently much-furrowed face.

"I am rather worryingly intrigued Ken. If it wasn't the Bible, and in hindsight I do concede that this was perhaps an unlikely choice, then what was it?"

Ken jumped off the desk and quickly checked around the corner for any signs of members of the management team. With no-one in the immediate vicinity, he excitedly returned to the desk.

"It was a, you know, a…sex book!!!" Ken sat up straight and started to nod approvingly at this piece of information he had just shared with Jack.

"A sex book?"

"Yep, a sex Book. A book…"

"about sex?" Jack felt he needed to interrupt.

"Exactly. A book about sex."

"Oh good. That's lovely to know."

"Oh there's more Jack."

"Really?"

"Oh yeah."

"How nice."

"Nice? Nice! Jack, you wait 'til I tell you how the word 'nice' doesn't even begin to describe just how nice it was."

Jack was beginning to regret entering into this conversation.

"So, to clarify, the word 'nice' doesn't begin to describe just how 'nice' it was?"

Ken nodded his confirmation.

"Yeah. It was nicer than nice."

"Nicer than nice?"

"Yeah, nice!!"

"Nice one."

"Nice one indeed Jack."

"I thought it was nicer than nice Ken?"

"Oh yeah yeah. It was Jack. It was nicer than nice."

"Wow," Jack felt compelled to continue, "nicer than nice? That's really nice."

"Ah mate, I'm telling you, it was really really nice." Ken nodded as he felt a real understanding develop between the two of them.

"Blimey. So, just to clarify once more, it was really really nice?"

"Yep, ah mate it really was."

"So, is 'really really nice', nicer than 'nicer than nice'?"

Ken paused as he tried to work it out.

"I'm not sure Jack, but what I can tell you, is that is was really.."

"Nice?"

"Nice!"

Ken could normally hold a reasonably good adult conversation. However, his obvious inexperience in matters of the flesh meant that conversations around that subject were not always as free flowing or articulate as his conversations around Banking Law and the pros and cons of PCs versus the Mac. Conversely Jack knew diddley squat about the latter subjects but could normally be relied upon to tell a good tale or two in the field of fornication, including one tale specifically about fornication in a field.

Jack paused as he tried to recap where they had got to in the last few seconds of bizarre communications.

"So, what exactly was 'nicer' than 'really really nice'?"

"The Sex Book!!"

"Oh gosh, yes, I had forgotten that's what you were talking about."

"It had loads of pictures!"

"Was it a Pop Up book?"

"No mate, don't be stupid. It's not for kids." Ken looked a little disgusted.

Jack stifled a laugh at the sight of Ken's ignominy.

"Of course not. How stupid of me."

"Jack, you're a bit weird today."

"So says the man sitting on my desk telling me about his nice sex picture book!"

"Yep, they were nearly real photos as well."

"What do you mean 'nearly real photos'?" Jack was getting a bit confused now and the regret he had felt earlier in the conversation was beginning to grow with the speed of an unwanted teenage spot. "How can you have a 'nearly real photo'? It's either a photo or it isn't."

"Well I think they were photos, but they were photos of drawings of people you know, doing 'it'!"

"So they were drawings then."

"Photos of drawings."

"But essentially they were drawings."

"Drawings of real people doing 'it'… which were photo'd."

Jack shook his head.

"Wow. Well thanks for that information Ken. I'm glad you felt you could share that with me."

"You wait 'til I let you know what we did when we read the book together!!"

"What a fantastic idea. Could I wait? Please? I've got a really busy day and much as I'd clearly love to know what you and Sharon got up to when you read your sex book with real photos of drawings of people having sex, I think that perhaps you should keep some of those details between you and Sharon?"

Ken looked a little thoughtful. Perhaps Jack was right. There were some things that you really shouldn't talk about. Intimacy is a wonderful thing in a relationship. You could be the wealthiest man in the world but if you never have intimacy, real intimacy, then you have nothing. What Ken had with Sharon was sacred to them. When he was alone with her then he was the richest man in the world. No-one could, or should, ever take that away from him. With this in mind Ken smiled to himself and puffed out his chest.

"You're right Jack. There're some things within relationships that should stay within the sanctity of that relationship."

"Absolutely." Jack was relieved.

"Relationships are about two people Jack. Relationships are about the intimacy between two people."

Jack had never thought he would see the day when Ken

would give him a lecture on the ways of Love. Okay, so it wasn't a particularly good lecture, but Jack gave him the courtesy of listening anyway.

"Intimacy is, it's, well, it's all about being.." Ken was struggling to find the word.

"Intimate?"

"Intimate! Exactly Jack, exactly. Intimacy is about being intimate. Intimate means keeping things between you and your lover. When you have intimacy, and I mean true intimacy Jack, then you don't need to tell anyone else because the only person that matters, and I mean truly matters, is your partner – the one who you are being intimate with."

"That's beautiful Ken."

"Cheers mate, I know I may not always share my thoughts. I'm one of those really strong guys who holds his feelings in, but I can be sensitive. I'm not afraid to admit that I'm in touch with my feminine side."

"Again, that's beautiful Ken." Jack was beginning to feel a tad uncomfortable and was convinced that in a moment Ken was going to ask him for a hug.

"Thanks Jack, it's good that we can talk about these things. Not that we've talked about 'things' specifically." Ken had made the speech mark signs with his fingers when he emphasised the word 'things' and had followed that by a further tapping of his nose.

"No, thank God, we haven't. As you said Ken, sometimes you know that there are some things that you don't share with others and, please, do feel free to keep it that way."

At this moment Karen, one of the cashiers, came around the corner causing Ken to hop down off the side of Jack's desk and straighten his tie.

"Morning Jack, morning Ken!" Karen smiled at the two men as she made her way past toward the door leading to the staff room and kitchen.

"Morning Karen." Jack nodded

"Morning Karen." Ken did the same and turned to return to his chair.

Karen turned back to face them as she reached the door.

"Ken, you really should tell Sharon that some things in a relationship are sacred you know." Ken's face dropped.

"Seriously," Karen continued, "she's told us she's going to put the video on You Tube later and wants us all to watch it at lunchtime."

Ken's face dropped some more.

"Would you like me to help you scrape your jaw off the floor Ken?" Jack felt a little sorry for Ken. Ken, whilst undoubtedly a bit of a plonker, meant no harm and was clearly well out of his depth with the raging sex monster that was Sharon.

Ken paced off towards the stairs.

Jack made a mental note never to go on You Tube again.

The rest of Jack's morning drifted by aimlessly. Pieces of paper were picked up, read and put down. E-mails were opened, read, and closed. The pieces of paper, already read, were read again and once more placed down. The e-mails were re-opened, re-read and closed once more.

How could Hayley be on a course for the rest of the week?

How could Jack's life have been turned so upside-down within a matter of weeks when seemingly nothing actually changed?

How could he keep on ignoring Imogen's texts that had now reached three in number?

The figures on the base of his computer screen eventually clicked over to 12.00.

Lunch. At last he could escape.

Jack pushed his chair out behind him and stood himself up. He felt the need to stretch himself high into the air in order to release some of the tension that had been building within his frame, a frame that had spent the majority of the morning hunched over his desk as he had busied himself doing nothing.

His phone rang.

"Fuck!" accompanied his sigh. However his annoyance swiftly turned to nervous, stomach-wrenching anxiety as he recognised the mobile number coming through on the phone display.

"Hi, good morning, in fact good afternoon, you're through to Jack Matthews, how can I help?"

"You knew it was me didn't you!"

"Absolutely, how's the course, yet another course I might add?"

Years of experience had enabled Jack to click into autopilot mode on the phone. Exchanging confident pleasantries was one thing, however, saying what he thought he had to say was another completely.

"Ah, it's as boring as hell! I've just been let out for lunch thank God."

"Hey, only three and a half days left!"

"Don't remind me, seriously, I don't think I can last 'til Friday."

"Come back now then." Jack's response was instinctive and, as such, quite honest.

"I wish! Anyway, how did it go last night?"

Jack's heart sank. He didn't want Hayley to ring up just to ask him how his date was. On the other hand, what if she wanted to check because she wanted it to go badly? Bolstered by this potential light gleaming at the end of this particular tunnel, Jack gave his answer.

"Oh, you know."

"No! I don't, that's why I'm asking."

"Honestly?"

"Yes!! Am I an ace match maker or aren't I?"

Jack was trying to hold his conversation whilst at the same time trying to interpret every inflection in Hayley's words as he tried to decipher their true meaning.

"It went alright I guess. We got on well. It was great to see her again."

"I sense a but?"

"Yeah, there is a bit of a but."

"I thought she had a nice butt!"

Jack laughed.

"Yes, she has got a nice butt, but then so have you." Jack didn't mean to let the last words go and turned to bang his head against the adjacent window.

"What's that noise?"

Jack hastily pulled away from the window.

"Er, nothing."

"So, what happened?"

"Ah, it's..it's hard to explain, well at least over the phone anyway. Listen can we meet up when you're back?"

"Yeah sure, we can do lunch on Monday if you like?"

"I was thinking sooner than that, what about Friday night? What time are you back?"

"Not 'til late I think. Is everything all right?" Hayley sounded concerned about her friend.

"Yeah yeah of course, there's just, just some things I want to talk to you about that's all."

"Okay."

"Nothing to worry about." Jack added quickly, sensing an uncertainty in Hayley's voice.

"Well, what about Saturday? We can grab a coffee during the day?"

"Well, what about in the evening? Do you fancy grabbing a bite to eat?"

"I'm actually out on Saturday, I've already got plans."

"Oh, listen to you, Miss Sociable! Where are you off to then?"

"Ah just out, with some friends."

"Okay, a coffee during the day it is then."

"Great, listen, I've got to run, hotel lunch is beckoning me. Call me."

"Yea, no p.." Jack pulled the phone away from his ear. Hayley had already gone and, with that, also the opportunity to ask her there and then why she had told him she'd set him up on a date before she actually had.

Still, at least Jack had arranged to speak with her at the weekend. All he had to do now was to keep himself busy for the next three and a half days and, during that time, somehow avoid thinking about his seemingly complicated love, or lack of love, life. A few days without having to shake all the thoughts clear within his head were just what Jack needed. If he could just clear his mind now and chill out then he knew he could get his life back to the calm order in which it was used to being lived. With these calming thoughts locked down Jack put his handset back onto his phone unit and stretched himself once more.

The tension eased its way out through his finger tips and for the first time in what seemed an eternity Jack felt relaxed.

The phone rang.

Jack looked down and recognised the incoming number again.

He reached towards the handset and clicked the button to forward the caller to his voice mail.

He turned and walked away from his desk; his relaxation was, it turned out, only fleeting as he was destined to spend the next day and a half plucking up the courage and finding the words he needed to return Imogen's call.

The Question is Asked

Saturday morning.

The sun was once more up bright and early, literally bright and early. Its comforting rays were beating on window frames encouraging people to get their lazy arses out of their beds and to get them out into the fresh air to enjoy and rejoice in the wonderful fruits that nature can behold on such glorious summer mornings.

Jack was one of those lucky few who had willingly taken up this kind invitation and was strolling into town to look for a few bargains on which to spend his hard-earned cash. Okay, 'hard earned' may be a slight exaggeration, Jack quite enjoyed his job but hadn't really got himself into 'career' mode as yet. Therefore, whilst he did at times work hard, he accepted that he generally worked within himself. Life is, after all, too short to bust a gut at work when to do so resulted in very little apparent reward for the efforts you'd need to put in to get anywhere.

Jack had seen several career minded people pass by him during his time at the bank, most on some kind of graduate accelerated training scheme. Most of these supposed high flyers had actually graduated in subjects as far removed from bank related subjects as you could imagine - Geology, Textile and Design, Travel and Leisure, Advanced Masturbation and so forth. In his early years at the bank, before he had given himself time to settle down on his own life path, Jack had found himself somewhat bothered by the idea that someone could queue jump ahead of him in the promotion stakes on the grounds that they studied how to embroider for four years. The answer given to him by his manager at the time was that people who had taken degrees had demonstrated the ability to learn and follow their goals and were, therefore, the sort of people a business would want to employ. Jack knew, of course, that this was bollocks. He knew plenty of people who had gone to university and their prime reasons for doing so were to:

a) Get laid

b) Get drunk

c) Avoid having to get a real job for as long as they could

d) Get laid and drunk some more

e) Repeat steps (a) through to (d) for as many years as they can get away with.

Jack had decided not to share this insight with his manager and had merely acknowledged that it was indeed useful to have someone who had majored in Marine Biology telling him how to lend money on the grounds that they would know all about loan sharks.

As Jack strolled through the streets, pleased with himself that he was up early enough to miss the hustle and bustle that would descend upon the town centre from mid morning, he reflected on his last couple of days since speaking to Hayley.

They had actually gone better then he had anticipated.

Much to his relief he had finally done the decent thing and returned Imogen's calls. They had met for lunch the previous day and had a frank and honest discussion, well reasonably honest anyway.

Jack had stopped short of naming Hayley but had told Imogen he was confused and not sure about his feelings towards someone else as well as Imogen. This was a generally honest interpretation of the predicament in which Jack had suddenly found himself, and certainly so at the moment he had felt the need to ease Imogen away and make his hasty escape on the previous Tuesday night. The mist that had shrouded his confusion since that night had faded away by the time he had seen Imogen again on Friday, however he felt it inappropriate to tell her that as they talked. He genuinely cared for Imogen. All of the thoughts and feelings that he had experienced when they had met up on that evening had been real enough at the time but had been generated at a time when he felt that Hayley was not interested in having a full relationship with him. At the moment he realised that there was hope he had also realised that he couldn't get involved with Imogen. This was as much to do with how much he cared for her, and as such he couldn't bear the thought of hurting her again, as it did with wanting to be with Hayley. It was this realisation that had suddenly turned Jack's view on his situation up on its head. He had realised that he was a good bloke. The additional unwanted weight upon his shoulders had been lifted and he was back just wrestling with his original dilemma. Buoyed by his sudden feeling of self worth Jack had steeled himself to talk to Hayley and just get all he wanted to say laid neatly on the table. He had recalled in his mind the conversation he had with Hayley on the night in the car after the wedding. In his mind he felt that she had tried to have the conversation with him then that he now wanted to have with her. On that occasion he had inadvertently blocked the notion of them being together. How different would things be now if he hadn't? That question was relevant then, however, the question that was going to be relevant when he met up with Hayley in a few hours for lunch was whether she was going to block the notion of them being together now?

This was a sobering thought but one which Jack, until now, had managed to keep nourished by a glass that was half full rather then half empty. Jack, however, was no fool, and he knew that as the minutes ticked slowly away his glass would become emptier and emptier.

Jack checked his watch. Nine fifteen. He stopped and reached for his mobile phone. Taking a deep breath he carefully and deliberately keyed in Hayley's number.

He stared down at his gently shuffling shoes as he waited to be connected.

"Sorry, the telephone number you are calling is not responding, please try later."

Jack tutted and placed his phone back in his pocket. He checked his watch again. Unsurprisingly it had not moved on too much; however, it did confirm to Jack that it was indeed still quite early in the day and therefore it's quite reasonable for Hayley's phone not to be on.

Jack, encouraged by the voice in his head, strode on into town with an action taken to try again at ten o'clock.

Ten o'clock had come and passed, as indeed had eleven, twelve, one, two and three.

Jack's glass was now completely empty and in danger of toppling off the edge of the table as he paced up and down his living room.

Why wasn't Hayley's phone on? Why hadn't she returned his calls from the messages he had left on her home answer phone?

Jack stopped.

Why hadn't he checked his own answer phone messages?

He practically fell over the sofa as his feet drove off towards the phone leaving his body struggling to keep up.

Jack sucked in some air through his pursed lips and gritted teeth as his machine advised him that he had two new messages.

"Hi Jack darling, it's your.." Jack hit the delete button and then felt a slight twinge of guilt. His mother, after all, may have had something important to tell him. There and again, she may not, so he clicked to pick up the next message.

"Hi Jack," it was Hayley. Jack felt the relief ooze through his body and he momentarily allowed himself to relax as the message continued. "I'm really sorry I haven't called you. I stayed over at the hotel last night so didn't get back until mid morning. Let's catch up on Monday."

The phone clicked off. Jack slumped down in his chair.

"Oh fuck it!" he declared.

He sat motionless gradually feeling his neck stiffen as he tried to set aside the frustrations he was feeling at yet again having come seemingly so close to actually addressing his problem. However fate, it would seem, was conspiring against him and doing all things possible to throw him off the scent as soon as he was in a positive frame of mind.

With this very thought trickling through his head Jack sat bolt upright.

"Nope, you little shit. You're not going to get in the way this time." The little shit to which Jack was referring was indeed 'Fate' and not Hayley.

Jack pulled himself out of his chair and looked himself dead in the eye in his lounge mirror.

"Right Mr Matthews, you're going to sort this out now."

Jack was impressed with his sudden assertive streak and nodded approvingly to the mirror. His reflection nodded approvingly back.

"But first," he continued, "you're going to have a strong coffee and be crystal clear what you're going to say to her."

Again his reflection affirmed this decision and followed Jack into the kitchen where it caught up with him as Jack stared at the glass microwave door whilst waiting for the kettle to bubble to a boil.

As the steam forced its way through the spout Jack spooned the second sugar into his mug and made his plans. It was nearly half past three. He would have a quick shower, get changed and go over to see Hayley before she went out for the evening. It was a simple plan and as such was compiled and confirmed by the time he had poured the water into his coffee. He leant back against his kitchen worktop and, as he slowly stirred his brew, he closed his eyes and tried to picture how the next few hours would unfold.

Hayley's flat wasn't too far away but, conscious of how long he'd taken to get ready, Jack decided to drive. Subconsciously he knew that this would give him somewhere to wait anonymously until he could summon up the courage to walk to her door. This proved to be a wise decision as he was paralysed in his seat for twenty minutes before he succumbed to the encouraging voice from within and got out of the car.

He stood up straight and tried to shake the anxiety from his bones.

"Come on mate, you can do it. Just get in there and talk

to her. Christ she's your best friend. It's Hayley. It's not some monster. Just go for it, everything will be alright."

His audible words of self affirmation delivered through gritted teeth gave further energy to his stride as well as drawing a puzzled and slightly alarmed gaze from a passing old lady.

Before he knew it, Jack was at the door.

Still under the will of his inner voice Jack raised his finger and, with only the smallest of hesitations, pressed Hayley's bell.

The ding dong echoing beyond the frame awoke Jack from his positive karma with a shuddering jolt, sending a heady mixture of paranoia, fear and panic descending with great delight down upon his burdened shoulders.

"Oh fuck off!!" Jack hurled his instinctive abuse at his demons and immediately tried to recoil the words as the door opened and a somewhat shocked Hayley stood before him.

"Jack!"

"Hayley! Hi!"

Both stood there, each seemingly as startled as the other at the sight of each other's presence.

"Did you not get my message?"

"No," Jack didn't mean to lie but once he had let slip the 'no' it seemed too late to retract it and replace it with the truth, "sorry, I didn't. When did you call?"

"This afternoon. Sorry, I didn't come back until late this morning so I couldn't really make lunch."

"Ah, okay. Did you try my mobile?"

"No," Hayley seemed a little hesitant, "I didn't think to."

There was a brief pause, long enough for them both to

get over the shock of seeing each other and for Hayley to remember her manners.

"Oh gosh, sorry Jack. Come on in." Hayley walked into her hall and Jack followed. He could see that Hayley had been preparing to go out and consequently felt a twinge of guilt that he had let the time slip away to its present position of a quarter to seven. Perhaps he shouldn't have elected to have a bath instead of a shower and to have checked out the final scores before doing so after all.

"I'm sorry I'm calling late." His apology was genuine enough.

"Ah not to worry, but I'm off out shortly so I might need to keep getting ready if that's alright?" The voice came from Hayley's bedroom where she was searching for some mascara.

"Yeah, of course," Jack called from outside the door. It seemed inappropriate to actually go into the bedroom.

"So, you alright then? Had a good week?" came the enquiry from opposite the dressing-table mirror.

"Yeah, not bad," lied Jack who couldn't believe he wasn't even in the same room as the person with whom he desperately needed to have possibly the most important conversation of his life. He took a deep breath.

"Actually, it's been a bit crap really."

"Oh good, mine's been alright too."

Jack banged his head on the adjacent wall.

"No, I said my week's been a bit crap." Jack called out a little more loudly enabling Hayley to catch his sentence on the second time round.

"Oh dear, that's no good. Was that because you missed me?" She leant into the mirror and started to carefully draw the brush across her lashes.

Outside the door Jack paused and looked up towards the ceiling. He then looked back towards the door and reached out to push it further open. At the very last moment he stopped himself and withdrew his fingertips.

"Yeah I think it was."

Whether it was the distance, or at very least the door between them, that distorted the meaningful tone of Jack's heart-on-his-sleeve honesty it was hard to say, but distorted it obviously had been.

"Ah, bless you. I missed you too."

Jack sighed and closed his eyes.

"No," he tried to sound a little more forceful, "I did miss you."

Hayley, again distracted by the final application which framed her beautiful eyes perfectly, stood herself up and walked towards the door.

Jack, distracted by the fact that his initial attempts to bare his soul were failing miserably, slouched back against the hall wall and hung his head in frustration.

"You alright?" Hayley was standing in the doorway and was a little shocked to see Jack's somewhat crumpled posture.

Jack slowly raised his head to face her.

"No," their eyes instinctively locked on to one another, "I had a crap week because I did miss you. I missed you."

"You missed me?" Hayley was beginning to pick up on the sincerity of Jack's voice.

"Yeah, as in, I really missed you."

The silence was held for a few seconds as indeed was their eye contact. Hayley broke the line of vision and, almost in a daze as she began to understand the significance of the conversation they were about to have, slowly slid down the wall until she was sitting by the door staring into space.

Jack, trying to regain the eye contact, followed suit and there they were, the two of them sitting in Hayley's hall staring at the wall.

"I'm a bit confused," Hayley honestly began, "when you say you missed me, do you mean as a friend?"

"Yes," Jack was also being honest and continued to be so, "and No."

"Yes and No?"

"Look, I know this may seem a little strange and trust me, I'm finding this a wee bit surreal, but I do need to talk to you about something, well, when I say 'something' I mean I need to talk to you about us."

Hayley had made fleeting eye contact with Jack during his last sentence but had nervously and quickly averted her gaze.

"The thing is," Jack was struggling to find the words. It had been so much easier in his head when he could plan what Hayley said as well, "the thing is, ever since we talked after the wedding I've kind of been finding myself confused."

Jack paused, hoping for Hayley to interject.

Hayley didn't know what to say but a familiar feeling of confusion that had clogged up her thoughts a few weeks ago was sneaking once more into her head.

"I mean, that night," Jack tried to get some momentum into his conversation, "it was a great night, wasn't it?"

Hayley nodded her agreement and the two exchanged a smile. The significance of the smile was not lost on either of them. Instinctively they looked at each other once more and the warm smile, the smile that let them both know that they were there for one another, was there and broadened across their relieved faces. It was as if they both knew that they need not be afraid and had been given the green light to lay their hearts out on the table, or hall carpet as was the case in this particular instance.

"All I had that night was my family telling me how great we were together and then, when we sat in the car, you started talking about that too. I know I said at the time that we were just friends but as soon as you got out the car and walked up to this place I wasn't so sure."

"Why didn't you say anything?" Hayley's response, like the smile, was instinctive.

"I've tried. Loads of times."

"When?"

"Oh, I don't know. Loads of time though."

"When?" Hayley was searching her mind to try and think of any time when Jack had tried to raise the subject.

"Oh, afterwards, the next week, a few times since, when we went out and met your friends."

"But you've never said anything!"

"It's hard! How to tell your best mate that you've got feelings for her when you're petrified that she might not feel the same? It's a bloody nightmare!"

There was a pause and Hayley lowered her head.

"I'm sorry Jack."

"That's alright, don't worry. You weren't to know. Like you say, if I didn't actually say what I was feeling how were you to know?"

Hayley's head remained bowed.

"No," her pause was deliberate but only as long as was really necessary to let her best friend down as gently as she could, "I'm sorry Jack."

This time she knew she needed Jack to understand what she was trying to convey even though at this precise moment she was not sure if it was completely aligned to how she felt. She slowly raised her gaze until she could feel Jack's stare penetrating deep into her eyes and deeper still into her soul. Jack felt the hall walls enclosing around him.

"I'm so sorry." Hayley, try desperately though she did, could not stem the tears as they prised their way past her freshly painted eyes.

"Don't cry." Jack edged himself along and offered his handkerchief and tenderly put his arms around her. His instinctive actions were those of someone who truly loved her, a truly selfless act indicative of the depth of their friendship and not the actions of someone whose attempted declaration of love had just been subtly and gently rejected.

"Jack, I love you, I do, but I think that I love you as a friend, my best friend." Hayley was wiping away her tears and so desperately didn't want to hurt her friend. At the same time she so desperately needed to be held.

"You said you 'think'," Jack clutched at the straw, "does that mean you're not sure?"

"No, I think it means I am." Hayley wiped away another stray tear.

"You realise you said 'think' again don't you?"

Jack wanted to comfort his friend whilst still clinging on to the tiniest of corners of the straw. It was a noble act. He squeezed her tightly and a small tear rolled forlornly down his cheek. He felt like his heart had been wrenched out of his chest in the flickering of an eye. In all the scenarios he had played through - the good ones and the not so good ones - he had always envisaged he and Hayley having long drawn out dramatic conversations but the reality had been anything but that. His dreams had been almost instantly quashed and yet bizarrely he found himself wanting to console his friend as much as he wanted to console himself.

The two of them, for a while, sat there in silence, holding each other so tightly so as not to risk letting go, as if by doing so they were somehow in danger of letting go their friendship.

"I'm really sorry if I led you on Jack." Hayley sat up a little straighter and felt for Jack's hand.

Jack responded and squeezed her fingers between his own.

"Ah, I dunno. I don't think you did Hayles. To be honest, I'm a little bit confused right now. It's as if I've spent the last few weeks thinking that I'm in love with you and in a few brief moments I've suddenly realised that I think it might have all been in my head." Jack turned to face Hayley. "I feel a bit of a twat to be honest!"

Both let out a stifled, but welcome, laugh.

"Jack, really, I am sorry. It's not just you," Hayley paused as she wiped away a stray tear, "I know I shouldn't have said those things in the car but everyone kept telling me how 'great' you were and that 'why wasn't I with you' and I guess I just wanted to check where you were with that."

Jack nodded and shook his head to himself at the same time.

"What would you have done if I'd told you at the time that I thought we should go for it?"

The eye contact that they had maintained during Jack's question was broken as Hayley looked away to contemplate his question. The truth of the matter was that she didn't really know but there was probably a really good chance that something may have happened. This was a recognition with which Hayley was really beginning to struggle.

"I don't know."

Jack found the courage to go on.

"So what's changed?"

Hayley still couldn't bring herself to look at him. The truth was that she wasn't sure what had changed. Her brain, the inner turmoils of which now resembled how Jack's own grey matter had been wracked in chaos over the last few weeks, was trying to race through her more recent memories to find an answer. The only one she could stump up was that Jack had re-assured her at the time of the wedding that they were just friends. Beyond that she had nothing and indeed, she was now finding herself sliding further into confusion as she contemplated that only a week and a half ago she set him up on a blind date on the grounds that she was actually feeling jealous.

"I don't know what's changed Jack. I know that when I got out of that car my head was clear and that I thought our friendship was right."

"See, you said 'thought' again! I think you're thinking too much about this don't you think?"

Jack smiled. This was probably not the greatest time to make a little joke but at the same time it wasn't the worst either. The two of them were tip-toeing around a sensitive issue and their relationship had, after all, been founded on their shared sense of humour.

Hayley smacked him on the arm and the two of them looked at each other. They could both sense that this felt like their relationship of old. There was a slight twist however in so much as each wanted to give the other a hug but this time each held back from doing so in case they suddenly felt the desire to kiss.

"Seriously though Hayles, what has changed?"

Hayley still didn't really know but didn't have to answer the question as the sound of the doorbell brought a swift end to the subject.

"Oh shit, sorry Hayley, I forgot you were going out." Jack started to stand up.

"So did I." Hayley got up but was clearly agitated and started to guide Jack into her living-room.

"You alright?" Jack was a little taken aback by Hayley's haste.

"Yeah, yeah, yeah," Hayley seemed to be almost panicking, "go and have a seat. I'll tell my friends I can't go out tonight."

"Oh don't be daft, don't let me spoil your evening. We can talk tomorrow, or later."

"That's fine, that's fine, just sit down, this is more important."

Jack did as he was told and sat himself down. He was actually quite touched that Hayley would dump her friends at the last minute in order to be with him.

Hayley pushed the living-room door shut and hurried to the door just as the bell resonated around the hall walls once more.

"Good evening, I have flowers and a bottle of wine."

"I can't tonight!" Hayley was trying to whisper.

"Are you okay. What's up?"

"I just can't go out tonight, I'm really really sorry, something's come up."

In the living-room Jack could make out the sound of a

man's voice at the door. His stomach started to turn as it dawned on him that there was a possibility that Hayley was actually going out on a date that night. He wasn't sure whether he should be flattered that she was dumping someone else for him, or jealous and angry that she could consider seeing someone else in the first place. The latter, he knew, didn't really make a lot of sense as she had every right to see someone else, well, technically at least.

"Well if you can't come out, why don't I come in and I can cook for us?"

"No!! Listen, I'm really sorry, I just can't tonight, I'll explain later, but right now you must go."

"Have you got someone here?"

Jack, still listening to the voices, had found himself drawn towards the door. He couldn't quite make out the voices but he suddenly felt that perhaps he should just go and let Hayley get on with her life. He took a deep sigh and walked out into the hall just at the moment the man at the door peered through past Hayley to see if anyone else was there.

The three of them stood there.

Jack stared intently firstly at the man and then at Hayley. Hayley could not return his look. With that, Jack brushed past them both and ran down the steps towards the sanctuary of his car.

"Jack, Jack, come back! Jack!!" Hayley called out and started to run off after him only to be pulled back by the arm of the man in the doorway.

"Let him go Hayley, it's all right, I'll speak to him."

"Why couldn't you just leave Danny, like I asked you to?" Hayley was almost crying.

"I'm sorry, I didn't know Jack was going to be here."

Danny was a little bit shell-shocked himself. This was not quite how he had imagined his first date with Hayley would start.

"Listen, I'll call him."

"I need to speak to him," Hayley was distraught, "just go Danny. I'm really sorry. I'm really confused. I just need to think."

Danny stooped down and put the wine and flowers just inside the door.

"Hey, no problem, and I'm really sorry, I didn't mean to mess things up. Are you okay?" he tried to extend a comforting arm out to Hayley but his gesture, genuine though it was in its intent, was shunned. "Okay, look, I'm going to go. If you need to talk give me a call. I'll get in touch with Jack and smooth things over with him."

Hayley nodded and slowly made her way back inside. She walked to her bedroom where she slumped down across the mattress upon which she would lie silently all evening until her tiredness finally got the better of the chaos within her mind and she would fall into a deep dream-riddled sleep.

Outside, Jack had reached his car and was trying to calm himself before driving off. Every sinew within him wanted to jam down the throttle and career off down the road at break-neck speed. Fortunately Jack was also a bit of a coward and the thought of crashing and/or hurting someone was sufficient for him to resist such urges so instead he took the alternative action of inhaling and exhaling the biggest breaths as he could manage in the hope that he could regain some control over his feelings and lower his blood pressure. He felt like his head was going to explode so such a course of action seemed an appropriate, if not the easiest of tasks to force himself to undertake.

Jack's mind, so crowded and jumbled over recent weeks, was surprisingly empty. He felt nothing other than the racing of the blood through his veins. Once he had brought his breathing under control, and the prospect of his forehead imploding had evaporated, he felt nothing at all.

He was numb.

Numb

Numbness is a strange state in which to find yourself. It feels like a place where you really have to make decisions but a place, by its very nature, where that's really hard to do. We all reach junctions within our lives on a daily basis. The majority of these junctions and the decisions to go left or right, or to go straight ahead or to reverse, are very minor and within the whole grand scheme of things are extremely unlikely to represent life redefining moments. Jack had encountered one such decision as he wandered aimlessly around his local supermarket on the Sunday afternoon when faced with the option of Salt and Vinegar or Ready Salted crisps. Not the most taxing of decisions that he had been faced with over the years but one which, whilst under the influence of the state of numbness, seemed to be more taxing than it perhaps warranted. Jack had picked up the Salt and Vinegar multi-pack and put it down. He had picked up the Ready Salted multi-pack, stared at this briefly, and then back at the Salt and Vinegar option, and swapped the two packs over. This in itself isn't too disturbing but by the time he had made the swap for the seventh time, whilst appearing blissfully unaware of his indecision, it had drawn the attention of the sweet plump mature shelf-stacker who was happily replenishing some stocks of half price Hula Hoops.

"You alright darling?" she had stopped meticulously arranging her crisp display and had carefully approached Jack.

"What? Eh? Hello." Jack opened and closed his eyes

rapidly in an effort to shift himself out of his malaise.

"Are you alright darling? You seem to have got yourself stuck like a record. You keep picking one pack up and putting the other one down and then swapping them back!" The woman, with all the best intentions, granted, was speaking to Jack as if he were a small child. This in itself was enough to spark a bit of life back into Jack's listless existence.

"N'n'n' No, I'm fine. I've only done it a couple of times." Jack was sure he had just got there; however, even as he was finishing his sentence he was beginning to doubt that this was the case, a fact the kind woman accordingly confirmed.

"No darling," she was still talking to him as if he had just asked if he could go to the toilet but hadn't put his hand up to pre-empt the request, "it's been a few more than twice hasn't it? It's been at least seven or eight times now and you're still doing it!"

Jack looked down at his hands which were still holding both packets.

"Ah, I think I must have been daydreaming a little!" Jack threw a warm smile at the woman in the hope this would re-assure her that he hadn't just wandered out of a warden controlled establishment.

"Ah, okay darling. Do you need any help with the rest of your shopping?" Clearly Jack's warm smile had done nothing to convince the woman that Jack was anything other than a simple lost soul. In many ways her swift analysis was not far off the mark.

"I'm fine thank you.." Jack looked at her name badge, "Nora - floor attendant - but I do appreciate you taking the time to come and wake me up! I think I'll go for the Salt and Vinegar!"

With that, Jack put the crisps into his shopping trolley and moved on to the next aisle. He did, of course, return a few minutes later when Nora had herself returned to the stock cupboard and swap them over for the Ready Salted.

Jack could console himself that such a decision had very little impact on his future. The same applied to practically all the decisions he made for the rest of that day, save a few obvious practical safety decisions around when to cross the road, when to stop filling the bath, how hard to hold his razor etc., but in the main nothing Jack did on that Sunday had any influence on how he would spend the rest of his life, and equally as relevant, with whom it would be spent.

Jack was aware that he needed to think about Hayley. He was aware that he needed to think about Danny. He was aware of all of this but he had reached the stage where, subconsciously, he realised he had to stop thinking. His brain was all thought out. His inner voice, so involved and vocal over the last few weeks as he struggled to make sense of his mixed emotions and feelings of anxiety, confusion and hope, had finally fallen silent.

Jack needed to be still.

He needed to do nothing.

Numbness was not a bad place at which Jack should stop for a while.

It was not a place that he should continue to reside for too long however, and fortunately for him his inner voice was screaming this at the top of its range on the Monday morning when Jack hit the snooze button for the third time.

"I'm not going to work!"

"What do you mean you're not going to work? How old are you? Six? You're not a child. Get up!"

"I don't want to! I don't feel like it!"

"Jack, Jack, Jack. You've got to go in. You've got to face her."

"I don't want to!"

"Jack – you've ignored her calls all day yesterday. Nothing's changed since you sat in her hall and held her on Saturday. She still loves you – even if it's not in the way you want."

Jack didn't answer himself back this time. He knew he was being petulant. He also knew that he had to get up and go to work. He didn't want to, but as he had reminded himself, he wasn't a child anymore. Reluctantly, he therefore dragged his sorry arse out from under the covers and stumbled wearily into the shower in the hope that the torrent of fresh water would help wake him from his slumber and ease his numbness to one side.

With some of his energy restored Jack had made the familiar journey into work where he had waited patiently for Hayley, or to be more accurate, where he waited with all the patience of a crack addict shuffling agitatedly outside a chemist's, waiting for it to open after the weekend, their crumpled repeat prescription for methadone in hand, only to realise that the chemist's opens two hours later on a Monday.

His waiting however, much akin to the fears of the late great Bob Marley's, had been in vain.

"What do you mean Hayley's not in!!!"

"Jesus Jack! Calm down mate. I'm just telling you." Ken shook his head and put his coffee down on his desk.

"Well where is she?"

"She's taken a couple of days holiday apparently."

"When? Why? She can't do that!"

Ken stared across at the stressed wreck of a man before him.

"Jack, what the hell's the matter with you?"

Any remaining ounce of numbness that had resided within Jack had now been hurled out with its cases never to return. He sat back down at his desk, his head once again pounding, and he closed his eyes, shielding them behind his hands.

"Jack? You alright mate?" Ken was a little concerned. He was not used to seeing Jack like this.

Jack took a deep breath and tried to recover some of his composure that had momentarily eluded him as it ran for cover, unaccustomed to seeing its master in such a state.

"Yeah, yeah Ken. I'm okay. When did Hayley arrange the holiday?"

"She called in and spoke to the boss this morning. Something about needing to go and see a relative."

"What about her appointments? That's a bit short notice isn't it?"

"She's only got a couple and we've been asked to cover them. I can pick them both up if you like, I'm not too busy?"

Jack nodded and returned his head to his hands.

"Oh apparently she said she was going to send us both an e-mail to give us the details."

Jack removed his head from his hands and immediately logged onto his computer, willing it to speed through its usual checks and docile set up so that he could access his messages as quickly as he could.

"I've got mine here," Ken, having been in the office for ten minutes longer than Jack and in a far more effective frame of mind, had found his message from Hayley, "it just says 'Hi Ken, sorry to have to take holiday at such short notice. If you could pick up a couple of my appointments while I'm off that would be great. Details are in my diary in my top drawer. I can't remember who they are - so I don't think there are any stinkers in there. Cheers Jack and send my love to Sharon. Please also tell her to stop publishing details of her sexual antics with you on Facebook, it's making it hard for me to look at you at work'. Charming!! I thought Sharon had stopped." Ken had read right to the end of the e-mail, despite the personal content at its end. This had brought a wry smile to Jack's face as he finally got access to his own mail.

There it was in his inbox, the second of three unopened e-mails. He held his finger gingerly over the Enter key and gave himself a moment to compose himself before pressing it down accordingly.

'Hi Jack.

I've been trying to ring you since Saturday night but I guess you haven't wanted to speak to me. I can't stand the thought of that being the case between us and don't think I could cope if I came in today and you couldn't bring yourself to talk to me or even look at me.

I've arranged to take a few days off just to give me some time to clear my head. I'm hoping that will give you some time to think as well so that when we next meet we can pick up where we left just before Danny called on Saturday.

I need you to know that I hadn't been seeing Danny behind your back. Saturday was actually going to be the first time we were going to go out. I was planning to tell you on the Monday but I guess that was a little stupid of me.

Not knowing that you felt the way you felt and thinking that you had been happy to see Imogen I kind of thought that when you found out about me and Danny you would have been really happy for us – your two best mates getting together. That's of course if we did actually get together. I'm not sure where that's heading now, to be honest, I'm not sure how I feel about anything right now, about me, about Danny, or about us. It's all a bit confusing!! I know that seems to have been a word we used a lot on Saturday but I think it's the best word to describe how I feel right now.

I remember you once giving me a bit of advice about when you're faced with a problem that the first thing you need to do is to step back out of the problem and look at it from a different perspective. That's what I need to do right now. I just need to get my head away from everything and work out how I feel. The only thing I'm certain of at the moment is that I can't afford to lose you as my friend no matter what happens. You mean far too much to me to ever allow that to happen.

I've got until Thursday off. I know we're due to be going to see Eddie Izzard on Wednesday but I'm not sure if it's a good idea for me to come along. I think the next time we speak it should be at a place where we can have a proper conversation.

So, there we go, I'm kind of glad I've written this note now. I've just re-read it and it kind of says all that I need to say and I'm not sure if I'd spoken to you on the phone that I would have been able to get all of that out. So, take care Jack. If I don't speak to you before I will be back on Thursday and perhaps we can go out at lunch or after work to catch up and see if we can get ourselves back on track.

Love Hayley

X'

Jack had read through the mail at the same pulsating speed at which his heart had been pounding, far too fast to take anything in properly. He took a couple of deep breaths and started to read it again from the start. He repeated this exercise twice more before forwarding the e-mail to his home e-mail address. Slowly he then got up from his chair and wandered into the kitchen to make himself a strong black sweet coffee. As he stirred the cheap steel spoon around his equally cheap mug he smiled to himself as some of the words that he had just read resounded around his head like a regal fanfare trumpeting the arrival of the beginning of his realisation and rationalisation of both how he felt and what he needed to do next.

Platonic?

Jack and Hayley loved Eddie Izzard. Jack had first seen his comedy hero on an old Benefit Gig video of his uncle's dating back to the early 1990s, prior to Mr Izzard's meteoric rise through the comedy establishment. From the moment he had seen the genius recounting his early childhood – how he was brought up in Nazi Germany in the 1930s and avoided persecution by escaping in a bullrush moulded U–Boat culminating in him being raised by wolves and hunting for their prey in a small red car – Jack had been hooked. He had shared the video with Hayley, and his extensive back catalogue, and Hayley too had joined the legion of action transvestite hero fans.

It was therefore with an understandable sense of excitement and anticipation that Jack was making his hurried way along the pavements towards his destination, a packed out auditorium eagerly waiting to be spun tales of the surreal and bizarre.

Across town Hayley had just finished applying a subtle application of make up and was admiring the rather stunning results in the mirror. She afforded herself a smile, an acknowledgement that she 'scrubbed up well', and then she too eagerly left her flat and started on her way. Her air of optimism was in stark contrast to the despondency within which she had languished over the weekend. Her malaise had continued through until Monday night when Jack, having read her e-mail earlier in the day, knocked on her door.

★

"Hi"

"Hi Jack, I wasn't expecting you." Hayley had looked surprised to see Jack standing in front of her.

"I know," Jack smiled warmly, "but I kind of guessed you weren't actually visiting a relative, and I kind of realised that I shouldn't have ignored your calls."

Hayley opened the door further and invited Jack through. He stepped inside and waited for Hayley to lead, which she did, and took him through to the kitchen.

"Coffee?"

"Yeah, that would be great."

There was an awkwardness about their initial conversation. This wasn't too surprising, of course, given the way their last face-to-face communication had ended. However, Jack, for one, had moved past that place.

"Thanks for sending me the e-mail."

"You're welcome." Hayley looked up from the mugs that had been the focal point of her vision whilst she was contemplating what to say.

"It really helped." Jack nodded.

Hayley finished making the drinks, offered Jack his mug and nodded towards the living-room where they both eased themselves down onto Hayley's sofa, albeit seeming to take care to ensure that there was a reasonable gap between them.

Hayley took a nervous sip of her hot coffee; it really was a little too hot to sip that soon, however Jack mirrored her actions.

"Cor blimey that's hot!" he pulled his lips away from the offending mug, "how can you drink that so soon?"

"I can't," Hayley at last raised a smile, "I just cope with pain better than you. You're a bloke after all!"

★

Jack's stride was a purposeful one. He loved the buzz of an expectant crowd. He was always the first person to shout down anyone who moaned about the cost of theatre tickets. 'It's as cheap as going out for a meal' was one such argument that he would hurl around as he chastised the guilty moaning party and pointed out that life was too short not to seize the chance to see the good and the great of your day and to have some memories upon which to look back when your years begin to catch up with you.

Tonight, he had decided, was going to be a good night. With that warm thought spurring him onwards he let himself drift back to the events of Monday evening.

★

"So," Jack sat forward onto the edge of the sofa, giving him a few additional moments to compose himself and his thoughts, "are you okay?"

Hayley nodded and squeezed out a smile, "Yeah, I'm alright. How 'bout you?"

"Yeah, yeah," Jack nodded his affirmation, "I'm fine."

Another awkward pause came and sat between them.

"I am sorry I didn't return your calls Hayles." There was a warm sincerity in Jack's tone that comforted Hayley.

"That's alright, I understand you must have been a bit angry."

"Yeah, a little bit."

"You know that wasn't my intention don't you, as in, I never meant to make you angry or upset you."

"Of course!" Jack was both touched by Hayley's concern and embarrassed to think that his behaviour would have caused her to think him so shallow. "I was only angry for a while, and I feel a bit of tit for feeling like that to be honest."

"Well, yes you were a bit of a tit!" Hayley hoped her comment would prompt a laugh from Jack and wasn't disappointed.

"How could I ever be angry with you for long anyway?"

"Well that's true, I am rather lovely."

They both looked at one another. This was how they had always been. This felt right. This was one of the reasons why both had questioned whether there was more to their relationship in the first place. Why can't two people who get on so well together take their relationship to the next level?

★

Hayley, as she made her way through the streets on the Wednesday night, found her mind wandering to the events of the last five days. She had not enjoyed the weekend at all. Jack may have been on his own rollercoaster of emotions but Hayley had experienced an even more unpredictable, topsy turvy ride which had taken her to the point of tears and desperate soul searching in a seemingly ever-decreasing circle. She had called Jack several times in order to try and make sense of it all but his rejection of her calls had merely served to push her further down her spiral to despair and ultimately to her decision to take some time off and avoid the whole issue as much as she could. She too needed to be numb for a while.

Her eyes, however, eyes that had sparkled in her mirror before she left her flat that night, were not the eyes of someone who was still in a land of confusion. She looked up into the late summer sky and sucked in some of the beautiful air that accompanies such glorious evenings. As she did so, she found herself smiling as she cast her mind back forty-eight hours.

★

"So," Jack began.

"So?" Hayley replied.

"So," Jack began again, accompanied by a strange sense of déjà vu.

"A needle pulling thread?" A small smile forced its way onto Hayley's face.

"Very good!" Jack acknowledged his friend's quick response, "but no, 'So' as in 'So, let's talk about the subject of 'us'."

The awkward pause was back again, trying to jump back up onto the sofa. Jack carried on,

"The thing is we need to talk about it don't we. Until we move past it one way or the other we're just going to get more and more confused and, I don't about you, but I've had enough confusion over the last few weeks to last me a year."

Hayley nodded as Jack continued.

"I was angry on Saturday, but I think I was more angry with Danny."

"It's not his fault Jack."

"The thing is Hayley, Danny knew how I felt about you. He should never have asked you out."

Hayley lowered her head to gather her thoughts.

"He didn't."

Jack hadn't been expecting that response.

"He didn't?"

"No. He didn't." Hayley tried to force herself to keep eye contact, "I asked him out for a drink."

"You asked him out?" Again, Jack wasn't expecting this response either, although logically it was the only other alternative to explain why Hayley and Danny were due to go out.

"Yes. We'd bumped into each other last week in town and got talking. I told him I'd set you up on a date with Imogen. He seemed really pleased for you. I kind of liked him, we got on really well, I'd had a couple of drinks, and I suddenly found myself asking him if he'd like to go out on Saturday."

"And he said yes?"

"Well, he was a little hesitant at first – which didn't make me feel that great, I've got to be honest – but then he said yes."

"Did he tell you how I felt?"

"No."

"Right."

"Not then he didn't."

"Not then?"

"No."

"So he has now?"

"Yes."

"When?"

"On Sunday. He called me to say that he was going to have talked to me about it when we went out on Saturday. He'd assumed it was okay because of the Imogen situation."

Jack smiled to himself – it was kind of comforting to see that it wasn't just his life that was confusing.

★

Jack checked his watch. He had another fifteen minutes before curtain up and only another couple of minutes before he reached the theatre. He always liked to get to a show at least ten minutes before the start just to take in some of the atmosphere. He couldn't stand being late and the mere idea that someone could leave their schedules so tight that they could risk turning up after a performance had started was completely alien to him, and yet, on almost every stand up comedian's DVD he had watched, he had witnessed people going to their seats after the start. The comedian always seems to enjoy this as it gives him a great opportunity to rip the piss out of these late comers as they stumble apologetically along their row, past the grumbling audience members who were courteous enough to turn up on time themselves, and who now find themselves having to either squeeze their legs to the side or stand up with the result that their folding chairs catapult backwards sending their coats, wallets, mobile phones and secret stash of Maltesers crashing noisily to the floor. If it were Jack sitting there he would find it hard to resist the temptation to trip the inconsiderate buggers up and stamp on their sorry arses – well at least that is what he once claimed he would do at the end of a particularly long spell on his soap box whilst under the considerable influence of his one time occasional friend Jack Daniels.

Tonight, however, he was sure that there would be no such issues. He reached into his pocket and pulled out his ticket to check his seat number. Not surprisingly it hadn't changed from the last time he had looked and he returned the ticket back to his pocket, assured that he had indeed purchased two of the best seats in the theatre.

★

"You can't blame Danny Jack, I'm sure the last thing he wanted to do was to hurt you."

Hayley extended her hand out and tenderly squeezed Jack's arm.

Jack knew he shouldn't blame Danny. In truth he had already forgiven him and his hesitation in responding to Hayley now was due to his embarrassment at having doubted Danny's intentions in the first place.

"I know," Jack nodded, "I guess everything's just got a bit muddled up. I work in a bank, I'm used to adding two and two together and making five."

Hayley smiled and squeezed Jack's arm once more. Their eyes met and Jack instinctively reached out his other hand, took Hayley's own hand gently off his arm, and nestled his fingers in between hers. Hayley responded by edging herself closer towards Jack.

"Everything has been a bit muddled recently hasn't it." It was statement rather than question from Hayley.

"It has indeed my dear. It has indeed."

Silence once more descended upon them both as they sensed the conversation steering its way around to its critical phase.

"Have you got things any clearer in your head since Saturday?" Jack needed to know.

"I think so." Hayley felt anxious. She squeezed her fingers tightly around Jack's. "Have you?"

"Yeah, I think so." Jack turned his body in to face Hayley and took hold of her other hand. He ever so gently caressed his fingers over her hands.

★

Hayley checked her watch. It was fast approaching a quarter to eight and she really didn't want to be late. She began to quicken her pace, almost breaking into a slow jog. Were it not for her two-inch heels she may well have reached such heady speeds but commonsense prevailed and she slowed back down to her brisk walk. She was almost there and literally just had to get around the next corner.

Jack was already making his way towards the usher standing guard outside the large double fire-doors signalling the entrance to the auditorium. He proudly held out his ticket which was duly acknowledged and accompanied by some mumbled instructions as to how to find where the matching seat was located. Jack nodded his thanks to the usher.

Jack had been to the theatre many times before and knew exactly where their seats were. He edged impatiently past a snooty upper class couple so far up their own backsides that, even though they were aware that their decision to stand in the middle of the aisle meant that they were holding up all those patrons wishing to enter the building via Door A, they were quite content to stand their ground until such time as they could attract the attention of an equally snooty twat, who eventually responded to the name 'Tarquin', sitting in one of the cheap seats towards the back of the auditorium. Jack consoled himself with the thought that they were probably genetically unstable, on account of years of rigorous inbreeding, and made his way towards his seat. As he got closer and found the correct row he saw that the seat next to his was empty. He checked his watch. It was just coming around to quarter to eight.

Hayley, breathing a little heavier, finally reached the bottom of the steps. She knew she was a little late but that was, after all, a woman's prerogative.

★

"The thing is Jack," Hayley had been over this conversation in her own mind on numerous occasions within the last twenty-four hours, having finally worked out what she wanted, "I just can't lose you as my friend. I'm scared that if we try and take it further, if it doesn't work out that's what would ultimately happen."

"Is that risk worth taking if the result is that we could work out and this could turn into something amazing?"

Hayley had thought about this. It had been the one question she had run over and over in her head.

"The truth is," she paused before delivering the truth, "I don't know. But I'm not sure that it's the right time now to find out."

Jack looked down to the floor and then back up to Hayley.

"I have been really mixed up recently Hayley. Probably the only one consistent thing that has remained in my mind is that I can't lose you. When I came round on Saturday I knew I had to tell you how I felt. A part of me thought that if we got it right we could have an amazing relationship. Who knows, that might still be true! But, when I was around here and then reading your e-mail, well it kind of made me see things for how they really are. I took your advice about the advice I gave you and took a step back. All I wanted to do on Saturday was to put my arms around you and tell you everything was going to be alright. Up until my cousin's wedding I had always felt we had the perfect platonic relationship. I love having you as my best friend. If everyone else had just shut up and let us get on with being ourselves then none of this would have happened."

Hayley had a tear in her eye and leant over to reach for a tissue. Jack waited until she had wiped it away before continuing to open his heart out.

"When you wrote that you thought I'd be happy if my best mates got together it was like a bolt through my head. Of course it should be okay for my best mates to get together. You're my best mates, I love you both. Okay, my love for you over the last few weeks may have strayed a little off the path on which it normally treads," Hayley smiled and playfully smacked Jack on his shoulder, "but the thing is I do love you both. It's just taken me a while to realise that if I want to keep that love for you for ever, then the only sure way of doing that is to keep it for you as my friend."

"Thank you Jack." Hayley leant forward and put her arms around him. She squeezed him so tightly that he thought she would never let go.

"You know I feel the same about you Jack?"

Jack smiled and nodded.

"It's weird isn't it," Hayley sat back, the anxiety that had grasped her body so tightly since she had opened the door to Jack a few minutes earlier evaporated, "if my friends hadn't gone on at me so much then I wouldn't have said anything to you and none of this would have happened."

"Friends and family eh? Who needs 'em?"

Hayley picked up her mug of coffee that was fortunately now at a temperature less likely to singe the front of her tongue.

"Friends and family!" she raised her mug high.

"Friends and family!" Jack picked up his mug and joined Hayley in their toast.

The two friends sank back into the sofa and snuggled up to one another.

"I've missed you!" Jack planted a kiss on Hayley's forehead.

"I've missed you too!"

Both stared ahead into space.

"What the fuck were we thinking?"

"I have no idea!" answered Hayley as she took another gulp of her coffee.

★

Hayley reached the top of the stairs leading to the entrance of the restaurant, checked her appearance in the dim reflection begrudgingly offered by the glass door and went inside. Danny was waiting at the bar.

"Hi, you made it!"

"Of course, I said I would." Hayley tilted her face to allow Danny to give her a chivalrous peck on the cheek.

"How's Jack?"

"Yeah, he's great. He says he's going to meet us here after the show for a drink if that's alright?"

"Of course, that'll be great." Danny handed Hayley a glass of wine and directed her towards a small table in the corner of the restaurant. "Is he definitely okay with us meeting up?"

"Absolutely. He might want to ask you lots of questions though – he's very protective."

"Is he going to ask me what my intentions are?" Danny

felt himself turning a little red after this last comment, a chemical reaction not lost on Hayley.

"I don't think he'd want to know."

"Indeed."

Jack too had taken his seat and had placed his coat and covert supply of snacks and drink in the adjacent seat vacated by Hayley. He had paused just before laying his coat down, his mind starting to outline the picture of the woman who should be sitting there next to him. He knew, however, that he couldn't dwell on what might have been and had quickly cleared his mind before the fog could squeeze itself under the door. He sat back and broke into spontaneous applause as Eddie Izzard made his entrance.

Throughout the first half Jack found himself being happily led along the surreal pathways that connected the seemingly improvised ramblings on the stage before him. Although he was not aware of it, and despite his initial waverings when he first sat down, the welcome distraction ahead of him meant that this was the first time in a while that he had not been preoccupied with thoughts of unrequited love and whether it was truly possible to have a platonic relationship with a member of the opposite sex who just happens to be your best friend.

The completion of the first half and announcement of a twenty minute interval prompted a mass exodus to the bar. Jack stayed in his seat and munched on a packet of Rolos which he had smuggled into the arena. These, however, didn't last long on account of them being so damn 'more-ish' leaving Jack with the dilemma of whether to sit in silence for the next fifteen minutes or force himself to have a quick half at the bar. This turned out to be one of the easier decisions Jack had been faced with of late and moments later he found himself standing at the end of a long line of people leaning over a ridiculously understaffed bar waving their ten pound notes in the belief that it would attract the bar staff to them more quickly than if they were to just wait there. Sadly, they were probably right.

Jack looked at his watch. Thirteen minutes to the start of the second half, and by his estimate, another six or seven minutes at least before he was likely to be served.

"Jack?"

Jack turned around to see the owner of a voice he recognised.

"Sarah! Blimey, how are you?"

Jack hadn't seen Sarah Michaels since she had been in to tell him of her impending engagement. This was a shame, as he was aware she'd been in since but he had not been around and he always enjoyed talking to her. Well, truth be told, this enjoyment was much to do with the fact that their conversations always seemed to run the fine line between talking and flirting.

"I'm good thanks, how are you?" Sarah leant in towards Jack so as to be heard above the bustling noise of the bar.

"Good thanks, although I'd be happier if I could get a drink!"

"I know what you mean, I've been waiting here for ages and can't get close."

"Yes mate?" a barman unenthusiastically responded to the ten pound note held aloft in Jack's hand.

"Just a bottle of Becks please and," Jack turned to Sarah, "can I get you and your other half a drink?"

"Just a glass of wine please."

Jack looked around for Sarah's partner who didn't seem to be in the immediate vicinity.

"What's your other half drinking?"

"It's just me tonight."

Jack turned back to the barman and placed his order. He turned back to Sarah and both gave each other that holding smile that people give each other where there's no point in starting a conversation just yet as you'll only have to stop in a moment. However, within a few of these moments they were walking away from the crowds of people seeking refreshment and over to the altogether more relaxed area where you could actually have a drink and hear each other speak.

"Cheers." Jack raised his bottle.

"Cheers, and thank you for the drink."

"Hey, you're welcome. It's all part of my extended service as your friendly account manager."

"Wow, I must recommend my bank to all my friends."

"You mean you don't already?"

"Well obviously I tell them I have a nice account manager but they don't seem to be swayed by that!"

Jack was enjoying the freedom afforded by meeting Sarah outside of the constraints of the professional workplace and was quite happy to step over the fine line and stand confidently in the flirting section.

"So, if you're not here with your other half then who are you here with?" Jack scanned the horizon for any other attractive women wandering around by themselves.

"Oh, no-one," Sarah looked a little embarrassed by the fact she had turned up at a theatre by herself, "I had two tickets but I only needed one."

"Your other half is in the forces isn't he. Could he not make it?"

"Er, no." There was hesitancy in her voice that Jack didn't quite pick up on.

"Oh gosh," Jack suddenly remembered the excitement in Sarah the last time they had spoken "how did it go? When I saw you last your boyfriend was coming to see you and a proposal was in the offing!"

This time the hesitation was a little more obvious and Jack immediately began to feel a bit of a fool as the realisation that he had rather 'put his foot in it' jumped up and blew a raspberry in his face.

"It didn't quite go according to plan." Sarah took a sip of her drink.

"Oh no, I'm sorry." Jack didn't know why he did it but it felt like the natural thing to do to reach out and gently, and ever so briefly as the realisation of what he was doing hit him, stroke her arm.

"You know what they say about sailors? A girl in every port?"

"Oh shit, sorry."

"Her name was Mary and the port was in Plymouth."

"What a git."

"Then there was Claire and the port was Gibraltar."

"Oh!"

"Mandy in Portsmouth."

"Ah, so literally a girl in every port."

Sarah shrugged her shoulders, "Yes, apparently he liked to 'drop anchor' whenever he could." She took another sip before continuing, "Well at least he had the balls to come down and tell me I guess."

"Yeah I guess. But if you ask me," Jack clinked his bottle against Sarah's glass, "the bloke's a fool."

"Ah, thanks Jack." Sarah was touched by the compliment. "So there's my sad old excuse. What's yours? Why are you here alone?"

Jack took a reciprocal drink from his bottle as he considered his response.

He stood there in silence for a moment.

"You seem confused?"

Sarah's observation was a good one.

"The thing is," Jack began, "I was due to be seeing my best mate – she's a she by the way," Jack felt the need to clarify this point, "but she's going on a date with my other best friend instead."

Both Sarah and Jack stared ahead for a while as they started to decipher the last sentence.

"I'm confused now," Sarah began, "so were you due to see your best friend – just as a best friend – and she's going on a proper date with someone else instead – oh, and that someone is also one of your best friends?"

"Well, yes and no," the furrows in Jack's brow slowly began to scrunch up his face.

"Yes and no?"

"Well, Yes, as in I was due to see my best friend and she's now going on a date with my other best friend, and No, as in originally I was hoping that we'd come here tonight as more than just friends."

For a second time both of them stared ahead as they deciphered Jack's latest offering.

"I'm still confused." Confusion was a popular condition affecting many people in Jack's life at this period of time, including now Sarah who continued, "So, you want to be more than just friends with your best mate but she's on a date with your other best mate."

"Yes," Jack nodded, "and No...I think."

Sarah shook her head.

"Yes and No again Jack?"

"Well it's confusing.."

"It sounds it. Well, if she doesn't want to be with you then she's a fool too Jack."

Jack smiled at Sarah. It was a nice compliment, particularly from someone as gorgeous as Sarah.

"Thanks Sarah."

"You're welcome."

Both of them stared ahead into space once more.

"So do you still want to be with her then?"

It was an unexpected question. Jack, his defences weakened by the combination of alcohol and talking to a pretty girl, had inadvertently taken his eye off the door in the back of his mind enabling the fog, previously so well contained on the outside, to slip itself through the cat-flap and swiftly engulf every other thought in its path. Did he still want to be with Hayley? Had he given up too easily? Why was she at a restaurant with Danny when she could be here with him?

"Yes."

Jack almost dropped his bottle. The voice in his head had picked up a megaphone and shouted his answer before Jack had even time to think it through. The overpowering force of the voice had scattered the fog leaving just a clear, vivid, all consuming realisation of how he truly felt.

"Yes," Jack sucked up the air into his chest and said it again just to make sure he had heard himself correctly, "Yes".

A huge broad excited smile flooded across Sarah's beautiful face as their eyes fixed upon one another.

"Then what are you doing here?"

"I have no idea!!" Jack, all fingers and thumbs as he knew he had to go, fumbled around in his pocket for his ticket.

"You're going to go for her aren't you!!" Sarah started to clap her hands excitedly.

Jack thought for a moment. If he had no idea why he was there and knew he still wanted to be with Hayley, surely the answer to Sarah's question was a simple one?

"Yes I am!" Jack looked at his ticket and then smiled back at Sarah who was jumping up and down on the spot with a smile that started at one of her ears and finished rather beautifully at the other. "Listen, I'm in row F seat 26. It's a great seat - will you sit there for the second half for me please? It's just if I fall flat on my face I think I'm going to need to come back and have a shoulder to cry on!"

"Yeah, of course," Sarah was clapping her hands again, "but you'll be fine! God, this is so romantic!"

"Do you think?" Jack hadn't even considered this as he awkwardly replaced his ticket into his wallet.

"God yeah," Sarah started to push Jack towards the exit, "so go, go!"

Jack started to do just that but was immediately pulled back by Sarah.

"Oo oo, just let me give you my number," she pulled her mobile from her rather stylish and compact handbag, "you must give me a call and let me know how it goes!"

"I will!" Jack smiled. Sarah had never looked more beautiful. Jack leant forward and embraced her. As he pulled away he paused, pulled her towards him and planted the most intense of kisses on her somewhat startled lips. The kiss was not a passionate one, it had no desire or intent behind it all, but it was heartfelt from Jack who had just been shown the light by the most unexpected source. The kiss was his sign of true thanks. Sarah just sighed. She felt like she'd just fallen into a Tom Hanks and Meg Ryan movie.

Jack turned and made his way out of the theatre. His heart was pounding relentlessly as he found himself unable to just walk. He broke into a brisk walk, and then into sporadic bouts of brief jogging, before the adrenalin could be contained no more and he found himself running at full pace through the streets, streets that were teeming with people moving from one pub to another, and onwards towards the restaurant.

The noise from the people around him was a distant hum in his mind. Busy though they were, the streets may have well as been deserted, as Jack could only hear the sound of his pounding chest and only see the clear path ahead that led the way to his destination. His mind had not even started to plan what he was going to say when he got there. It didn't have to. Jack knew what he had to say. He knew he had to lay his soul on the line this time. To do anything else simply wasn't an option. He had to, he simply had to be with Hayley.

★

The noise came crashing down from the cool night air like a firecracker exploding at Jack's feet.

The pathway that had been so apparently clear and easy to navigate was now crowded by groups of giggling women and swearing men moving between their watering holes. The pounding of Jack's heart was now just a back beat underpinning the evening ambience of laughter, raised voices, clicking of stilettos against tarmac and the latest chart hits emanating from the latest microscopic mobile phones.

The sudden change was due to Jack's current extreme close proximity to the restaurant door. He had stopped his charge as he had reached the steps leading up to its entrance and, having decided to pause to gather himself, had inadvertently allowed himself to feel some twinges of self doubt. He knew he had to be with Hayley. At the same time the thought of ruining things forever and therefore not being with her was suddenly a very real, and potentially an immediately impending, possibility.

Jack closed his eyes. He had to focus. He had to listen to his inner voice. He needed to get this right. The hustle and bustle of the street around him faded into the background once more as the voice in his head delivered its verdict.

"You love her."

Silence. Silence in Jack's mind. Silence, it seemed, all around him.

He loved Hayley.

It was as simple and as clear as that. The reason he had to be with her was because he loved her.

He skipped up the steps and pushed through the door and into the restaurant. People were everywhere, seemingly all the tables were taken and the numerous staff were busying themselves around these taking orders and serving large trays of drinks and various courses of meticulously prepared food to their satisfied customers. Trying to see Hayley in this continually moving haystack was a frustratingly difficult task.

"Can I help you sir, I'm afraid we are fully booked at the moment."

Jack hadn't noticed the rather impatient door host

standing there with his clipboard and false smile.

"Er, yeah, please, I'm looking for my friends, but," Jack cast his eyes around the restaurant again, "I can't see them."

"Indeed. We are, as I said Sir, fully booked. We are rather busy tonight."

Normally Jack would feel the need to respond to such sarcasm, however tonight his mind was very much elsewhere.

"Yeah, I understand." Jack looked at the clipboard in the man's hand. "Could you tell me where they would be sitting please?"

The man sighed but looked down at his list, "Name?"

"It would either have been Danny or Hayley."

"Surname?"

"Hayley Smith or Danny Wilding."

The man perused through the names.

"Would it have been a table for two or a group booking?"

Jack was beginning to get a little frustrated.

"Two, table for two."

The man flipped over one of the sheets on his clipboard and ran his finger down the list of pencilled in names.

"Ah, here we are. Wilding, table for two, 8 o'clock."

"Great! Where are they?"

The man referred back to his sheet once more and then surveyed the restaurant. Much to Jack's further annoyance the man then repeated this exercise.

"Well?" Jack was thankfully resisting the temptation to grab the irritating little twat by his over-starched collar.

"They are over in the far corner just beyond the pillar there in the bay."

"Thank you."

No response from the waiter other than to move past

Jack and on to the next waiting customer whom he could look down upon.

Jack paced through the maze of crowded tables towards the small hidden bay in the corner of the restaurant. The high backed seating of the booths in this particular corner meant that he wouldn't get a good view of Hayley or Danny until he would be actually standing at the table. He wasn't sure if this was a good thing or not. Having not been in a position before where he was going to pronounce his undying love for his best friend it was hard to say whether the addition of the element of sudden surprise that he was there interrupting her meal – whilst she was on a date with his other best friend – would make any further difference to the surprise that he was making such a declaration in the first place.

The voice in Jack's head quickly skipped over this final stalling tactic and drove Jack forward towards the bay. Before he knew it he was there.

"Jack!"

"Danny."

"What are you doing here?"

"Er, where's Hayley?"

Jack was looking at the empty chair opposite Danny. A half empty glass of wine indicated that she might have made a trip to the restroom.

"Do you not know?" Danny, who was in the middle of making his way through an extremely large platter of ribs, looked startled to see his friend.

"No," Jack looked around to see if Hayley was making her way back to the table, "why would I know?"

Danny's look of surprise was replaced, much to Jack's initial bewilderment, by a broad smile.

"Quickly, sit down. Read this."

Jack hurriedly sat himself down and took hold of the napkin presented to him from across the table.

★

The audience erupted into laughter once more. Sarah found herself having to massage her cheekbones as they literally began to ache.

"Oh, don't worry, we haven't started yet, we were waiting for you to get back."

Another laugh from the audience as their attention was drawn to the late-comer making her way along the sixth row from the front of the stage accompanied by a slightly confused look as she double checked her ticket number.

Hayley paused as she found herself doing a double take before she recognised the lady sitting in her seat as Sarah Michaels.

"Sarah?"

Sarah turned around. It took a moment for her to work out where she had seen the bemused lady saying her name before. Once that moment had passed, and she had put two and two together with admirable speed, Sarah clapped and let out a high pitched whoop.

"In your own time ladies." Eddie Izzard looked on from his vantage point.

"What are you doing here? Have you seen Jack?" Hayley was oblivious to the fact that the entire performance had ground to a halt as she stood there questioning Sarah.

"Oh my God! You're his best friend aren't you?" Sarah clapped and whooped again.

"Yes…and no."

"That's what he said!" Sarah started to stand up, much to the initial momentary annoyance and then amusement of the gathered masses.

"What?" Hayley, confused, puzzled, bemused, didn't understand what was going on at all. "Where is he?"

"He's gone to find you!" Sarah was beaming.

"What?"

"Oh shit." it suddenly dawned upon Sarah that Hayley might just have turned up late for the performance and actually had no reciprocal feelings for Jack. "Why are you here? Weren't you on a date with Jack's best friend?"

"What, how did you know about that?"

"Jack told me before he…" Sarah paused again, in a concerted attempt to keep herself in check and avoid letting the romantic picture that was being played out in front of her evaporate, "erm, Jack, told me. So you were on a date with his best mate then?"

Hayley had no idea how Sarah knew all this but felt compelled to answer.

"I was but…"

"You realised you should be with Jack?" interrupted Sarah with a mixture of expectancy and absolute hope.

There was an audible intake of breath from the rows of seats around them which suddenly made them both extremely aware of their surroundings and the fact that well over a thousand pairs of eyes were upon them and well over a thousand pairs of ears were straining to hear Hayley's response.

Hayley looked around, the proverbial rabbit caught in the headlight, or spotlight as was now the case thanks to the lighting engineer and direction from the stage.

Hayley returned her gaze to Sarah who was biting her lip

as she waited for Hayley to confirm or deny her last question.

"Yes." Hayley's grin mirrored Sarah's and indeed all those within earshot. It was a weirdly liberating moment to publicly admit that she knew she should be with Jack. She found herself uttering "Yes" again just to confirm her answer.

Sarah, for her part, was now jumping up and down, much to the amusement of the audience. She jumped forward and hugged Hayley.

"So, where is he?" Hayley managed to pull herself away from the enthusiastic embrace.

"He's gone to find you," Sarah paused to take a breath, "he's gone to tell you he loves you."

A smattering of applause came from the seats around them, and from the stage.

"Well, are you going to go and find him and let me carry on then?" came the question through the sound system – which was also met by a smattering of applause from the members of the audience who were not fully aware of the drama unfolding in row F.

"Yes, yes, sorry Eddie." Hayley raised her hand in apology and started to ease her way past the various wellwishers along her aisle.

"You can sit down now sweetheart."

Sarah did as she was asked. Her cheekbones were more painful than they had ever been and by the end of the show she would barely be able to move her head.

Hayley rushed through the theatre and out into the evening. Just as Jack had struggled to keep himself from breaking into a mad dash so Hayley struggled; her heels had not undergone a miraculous metamorphosis into a pair of Nikes and therefore she had to keep her speed down to a painful brisk walk.

She then suddenly stopped and reached into her handbag for her mobile.

She dialled Jack's number and waited.

It was unavailable.

★

Jack, prompted by a nod from Danny, opened up the napkin. He felt his chest jump as he recognised Hayley's hurriedly scribbled writing.

"Danny,

I'm so sorry. I know this is really terrible – and forgive me for writing this while you're in the loo – but I know I just need to go.

You're a really nice guy. You make me laugh, you're great company, you're sensitive, you're good looking too! (thought I'd put that in to help soften the fact that I won't be here when you get back!!)

But, for all the great things you are, you're not Jack.

Sorry Danny, I'm hoping I can get there before the second half of the show. I will call you.

Love

Hayley

X"

Jack re-read the note. He then sat back in his chair and looked across at his friend. Jack had been expecting Danny to look annoyed but he didn't.

"Sorry mate," Jack apologised.

"What? Don't be daft Jack. It's me who should apologise. You were right."

"I was?"

"Yep, she felt the same way after all Jack."

For some reason the letter hadn't fully registered with Jack. He had read it as Hayley not wanting to get involved with Danny. The implication that this was because of her feelings for Jack had somehow gone over his head. Therefore to now hear his friend tell him that Hayley felt the same way as Jack did was almost like a thunderbolt shuddering into his senses. He grabbed the napkin and read it again.

"What the hell are you still doing here my friend? Go and get the girl!" Danny stood up with Jack and they shook hands before giving into the moment and exchanging a brief man-hug - something they had always agreed they would never do. This prompted a slightly awkward withdrawal from the pose and a nodded acknowledgement that they would not make mention of the hug in the future.

"How long ago did she leave?"

"About twenty minutes."

"I must have missed her on my way in. Oh, actually," Jack took out his wallet and pulled out his ticket, "if you get to the theatre too there's someone there I'd like you to meet."

Danny looked confused but took the ticket.

"Trust me! Just go and tell her Jack sent you and told you that you have to buy her a drink after the show."

Danny nodded his appreciation for the tip.

"I know you'll finish your ribs first." Jack looked towards Danny's plate.

"Absolutely." Danny concurred, patted Jack on the back, and sat back down.

Jack ran out of the restaurant and skipped down the steps onto the pavement.

He reached for his mobile phone and stood impatiently waiting for the connection.

Her phone was unavailable.

"Shit!" cursed Jack and he started to re-dial whilst navigating his way back towards the theatre. His re-dial attempts were, however, in vain.

Of course what he didn't know was that Hayley was experiencing the same difficulties as she continually hit the re-dial button. By now she had had to slow down to a very sedate walking pace - her heels were clearly not designed to run in, however she consoled herself with the fact that they looked great.

She was only a couple of blocks away from the restaurant when it suddenly occurred to her that Jack may not even be there. With this rather worrying thought running through her mind she decided to stop, take a seat in the old market square, where she now found herself, and try Jack's phone once more.

She hit his contact details and held the phone close to her ear.

She jumped.

It started to ring.

"Hayley? Is that you?"

"Jack! Yes, where are you? I've been trying to phone

you for ages." Hayley's voice was excited, nervous, exasperated.

"I've been trying to call you too!" Jack had slowed his own pace now so he could concentrate on his call.

"Where are you, I think we need to talk," Hayley started to ramble as her head became overwhelmed with all the things she wanted to say, "as in I know we need to talk. Jack, the thing is, I need to see you as there's something I need to tell you. I've left the restaurant and have been to the theatre to find you but you weren't there, so I'm making my way back to the restaurant, oh God, have you already been there? Is Danny okay, I can't believe I left him a note, but I'll tell you about that when I see you. Oh shit, I hope he's not angry. Oh my God I'm turning into a heartless bitch. Anyway I'm on my way back so if you're not at the theatre yet then tell me where you are because, Oh God, I've just got to see you. Where are you? Oh shit, are you still there? Say something Jack!" Hayley pulled her phone away from her ear just to check she still had a connection.

"I'm here."

The voice hadn't come from the phone.

Hayley turned around to see Jack standing in front of her, his phone in his hand.

"God you go on don't you!" His warm smile lit up Hayley's face.

"Sorry, I guess I just had something that I needed to tell…"

Their lips met before the final words of her sentence could escape. Jack felt himself pull her into him so tightly knowing that he never wanted to let her go. Hayley's hands cupped the back of Jack's head ensuring that the kiss, this magical earth-shattering kiss, would last long in their memories as she held his face to hers.

★

We all travel down our own paths. Sometimes the path we are on can cross or run so closely to that of someone else that it allows us to peer over upon it just to see if it's one we would like to tread for a while. Sometimes we find ourselves at a junction where two such paths meet at their end. One route takes the two paths along together and the other route divides them once more. It's at such forks in the road where life defining decisions are often made.

As Jack and Hayley kissed under the bright lights of the bustling square, the gentle summer evening breeze circling them approvingly, they had reached such a fork. As they finally pulled themselves apart and held each other's hand, they walked off, literally into the sunset, knowing that they were, at last, walking down the same path together, their path.